P●

THE EAST END MURDERS

A Family Affair · End of the Line

Anne Cassidy

■SCHOLASTIC

Scholastic Children's Books
Commonwealth House, 1-19 New Oxford Street,
London WC1A 1NU, UK
a division of Scholastic Ltd
London ~ New York ~ Toronto ~ Sydney ~ Auckland
Mexico City ~ New Delhi ~ Hong Kong

A Family Affair first published by Scholastic Ltd, 1995
End of the Line first published by Scholastic Ltd, 1996
This edition published by Scholastic Ltd, 1999

Copyright © Anne Cassidy, 1995, 1996

ISBN 0 590 54448 9

All rights reserved

Typeset by TW Typesetting, Midsomer Norton, Somerset
Printed by Cox & Wyman Ltd, Reading, Berks.

10 9 8 7 6 5 4 3 2

The right of Anne Cassidy to be identified as the author of
this work has been asserted by her in accordance with the
Copyright, Designs and Patents Act, 1988.

A Family Affair

Contents

1

Anthony Hamer
Investigations Inc.

The girl had been kidnapped.

That was what my uncle Tony had told me.

The parents were due to come into the office at about eleven. I was to bring them a cup of tea and some biscuits; digestive or raspberry wafers, whatever I thought suitable.

Tony thought he might be slightly late so I was supposed to sit them in the office and ask some general questions, about the weather, the traffic, whether they'd found the office easily or not.

"Whatever you do," Tony had said, "don't ask them about the kidnapped girl. Leave that to me; I'm the detective, you're the office clerk."

"Remember that," he'd said.

I looked round at the tiny office that I'd spent the

last week in, at the filing cabinets that I'd sorted out and the coffee machine that I'd come to know so well.

How could I forget? Tony made a point of telling me at least once an hour.

"I want you to answer the phone and take messages; sort out the filing cabinets; type up those letters; make me tea and coffee when I want it; run messages for me.

"On no account are you to involve yourself in the work of the agency: I'm the detective; you're the clerk."

So I'd busied myself with bits of paper and phone calls. I'd been sent to buy Italian coffee and Earl Grey tea as well as assorted biscuits. I'd watered the plants and shown people into my uncle's office. I'd smiled and offered tea or coffee.

Twice, my auntie Geraldine had popped in and chatted to me about her daughter Sarah, who was working in an insurance company (a very reputable firm), and her son, who had gone into the RAF (marvellous opportunities for young men).

A couple of afternoons, when the smile on my face had become too heavy to carry, I'd gone into the tiny toilet, sat down on the floor, taken off my glasses and put my head in my hands.

The job that my uncle had so generously given me was beginning to feel like a prison sentence. The huge oak desk that I sat at seemed to hem me into the corner and the filing cabinets stood guard at each side of the exit door. I found I only had to sit still for more than thirty minutes and a head-ache would start to develop. I wasn't allowed to go out without saying where I was going. I wasn't allowed to go into my uncle's office unless I knocked first. From time to time I looked down at my foot and imagined a long brassy chain attached to my ankle.

I couldn't leave the job though. I'd promised my mum I'd give it three months.

So, on the Friday morning, just before the family of the kidnapped girl were due to come in, I crossed out one week on my own personal calendar. One down, only eleven to go.

They came at about ten. The man walked in first.

"Mr Cooper?" I said in my best voice.

He was big; tall and heavy, maybe about fifty. He had a leather jacket on that was just too small and I couldn't help noticing the small gold ring in his ear.

"We're here to see Mr Hamer," he answered and walked past me; in his hand he had a mobile phone and he was pulling out the aerial and pressing the buttons.

The woman, Mrs Cooper, followed.

She looked much younger than her husband, in her thirties probably. Her hair was deep auburn and she was meticulously dressed in a cream mac and trousers. Her face was pale, looked white, in fact, against the redness of her hair.

She stood still for a couple of seconds and then looked round at her husband.

"That you, Harry?" he was shouting into his mobile, as though the person at the other end was hard of hearing. "I'll be in a bit late. You make a start on the rents."

Mrs Cooper drew a long slow breath in between her teeth. Her eyes caught mine for a moment and then she looked away. Her husband's voice seemed to get louder.

"I'll be about an hour," he said, then lowered the phone and pushed the aerial in. He looked at me, puzzled, as though he'd momentarily forgotten where he was.

"If you could just come this way," I said, showing them into my uncle's office. I went through the allowed conversation subjects. The woman spoke: yes, it was a nice day; the traffic was heavy but they had left early; yes, they'd found the office with no problems.

The man, seating himself at the far end of the sofa, said nothing, but looked disgruntled.

"Mr Hamer is out on a case at the moment," I said, even though I knew he was at the barber's. "I expect him back any minute."

That was when the door opened and he came in.

"Thank you, Patricia. I'll see Mr and Mrs

Cooper now. Could you continue sorting through the accounts? Thank you, dear."

And I was dismissed.

I sat down at my desk and thought about the people that my uncle Tony was talking to. I'd copied the original message from the answer-machine, first thing that morning. I got out my pad and flicked back to the page that I'd written the details on.

"Mr Cooper ... eighteen-year-old daughter hasn't been seen for three days ... further developments that he'd like to talk about..."

My uncle had presumably rung Mr Cooper because he'd started talking about his "kidnapped" daughter. When I'd asked him about it he'd said:

"This is England. People don't get kidnapped here!"

I looked down at the bit of paper again. Mr and Mrs Cooper and their missing daughter.

Kidnapped.

I let the word settle in my mind for a few seconds.

A picture of a masked man came into my head. He had a Balaclava on with only slits for eye holes. I imagined him walking behind a young girl and then, just as she was about to turn round, putting his hand across her mouth and whispering harshly in her ear: *do what you're told and I won't hurt you.*

A light flashed on the intercom; I reached across and turned on the play button.

"Patricia," Tony said, "can you hold my calls for, say, twenty minutes?"

I was about to answer him when he began to talk to Mr Cooper again. I reached across to flick the switch off but stopped half-way when Mr Cooper began to speak, his voice louder than it needed to be.

"You see, Mr Hamer, Judy is my wife's daughter, my stepdaughter. We married four years ago when Judy was fourteen. Things have always been difficult between Judy and me."

Mrs Cooper butted in.

"Judy and I have always been very close. Even though George and I were married she, she…" There was a brief silence. Then Mr Cooper came in:

"She always made it very clear, Mr Hamer, that I was in the way. The fact is, although I'm very fond of the girl, she doesn't like me."

"Her brother, Paul, still lives with his father. Judy misses him I think and she takes it out on…" Mrs Cooper's voice was croaky.

"No, let's be plain, the girl can't stand the sight of me at times."

My uncle Tony's voice came in at this point:

"So you haven't seen her since…"

"Monday morning," Mr Cooper said.

A light started flashing on the telephone and I reached across and gently pushed the off switch on the intercom before I answered it. It was a local solicitor's office that my uncle did business with. The clerk proceeded to give me a long message about the court times my uncle needed to know about.

I took the message, wrote it in neat long-hand, but all the while I was thinking of the Coopers and wondering who had kidnapped their daughter. When I finally put the phone down I picked up my glasses and began to polish them. After I'd finished I reached across and carefully flicked the intercom switch again.

"But why haven't you gone to the police?" my uncle was saying. "I can assure you that they would take a kidnapping case very seriously indeed."

There was silence for a few seconds, then Mrs Cooper spoke:

"My husband doesn't think…"

"What my wife is trying to say is that I don't think this note is from a kidnapper. I think that Judy, and possibly her boyfriend, are trying to make some money out of me. My wife just can't see that the girl could do any wrong."

"George…" his wife was crying.

"That's why I've not gone to the police. This is a family affair, Mr Hamer. My stepdaughter is trying to make a fool out of me! If I go to the police and it turns out that I'm right, then she'll go to prison. No, Mr Hamer, for all her faults my wife adores her daughter. I want you to find her and put a stop to this nonsense. Threaten her with the police if you like, but then she should come home. Her mother needs her."

"But why are you so sure that the note isn't real?" My uncle spoke softly.

"Look, Mr Hamer. My stepdaughter didn't come home on Monday. On Wednesday morning my wife got this note saying that she had been abducted; asking for the money. Lo and behold, I'm driving along on Wednesday afternoon and who do I see disappearing down the steps of the tube station? The lovely Judy."

"But…" My uncle's voice again.

"I know it was her, I'd recognize those long legs anywhere. No, Mr Hamer, my stepdaughter is playing a little game here and I want you to put a stop to it."

There was quiet for a minute and then a voice interrupted my thoughts. It came from the intercom and it was addressed to me.

"Patricia dear, could you bring in our contracts file."

And then it snapped off; without even waiting for an answer.

I sorted out the file and went into the office. All the while I was thinking of Judy Cooper and wondering what had made her hate her stepfather so much.

Mr Cooper looked more relaxed than he had been earlier, but Mrs Cooper had her legs crossed tightly and her arms folded across her chest.

I was putting the cups on to the tray when I heard my uncle say:

"Your stepdaughter's full name, Mr Cooper?"

Mrs Cooper spoke quickly.

"Judy Ann Hurst. She kept her father's name, my first husband."

I walked out of the office carrying the cups. I sat down at my desk.

Judy Hurst! Judy with the red hair and freckled skin. She'd been in my class at school. We hadn't been friends as such but I remembered her quite well. She'd left before A-levels and someone had said she'd got a job in a hairdresser's.

Judy Hurst! She was part of the gang of kids who hung around the pubs and clubs down by the docks; the well-dressed mob who drove around in their dads' cars. At least that's what Billy told me and he knew some of them quite well.

Judy Hurst kidnapped! Or faking it to get money out of her stepfather!

After Mr and Mrs Cooper had left I started to tidy up the mail and continued to think about the missing girl. I knew a lot of her friends, at least had known them when they were at school. I had been to some of the places that she went to, the clubs and the pubs. I could probably find out some things about her, about her life and her boyfriend.

I took my glasses off and put them on the desk. I

thought that maybe I should go into Uncle Tony's office and offer to find out what I could.

But I knew what he would say.

"Don't be silly, Patricia. You're an office worker. Don't get involved in the investigative side of the business."

So I didn't bother.

I thought about ringing Billy and arranging to go out that evening to one or two of the pubs that Judy and her friends used.

Just for a change, I told myself, nothing else.

2

A Night Out

Billy said that he would meet me down by the docks at about seven.

I got home from work about six. My mum was in the hall, talking to my dad on the phone. I could tell it was him because she was standing stiff and erect and pointing her finger into mid-air. I gritted my teeth. It had been weeks since he had rung her. She mouthed "hello" at me and I dashed up the stairs before she could grab me for a report on the daily workings of my uncle's private detective agency.

I threw off my skirt and top (matching, Peter Pan collar), my tights (20 denier) and my black court shoes (leather soles and uppers).

I put on my cotton trousers, a sweatshirt and my DMs. For the first time that day I felt comfortable.

No more breathing in to make sure my stomach wasn't sticking out; no more straightening my skirt every time I sat down to make sure it didn't end up a mass of wrinkles underneath me.

I hung the skirt and top carefully on a hanger. My mum had bought them for me and I knew that she would check to make sure they were there for Monday morning.

I tipped up my shoulder bag and watched my belongings spill on to the bed: my provisional driver's licence, my glasses case, my purse, my cash card holder, my make-up bag, my dental floss, a couple of scrunched-up tissues.

I put my purse and my dental floss in my pocket. I picked up the make-up bag and held it for a moment. Then I tossed it back on to the bed.

Don't get me wrong, I have nothing against wearing make-up. I quite like sitting in front of a mirror and colouring in bits of my face. Blues and greys, like pale water-colours on my eyelids, eye-liner that looks like felt tip, and lipstick, pillar box red, painted carefully round the edge of my mouth.

Sometimes, I just do a quick sketch with some mascara and a handy spot stick, maybe a touch of pale pink lipstick and a spot of blusher.

A lot of the time though, I like to go naked, no make-up at all. I like to feel the air against my skin. I like to rub my eyes furiously and not worry about mascara all over my cheeks.

I stood on my bed and looked at the hats on top of my wardrobe. I had about a dozen that I'd collected over the last year. There was a row of hat boxes my mum had found for me that held the more fragile ones, and on top were the hardy felt boaters and berets I mostly wore. I picked a straw hat with a floppy brim.

I put it on my head, glanced in the mirror, and decided to make my way to the docks.

When I went downstairs my mum was on the phone again. This time it was to her friend and I could hear her telling her that my dad had phoned and about time too. I kissed her quickly on the cheek and she mouthed goodbye, while at the same time rolling her eyes at my outfit.

I waved and got out quickly before she could give me the benefit of her advice on How a Young Lady of Nineteen Should Dress.

Billy was there when I arrived at the pub. He had already bought me a drink and it was sitting on the table beside him. He was reading a car magazine and just nodded to me as I went over and sat down.

I sipped my drink and Billy read on. If anyone had been watching us, they would have sworn that we were an old married couple.

Billy was my oldest friend. We'd been mates since we sat on the same desk at secondary school. I was eleven and wanted to be the second woman prime minister. Billy was never young. William, as he liked to be known then, was eleven going on nineteen, as sensible as the well-fitting shoes he wore. He hadn't known then what he wanted to be; let's wait and see what's available, he'd said, and that had been the end of the conversation.

He was one of those kids who knew all their rights and spoke up for himself. He was often telling the rest of us to "make a formal complaint" if a teacher was rude or shoved us. Or if someone was unpleasant and called me names, he would tell me to sue them for defamation of character.

The shoes wore out eventually and he bought a pair of trainers and let people call him Billy. His big love was computers and he spent all his free time on his PC. While we were all playing martial arts and war games he was trying to write programs for designing cars, his other great love.

Billy had a great future, everyone said. All his teachers predicted that he'd walk the exams and go straight to university.

But when his mum and dad were killed he dropped out of school. That's when he and I became close. He'd looked bewildered at the funeral, his eyes moving frantically here and there. He'd said afterwards, with an awkward laugh, that he'd been looking for someone to blame; someone to complain to.

Now he was nineteen going on forty-five. His

computer mostly sat untouched. He spent his time buying and selling cars. He took weeks doing them up; so much so that I often thought he would keep the one he was lovingly working on. He never did though. Once it was finished, we would take a couple of rides in it and he would sell it and buy another.

After a few moments I said:

"Remember Judy Hurst?" (Billy and I didn't usually bother with small talk. Whenever we met we always started to talk as though we were in the middle of a conversation.)

"Yes," he said, turning a page of his magazine.

"You'll never guess," I said, feeling momentarily thrilled with the information I had ready to reveal.

"She's gone missing," he said.

I was stopped in my tracks.

"How do you know?"

He folded up his magazine and took a mouthful of his drink.

"I saw a couple of the kids she hangs around with at the auction yesterday. They said she'd been missing for a couple of days. Disappeared!"

"Any idea who she was seeing? I mean her boy-friend?" I was remembering Mr Cooper's last words.

"Last I heard she was seeing Terry Hicks."

"Terry Hicks?"

"Mechanic, works in that Classic Car Care place

off the High Street. Nice-enough bloke, about twenty-five, going a bit thin on top, wears a ponytail. I sometimes have the electrics in my cars looked at there. What are you so interested for? I didn't think Judy Hurst was one of your crowd."

"She isn't," I said. I was going to go on and tell him about her parents coming into the office when he suddenly said:

"I went out with her once."

"Judy Hurst. When? You never told me!"

"I don't tell you everything," he said.

This wasn't true, Billy usually did tell me everything. When it came to girlfriends I usually got most of the details, just as he spent many an hour listening to stories about my meagre love-life.

Both of us had had fleeting relationships over the years. A couple of months was the longest I'd ever been "going out" with anybody. Billy had had one girlfriend for about a year but that was before his mum and dad's death. Since then it had been some evenings out with girls from school or, once, with a cousin of his.

Most people thought *we* should get together, he and I. It was true we had everything most people in a relationship had – except the kissing.

The previous Christmas we had almost had that.

I felt a pang of jealousy.

"When did you go out with Judy Hurst?"

"Oh, a couple of years ago. Just to see a film, I

think. I can't remember why I didn't tell you."

I looked across the table at him. His hair was a mess and his shirt collar looked as though it hadn't been ironed. I remembered, for a second, the moment we had kissed under the mistletoe in my mum's kitchen.

It had been Christmas Eve and we'd been watching a video while my mum was out. We'd just had some coffee in the kitchen and he'd stood up to leave. Sellotaped to the frame of the door was a piece of mistletoe.

"Give us a Christmas kiss then," he said, turning to me.

I'd puckered up my lips to kiss him and he'd done the same. It had been a very brief kiss, our lips hardly touching. His hands had been on my shoulders though and I could remember feeling the warmth radiating from them. After the kiss, instead of moving back, away from each other, we'd stayed in the same position and that had been the point at which one of us – I'm still not sure which one – had leant over and kissed the other gently on the mouth.

I'd closed my eyes and let his mouth move from side to side across mine. One of my hands came up and rested on his face. I had just been about to bring the other one up when the key scraping against the door outside had made us both jump apart.

My mum and a friend had come in, laughing and saying "ssh" to each other, unnecessarily. He'd gone home straight after that and we'd not mentioned it again, ever.

"Look who's here," Billy suddenly said.

I looked away from him to the door of the pub.

Two girls and a young man had just walked in. Sharon and Debbie Bradley. The terrible twins. They ignored us, walking straight over to the bar. The man, younger by a couple of years, followed them.

I began to get excited. The twins were part of the set that Judy Hurst hung around with.

"Do you want a drink?" I asked Billy. He had gone back to his magazine.

"Um," he said, handing me his glass. I walked over to the bar and stood beside Sharon Bradley.

"It's Sharon, isn't it?" I said, in my nicest voice.

The girl turned and looked at me, from my straw hat to my DMs and back again.

"Yes?" she said. The young man was whispering and laughing with the other twin.

"I thought it was!" I said, a wide smile on my face, throwing in as much pleasantness as I could. "I said to Billy, my friend, I'll bet that's Sharon and Debbie Bradley there, from the old school. It's me, Patsy Kelly, remember? We were in the same form."

Sharon looked at me for a minute, then raised her pencilled eyebrows.

"So it is," she said, turning away from me, towards her sister. "Well, look here, Debbie, it's someone from school; Patsy Kelly."

"Yes," I said, ignoring her body language. "Who was it you used to hang around with? Judy, Judy Hurst, that was it."

"That's right," Sharon said. Her sister, Debbie, stopped what she was saying to the young man and turned to face me.

"Poor Judy," she said and, looking at her sister and the young man, spluttered out some laughter. The young man joined in:

"Yes," he said, "she's gone missing!" and continued laughing.

"I'm sorry," I said, watching the three of them sharing the joke. I wondered what Mr Cooper would make of it.

I paid for our drinks and took them back to the table. Disappointment was needling me.

What had I hoped for? To find out some juicy piece of information that I could bring back to Uncle Tony. To show that I could help with the investigation? I had heard nothing new. Judy Hurst and her friends appeared to be doing exactly what Mr Cooper thought they were doing.

I put the two drinks on the table, disgruntled. It had been a waste of time coming here.

"There's a coincidence," Billy said, looking across at the group.

"What, Sharon and Debbie using this pub? I knew they came here. That's why I suggested we…"

"No," Billy said. "There we were talking about Judy Hurst and who should walk in but her brother, young Paul."

I looked back at the group at the bar. The young man had his arm around Sharon and was whispering something in her ear. His hand was resting on her shoulder and I could see his fingers tapping out the beat of the song that was playing on the jukebox.

He looked perfectly relaxed and happy.

"That's Paul Hurst?" I said.

"Yes, and doesn't he look upset about his poor, disappeared sister."

I sat back, my glass in my hand.

Was a member of Judy's family involved in the deception, as well?

Perhaps it hadn't been a waste of time coming after all.

3

Monday Blues

I ran as far as I could. I went along our street and into the next one. I passed the milk float three times and four times it passed me.

I kept thinking about Judy Hurst and her brother Paul. They'd been in my mind all weekend.

Every hundred metres or so I had to slow down and walk; my heart seemed to be throwing itself against the wall of my chest. Once, I stopped completely, leaned over a garden wall and took great lungfuls of air.

I could have rung my uncle Tony and told him what I had seen. A couple of times I went to the phone and started to dial. I'd stopped though; I kept remembering his words on the Friday evening before he'd left.

"It's hardly worth me starting to make enquiries.

This Judy will probably turn up on her front door-step at the weekend. It'll be all 'sorries' and 'I'll be a good girl' and that will be that."

He'd been looking in a tiny mirror at the time, combing his hair with his fingers and using his thumb to straighten his eyebrows.

He wasn't taking the Coopers' case terribly seriously.

"Nine times out of ten missing girls turn up," he'd said, before locking the office door behind us.

If Judy Hurst did return home at the weekend, then it might stir up more trouble if I suggested that her brother was involved. I jogged back to the top of my street and turned the corner. I held my elbows up and wiped the strained expression off my face; it wouldn't do to let my mum see me so exhausted.

I looked at my watch. It was seven-forty. Another hour and a half and I'd be at work. Then I'd know if Judy Hurst had gone home or not.

When I got to the front door my mum was warming up. She wore matching leggings and shorts and a long grey top that covered her bottom. She was standing in one spot leaning over to each side and letting her head wobble on her shoulders.

I managed a smile in between the breaths.

"Well done, Patsy!" she said, hugging one of her knees up to her chest, then letting it go again, "I told you a short run would make you feel better!"

"Yes," I smiled, and she cantered off out of the

front gate and along the street.

My mum is a health fanatic. She jogs every day, plays badminton and tennis, goes for long country walks and eats sensibly. Myself, I prefer riding around in cars and eating burgers. Every now and again Mum talks me into some sort of vigorous exercise. I usually do it just to please her but this time, with my new job, I had decided to get fit.

Inside, I collapsed flat on the settee, my arms dipping into the carpet, my legs hanging like lead weights. There was a vague unease in my head that was nothing to do with my general level of unfitness. I tried to put it out of my mind by thinking of Uncle Tony's words.

"Remember Patricia, I'm the detective, you're the office clerk."

When my breathing returned to normal I struggled up off the settee and went to get my office clerk disguise which was hanging in the wardrobe where I'd left it on Friday.

Mrs Cooper was at the office when I arrived. She was walking up and down in a state of great agitation. I could feel her heels digging into the floor every time she turned around. Uncle Tony was on the phone. Putting his hand over the mouthpiece he said:

"Patricia, get Mrs Cooper a cup of tea. Get her to sit down, she's a bit upset."

"Of course I'm upset," she said, throwing a look of daggers at my uncle. He had already turned his back though and was speaking to someone on the other end of the phone.

Mrs Cooper was wearing a deep blue jacket and trousers and her auburn hair was pulled back into a plait that crept down the back of her head. Her face was still pale but she had a touch of eye-shadow and mascara on.

"What's happened?" I said, taking my hat and jacket off and laying them on top of the filing cabinet.

"This!" Mrs Cooper thrust a brown envelope at me. "This is what's happened. It arrived this morning in the post."

I took the envelope from her. It was unexpectedly light, as though there was nothing in it at all. On the outside, the Coopers' name and address had been scrawled in a thick black felt-tip pen.

I could smell her perfume as she came and stood close by me. On her hand she had a single gold wedding ring that seemed to weigh her fingers down.

"Inside!" she said tersely. I decided I didn't like her at all; not one bit.

I tipped the envelope on to the desk. At first nothing came out but when I shook it more vigorously small curls of red hair fluttered out.

"It's Judy's hair!" Mrs Cooper said. "Look at it.

All her lovely hair cut off."

She fingered the back of her own hair and looked away, over at Uncle Tony's back, over to the door, as if she was expecting someone to walk in.

On the desktop sat the small pile of red curls. I touched the hair. It was wiry and felt harsh. Each clump of it was only about three centimetres long but there were dozens of them, as if someone had given Judy a complete short back and sides.

"Was there a note?" I said. I could hear my uncle Tony talking rapidly to someone on the telephone.

"Here," Mrs Cooper pushed a bit of paper in my direction. "I don't know why I'm showing this to you. It's *him* we're paying, not his secretary!"

I didn't bother to tell her that I wasn't even important enough to be his secretary. I just looked at the note and let her mumble on.

"NEXT TIME IT'LL BE SOMETHING MORE PAINFUL THAT WE CUT OFF."

That was it. No demands, no instructions, no warnings not to contact the police. I even turned it over, as though I might have expected there to be a PS, or a clue, like a whacking great ink fingerprint.

I didn't get any more time to look at it though, because Mrs Cooper plucked it from my hand and followed my uncle into his office. I could still hear her voice, cross and continuous. As soon as the door closed the intercom light flicked on and I heard:

"Patricia?"

"Yes?" I said, rising from my desk slightly. In front of me was the red hair, looking for a moment like a pile of copper wood-shavings. Maybe this was the time to go in and tell them about Paul Hurst. Then I heard:

"What happened to that cup of tea?"

I sat down on my seat again and, cupping my hand, I swept all the hairs off the table and into the envelope.

I was getting the china out of the cupboard when the outside door burst open. Mr Cooper stood there for a brief moment, looking distractedly at me. He was talking into his mobile phone again saying, "Yeah? Yeah? Well get them out!" He gestured at me with his finger and continued talking.

I looked him over. He was overweight, his stomach poking out through the opening in his blouson jacket. He wore fashionable trousers and a silk shirt. There was something not quite right about him though; the gold ring through his ear sat awkwardly against his thinning hair; he looked as though he'd be more comfortable in an old pair of jeans, sweatshirt and a woolly hat.

"Threaten them with the bailiffs, Harry. That's all you need to do." He was rolling his eyes, making fun of the person on the other end of the line. When he rang off he took a look around the office. Then he stopped for a minute and sniffed the air. "She already in there, is she?"

"Yes," I said.

He pushed the aerial back and clicked his tongue a couple of times. Patting his wispy hair into place he pocketed the mobile and went into my uncle's office.

"I'll get another cup then," I said wearily, to myself.

They were in my uncle's office for about thirty minutes. I turned the intercom on a couple of times but all I could hear was a one-sided argument that seemed to go on and on. It was mostly Mrs Cooper's voice, once or twice breaking into tears. Occasionally I heard Mr Cooper dismiss something she said or try to placate her. My uncle's voice was soft and whispery, and I could hear his chair legs scraping as he got up, presumably to go and comfort Mrs Cooper.

When I took the tea in they were sitting on opposite sides of the room again; she with the palm of her hand over her mouth, her eyes clinging on to my uncle. Mr Cooper was staring straight ahead, his mouth puckered in annoyance. My uncle was furiously writing things down.

It went quiet while I handed each of them a cup of tea and offered them a biscuit. It was on the tip of my tongue to tell them that I knew Judy and that I'd seen her friends and her brother in a celebratory mood the previous Friday.

Something stopped me though. The heavy atmosphere sat in the room like an invisible wall. My uncle Tony finally broke the silence by saying:

"Thank you, Patricia; now if we could recap…"

I went back into the outer office and quietly switched the intercom on.

"…I deal with a local forensic lab; they will look at the envelope and the hair. If there's anything interesting there, I'll let you know. Meanwhile, all you can do is to wait for the phone call that will inevitably come. It's like I said on Friday. We can do nothing to find Judy until either she or her friends contact us. If it transpires that she has been abducted, then similarly, we can do nothing until the kidnapper contacts us with instructions.

"My colleague, Bob Franks, has already attached the recorder to your telephone. That way we'll have the voice and every detail of the caller. When the instructions come, we'll follow them to a T. If it turns out to be your daughter's friends, then we'll catch them. If it is a real kidnapper, we'll have a head-start on him.

"I think this is our best option. Truly I do.

"I also think this delivery, the hair, means nothing. If Judy is playing tricks, then she's got herself a new haircut. If she's not, at least it shows that the abductor doesn't intend to hurt her, at least for the moment."

There was a mumble of voices. I thought I heard

Mr Cooper say something like: "exactly what I think"; and Mrs Cooper say: "I hope you're right."

When they came out, they were together. One of Mrs Cooper's arms was laced through her husband's. Her hand hung limply over his wrist though and her expression was stony.

My uncle Tony said:

"This is an awful business. It's so upsetting for you and your husband."

"And for my son," Mrs Cooper suddenly said. "My son Paul is devastated. He's been unable to go anywhere or do anything all weekend."

"I can imagine," my uncle said.

"There, love." Mr Cooper put his arm around his wife's shoulder. As he went out of the door he turned back to my uncle and said:

"Let us know if you hear anything."

After they'd gone I visualized Paul Hurst laughing and giggling with the terrible twins. I looked at the envelope that held the short red curls of hair and wondered what it all meant.

Paul Hurst devastated. My foot.

4

Judy Hurst

When my uncle Tony went out I rang Billy. I hadn't seen him all weekend and I wondered what he had been doing. I also intended to tell him about the latest developments in the Judy Hurst Case.

As the dialling tone sounded, I thought about what he'd said about Judy Hurst, about his date with her.

"Pretty girl, quite bright too, but not really interested in other people."

"You mean she didn't fancy you," I'd said mischievously.

"I don't mean that, but that's probably true as well. I mean that she had a couple of topics of conversation. Judy Hurst and Judy Hurst."

I let the phone ring and ring. I took my glasses off and rubbed my nose. Sometimes Billy was out in the garage working on his car and it took a while for him to register what the ringing was. I'd told him to get an answer-phone but he wouldn't.

He was right about Judy Hurst though.

I wasn't close to her at school but I did remember a few things.

She was one of those kids who grew up early. While the rest of us were still collecting stickers and packets of felt-tip pens, she was plucking her eyebrows and shaving her legs. She always had serious boyfriends, older lads who were already at work or college. While we were venturing out on the odd date or frantically snogging in the alley between the dining and the sports hall, she seemed to have some good-looking, well-off boyfriend meeting her outside the school gates. We could see them walking up the road together; the young man with his arm proprietorially around Judy's neck and Judy, throwing a quick glance over her shoulder, to see just who was looking.

It was her red hair that made her stand out so. It was dark auburn, not the carrot colour that some kids had to endure. It was thick too and she kept it carefully cut and shaped. That was in keeping with her whole personality really: careful, planned. The rest of us were always growing our hair, or having it permed or trying some new style that would enhance our looks, make us look a couple of years older, improve our love-lives. She was satisfied with what she had – a geometrical cut with no loose or flyaway ends.

The phone was still ringing. I looked at my watch. I decided to give it another twenty rings. If he didn't answer then, I'd hang up.

I had never spoken to Judy Hurst much, but then nobody really did; they listened. Judy spoke a great deal; about her clothes, her house, her mum's new car, her mum's new boyfriend, her intended holiday in the Seychelles or wherever it was. As soon as I'd heard it all once or twice I moved on, looking for someone with half a brain to talk to. Judy Hurst never seemed to notice, she just flicked her red hair in the direction of some other kid and started the whole story again.

Why Billy went out with her I'll never know. What is it that men look for in the opposite sex?

I'd counted to nineteen and was just about to put the receiver down when I heard the click of it being picked up.

"At last!" I said, in a mock angry voice. "Where have you been?"

"I'm sorry, do you want to speak to Billy? He's not here at the moment. Can I take a message?" It was a female voice. A soft whisper.

"Er…" I said, lowering my voice. Who was she? "…Just tell him…" Why had Billy got a *girl* answering his phone? "Yes … say that Patsy phoned. I'll call again later." I said it quietly, not wanting to sound loud and uncouth.

The phone clicked and I heard the heavy purr of the tone.

Billy Rogers had a girl in his house that he hadn't told me about. Maybe I didn't know him as well as I thought I did.

I was still thinking about Billy's mysterious girl as I walked along the Parade to the High Street. My uncle had given me an envelope file full of papers to deliver to a local solicitor's.

I pulled on the brim of my felt hat to stop the breeze from swiping it. I'd lost a hat like that before; one minute it had sat demurely on my head and the next it catapulted across the road. It had been red velvet, but when I picked it up from the pavement a few minutes after, it was damp and the crown had collapsed where someone had stepped on it. It was a dead hat. I'd buried it at the bottom of my wardrobe and been more careful since.

The papers were to do with a court case and my uncle said they had to be there by eleven o'clock. I hurried my steps.

What if Billy actually had a girlfriend? Someone he hadn't told me about?

I shook my head. Billy would tell me.

He hadn't told me about his date with Judy Hurst though.

There was a disgruntled feeling somewhere at the bottom of my ribs. I couldn't know everything about Billy's life; we were close friends, that was all.

It wasn't quite true though. My fingers rose up to my mouth and moved slowly up and down. The kiss came into my head again like a song I couldn't forget. I remembered Billy's hands on my shoulders, moving down my back a few inches and pushing my chest against his. Above us had been the sprig of mistletoe, dangling from a piece of Sellotape.

He'd never referred to it again though and now there was a strange girl answering his phone, taking messages for him in a breathless voice.

Feeling inexplicably sorry for myself I walked up the steps to the solicitor's.

The clerk took hours (or so it seemed) checking through the documents I'd brought. He kept stopping off to have a conversation with a woman at the other end of the office about a blocked drain he'd had. A hundred and twenty pounds the estimate had been and when it was finished the plumber had tried to charge him two hundred. He'd soon changed his tune when he'd found out he was in law, the clerk said. The woman had a habit of repeating odd portions of what the clerk was saying – *two hundred pounds … changed his tune … in law…* Her voice was like a sad echo.

Finally the clerk handed me a notarized receipt and as I left I could hear him retelling parts of the story – the plumber came in a resprayed British Telecom van; you could tell because parts of the logo were still showing through. *Resprayed van...* the woman's voice chorused. I let the door swing quietly behind me.

Outside it was still windy.

I'd stopped thinking about Billy and it was only then that I recognized the road I was in. It was the parade of shops that was quite close to our old school. There was the chip shop where we used to buy our lunch, and the Greek baker's that sold baklava and sandwiches.

I began to feel saliva forming in my mouth and I looked across the road at the sweet shop that still had the old handwritten notice in its window: only three schoolchildren at a time. I noticed a couple of kids in dark grey uniform hanging around the corner.

I'd only left school three months ago and already it was like another land, a different time. It was as though I had never worn that stiff grey skirt and shapeless blazer, as though the hours and days and weeks sitting inside the high-ceilinged classrooms had never happened.

Don't get me wrong, I wasn't disowning school; I had good feelings about it, mostly; but it was as if it had happened to someone else, some young kid who laughed and giggled her way through lessons, who got excited on school outings and who spent hours on projects about dairy farms in Holland.

That kid wasn't me; it was someone else.

It was while I was philosophizing on these matters that I noticed Paul Hurst standing across the road.

The traffic was crawling past and a bus came to a stop between us. When it finally moved on he was still there, facing me, in conversation with a young man who had his hair drawn back into a ponytail.

For some reason I stepped back into the doorway of a shop, as though I was afraid of them seeing me. I pulled the brim of my hat down and looked through the traffic. After a few seconds the man Paul was talking to turned and I saw his face. It wasn't anybody that I knew.

Then I noticed the shop they were standing in front of: "Classic Car Care". It was the shop that Billy used; he had his car electrics checked there.

The boy that Paul Hurst was talking to was Terry Hicks, Judy Hurst's boyfriend. It had to be. His front hair was thinning and he had a ponytail.

The young man turned suddenly and walked off. Paul Hurst shouted something at him and above the wheezing engines and grumbling exhausts I heard the words: "...later, Terry." The young man didn't look round, he simply raised one arm in a kind of backward wave. Paul Hurst waited a few seconds then shrugged his shoulders and walked off.

It had to be him; Terry Hicks, Judy's boyfriend.

I watched his back grow smaller in the distance. Where was he going? Was he going to meet his kidnapped girlfriend?

Inside me there was about ten seconds' indecision.

My uncle's face came into my head. His words sounded in my ear, as though he was standing behind me and whispering them:

"I'm the detective; you're the office clerk."

That was when I decided to follow Terry Hicks.

5

Shadow

Terry Hicks had a long stride. He was already a good bit ahead of me when I started and as the seconds moved on he seemed to get further away. Keeping my fingers crossed that he wouldn't turn around I broke into a slow run, dodging in and out of the shoppers, and covered most of the distance between us. When I was about twenty metres or so behind him I slowed down to a walk again.

After we'd covered about a kilometre he took a sudden left off the High Street. He was heading in the direction of the river. I turned the corner and followed as inconspicuously as I could, keeping a number of people between us.

He turned again, off the more busy road into a side street full of small terraced houses. There were fewer people and I began to feel too close to him. I slowed down and dropped further back, letting an old woman with a shopping basket on wheels overtake me.

At that moment Terry Hicks looked back over his shoulder. I kept going even though I felt my mouth fill up with saliva. He turned back though and continued walking. I swallowed and carried on. I looked up briefly and saw that we were in Primrose Street and then, turning left, we were in Rose Avenue. There was a group of kids on bikes lounging by the side of the road. As Terry Hicks passed them a couple broke off from their friends and started to walk in the same direction. It meant that there were four people between us: the woman with the shopping trolley, a man and his dog, and the two boys.

I relaxed for a minute and watched Terry walk ahead. It was a long, curving, avenue and I knew that it led down towards the river.

I wondered if he was going to see Judy Hurst; going to the place where she was hiding out. It made sense for her to stay in one of the houses along by the old industrial estate.

The streets in that area had been dilapidated and run down for some years. Rows of houses and old factories had been bought up for redevelopment; some flashy marina, I think, but it hadn't happened. The company had run out of money and the houses and buildings had been left to crumble. Billy and I sometimes drove round that way when he was testing his cars. The houses were a mixture of rambling Victorian semis and terraced cottages that had been condemned as uninhabitable by the local council even though many people in fact still lived there. They were a mixture of squatters and the homeless and down-at-heel families. It was a rough area; people minded their own business, looked after themselves.

It was the perfect place to hide out in.

I walked on, to the point where the only two people in the street were myself and Terry Hicks. At some point he was going to turn round and notice me; I needed to look different, quickly.

What did *real* detectives do? Did my uncle Tony carry a small case of disguises with him? A fake moustache? I almost stopped and laughed. I imagined him with a flat black attaché case stopping at the corner of every street, emerging seconds later with round black glasses and a beard, or a red wig and a monocle.

I had to think quickly; Terry was moving well ahead.

I went into a corner shop and bought a news-paper. I took off my hat and tucked it inside my coat. I walked out of the shop with the newspaper held up, not covering my face, but so it looked as though I was concentrating on it. My hair, previously held down by my hat, was flying about wildly in the breeze.

A couple of Asian women in saris came out of one of the houses, and I let them walk between me and Terry Hicks. After a few minutes I got out my glasses and put them on, tucking the back of my hair into my collar.

Terry Hicks looked round again but I just continued to walk, hoping that I looked different enough. He stood for a few seconds and I groaned inwardly, realizing that within a few moments I would have to pass him. He turned back though and started walking again. I was closer to him than I wanted to be, so I waited for a few seconds and then bent down, as if to tie up my shoe-laces.

The end of the avenue was in sight and he turned right, towards the river. I dropped the newspaper and took off my glasses and jacket. As I walked along I noticed a cardboard box that had been dumped by a wall. I picked it up, put my jacket and hat and bag inside it and carried it in front of my chest. Then I started to walk towards the road that led to the river.

When I turned the corner I almost skidded to a halt because there, half-way down the road, was Terry Hicks, knocking at the door of one of the houses. He looked casually in my direction and I had no choice but to walk on down the road. As I passed the house I bowed my head as if looking into the contents of my box. I walked briskly and just as I was a few metres on, the front door clicked open and I heard a female voice.

I didn't hear either the words or Terry's reply. All I heard was the bang of the door as it shut after him. I turned the corner of the street, put the box down on the pavement, and wondered what to do.

I looked at my watch. It was one o'clock. I'd been due back at the office ages ago. If I went back now, with no information, it would have been a complete waste of time and Uncle Tony would be angry with me for having stayed out so long.

I needed to go back to that house and see who Terry had met there. In my head I already knew. It had to be Judy Hurst, hiding out, waiting for her stepfather to pay a ransom for a fake kidnap.

I had a stroke of luck.

A small lorry came up behind me and turned into the road. From where I was standing I could see that it had pulled up almost opposite the house that Terry had gone into. The driver got out and went into a house nearby. Without thinking, I walked back across the road and within a couple of seconds I was standing, hidden by the lorry, looking directly at the house that Terry had gone into.

What I was going to do if the driver came out again and wanted to take his lorry away I didn't know. I just hoped I wasn't going to be there for very long.

The house was one of the big three-storey ones, semi-detached. Its window frames appeared to be hanging in shreds and the roof was visibly bowing. It had a small front garden which was overgrown with ivy and weeds. Along the wall outside someone had painted the words: HOMES BEFORE PROFIT.

My eyes flicked up and down the building. Then I saw them, in the upstairs front room window; Terry Hicks in a deep kiss with a girl. She had her back to me but I could see that she was shorter than him. Her hair was close into her head and I could see the familiar flash of auburn, even through the grimy windows.

That was where Judy Hurst was hiding out.

I began to walk back towards town and my uncle's office.

6
Found

My uncle was out when I got back to the office. There was an angry note pinned to the door. It said:

Waited for you to come back from the solicitor's. Where the hell have you been? Had to go and see the path. lab about the Hurst hair. Will be back about four. Keys are with Mrs Johnson from the baker's.

I almost stamped my foot with frustration. I had found Judy Hurst. I was desperate to tell my uncle, to see the amazement in his eyes. I wanted to see the look on my mum's face when he told her that I had cracked the case.

I was bursting with news and there was no one to tell it to.

I went along to the "Crusty Bake" and got the key

from Mrs Johnson. While I was there I bought a tuna mayonnaise roll and an iced finger. I went back into the office and put the kettle on. It was quarter-past two.

While the kettle was boiling I switched the answer-machine on and got my pad out. There were a couple of messages from the solicitor's and a call from Auntie Geraldine. I looked at my watch. It was almost three o'clock. Uncle Tony had said he would be back about four. I bit into my tuna roll and sat down to wait.

My uncle Tony got back at about ten to five. When he heard the story he was furious.

He stood up and sat down. He walked across to the filing cabinet and opened the drawer; then he slammed it shut.

At first I thought he was angry with me for getting involved at all.

But he wasn't. It was quite the opposite.

"You mean you've known since *Friday* that her friends and her brother might be involved in this deception and you didn't say anything? What if Mr Cooper had paid over thousands of pounds at the weekend?"

"You said she might go home at the weekend…" I said weakly. I was surprised at his anger. It hadn't seemed to me as though he'd been bothered about the case at all.

"*Thousands* he might have been swindled out of and you've known this since Friday."

He stopped for a moment and looked murderously at me.

"I'm sorry…"

"No time for excuses now! We'll discuss it later, after we've got the Hurst girl. Then we'll see, my girl, then we'll see if you've still got a job."

I closed my eyes and grabbed my jacket. My hat was sitting on top of the filing cabinet and I put it on, for once glad of the shelter it seemed to give me.

In the car I sat close to the window, as far from my uncle as I could get. He said a few things at first and I answered, making excuses and then giving directions. After a while there was complete silence.

At the best of times I felt uneasy with my uncle Tony. My mum said it was because I wasn't used to being around an older man. That was possibly true; it had been over four years since my dad had left home. I still saw him, although his job meant that he travelled a lot and was often out of London. When he was around we went to the theatre or to concerts. But he wasn't like a parent, he was like a good friend. I couldn't remember any time during the last few years when he and I had rowed seriously about anything. It was something that annoyed my mum intensely: the fact that my dad wouldn't act the way she thought a responsible parent should.

So my uncle Tony became a bit like a replacement.

My mum always made sure that he saw my school reports, and he was always invited to family occasions like my birthday or Christmas. Frequently, if there were problems, my uncle would sit in the biggest chair in the living room while my mum explained it all to him. Then he would pronounce, like a stern father.

It was funny really. My dad was like a sweet uncle who pampered me, and my uncle was like a stiff and awkward father who didn't.

I looked across the car at his profile. He was muttering something under his breath and I could see by the way he was gripping the steering wheel that he was still angry with me.

I tried to make myself feel better by imagining the scene an hour on. We'd take Judy home to Mr and Mrs Cooper. There might be some angry words and recriminations but that would be their business; we would have done our bit.

It was getting dark when we pulled up outside the house. The door was closed and it looked as though it was pitch-dark inside. I wondered if Judy Hurst had spent the nights here. Perhaps her boyfriend or her brother stayed with her, or even the terrible twins, Sharon and Debbie.

There was an old-fashioned metal knocker on the door and my uncle banged it loudly. There was no answer so I walked backwards into the middle of the street to look up into the room where I had seen Terry Hicks and Judy a few hours before. That was when I noticed the number on the door, 150, scribbled above the letterbox.

"Are you sure this is the right place?" Uncle Tony looked at me.

"Yes…" I said, certain in my mind but looking around just to please him.

"Did you write the name of the street down? The number?"

No I hadn't. I said nothing.

"First rule, young Patricia –" I hated it when he started to talk to me like that – "write everything down: times, places, faces, street names, phone numbers…" he continued, mentioning every possible detail of information he could; at the same time he walked into the untidy front garden and looked in the bay window. His voice was low and it was as if he wasn't talking to me but reciting his times-table: "…hospital numbers, opening times, closing times, car registration details…"

That was when the front door sprang open and a man stepped out and stood, stock-still, a few metres from us.

My uncle stopped in the middle of his next word and for a mini-second the two of us looked at each other with surprise.

The man stood rigidly, his hands in mid-air like fists, as though he were about to offer either of us a fight. He was wearing a massive overcoat with a duffle bag over his shoulder.

"What's the matter…" I started to say but he looked at me and then said:

"I never done nothing."

And he turned and started to walk away, breaking into a run a few metres up the road. We were still standing there as he merged into the darkness.

When I looked back my uncle had already gone into the house and had switched on a light. I stood at the door. The hall was a dull yellow colour and the place smelt of damp. I leant against the door jamb and felt the cold penetrate my jacket. It was a dreary place and there was a bad feeling there.

My uncle had run up the stairs. I could hear him calling out Judy's name. I walked gingerly down the hall taking care not to brush against the damp-looking walls. I pushed against the living room door and it opened on to an empty room with only the light from the street outside shining in. The back room was the same but darker. The light-fitting hung emptily from the ceiling and there was a single chair in the corner.

I came back into the hall and saw the cellar door under the stairs. I pulled on the handle but it was tightly closed. All sorts of forebodings went through me as I imagined a stuffy, underground room.

I could hear my uncle's footsteps coming down the stairs and I stood back as he came over to the door and yanked it open, all the time muttering under his breath. I stepped away as he shone his torch into the cellar and disappeared down the stairs, enveloped by the blackness. I turned, and a few metres away was the kitchen door, slightly ajar. The room was in darkness and there was a powerful smell in the air, like paraffin or petrol.

"There's some old rubbish down there, nothing else. I'm sure you've got the wrong place," my uncle's voice came from behind me. It had a hint of superiority about it. He had been right, I had mucked it up.

"No," I said.

I was about to argue with him but I stopped because I saw something in the gloom of the kitchen, a shape I hadn't been able to make out before.

"What's in there, Patricia?" Tony was looking at his watch, doing up the buttons on his coat. He had finished his search.

I used my free hand to push gently against the kitchen door so that it opened a few more centimetres. The light from the hall threw a yellow glow into the room.

I held my breath, not wanting to look. In the end I forced my eyes to move into the room and search out the shape that I had seen.

It was on the floor, small and white. An outstretched hand.

I closed my eyes and opened them again.

It was still there, lying palm up, its fingers curled.

I felt my uncle behind me, his breath on my neck.

"What's that smell..." he started to say and then was struck silent.

After a few seconds of looking at the long, curled fingers, the painted nails, he said:

"My God. My good God, what's happened here?"

7

Dead

I'd never seen a dead body before.
For me, death was about flowers and dark wood
coffins, women whose pale faces were covered with
black netting and men with strained expressions
patting each other on the shoulder, unable to speak.
It was a TV version and it didn't prepare me for
what I saw that night.

My uncle turned on the light. It was one of those
strip fluorescent bulbs that took a few seconds to
light up. It gave a couple of lightning-like flashes
and then it was black again before it filled the room
with brightness.

It was during those two or three flashes that I got
my first look at Judy Hurst. She was lying on her
back with her eyes staring up at the ceiling and her

mouth open. It was like a couple of slides being shown in quick succession, then darkness. In the first I saw her white face and neck. In the second I just saw her eyes, like two glass replicas, fixed on some point directly above.

I'd known she was dead when I'd pushed the door open and looked into the room. But the sight of her was still a shock. Her expression was frozen and her face looked like that of a plastic doll. She was like a shop window dummy that had been discarded from a display. She'd been buried by the darkness and by putting the light on we'd unearthed her. It didn't seem right.

Even though I hadn't liked her much, had no feelings for her, there was a sensation of dread forming in my stomach and my knees felt weak. I put my arm out to lean on the door.

All the time I could smell the petrol. It was that pungent smell that hung around Billy's kitchen, from his overalls and from bits of cars that he insisted on working on inside the house. My uncle walked around me. He kept saying: *my God, my good God*, and shaking his head.

I stepped closer and looked at Judy's clothes; dark leggings, some kind of black sweatshirt. Up on her neck there was a dark stain. It was dried and looked like reddish mud but I knew that it wasn't. I squatted down and touched her arm. It was cool but not cold.

Still she stared up at the ceiling. I wanted to shake her arm and say, *wake up Judy, wake up*.

My uncle was tiptoeing around the body and I stood up and looked away. On the floor, a few metres away, was a large black metal spanner, the type that was used in car maintenance. Billy had loads of them, all different sizes.

The smell seemed heavier since the light had come on. My uncle looked up, his face puzzled, sniffing the air. I looked around the room and saw, over by the back door, a can that had tipped on to the floor. A colourless liquid had spilled from it. My uncle saw it at that moment as well and said:

"He was going to set the place on fire as well. Let's get out of here. We'll call the police on the mobile."

Within ten minutes there were three panda cars and an ambulance in the street. I was sitting on a wall beside Tony's car trying to take in what had happened. Judy Hurst was dead on the floor of that meagre little kitchen. The murderer had already sprinkled the room with petrol, intending, no doubt, to cover up evidence, to make it look as though she had died from the fire.

Only four hours before I had seen her kissing Terry Hicks in the upstairs bedroom.

The question that kept forcing itself into my mind was: *if I had contacted my uncle more quickly, would she still be alive?*

There was a procession of police in and out of the front door. They carried stuff in and came back out again, sometimes talking into their radios, sometimes just walking a few metres and looking up and down the street. I heard them saying things to each other: *nice-looking kid ... hit on the back of the head ... path. on his way...*

My uncle Tony fidgeted the whole time; in and out of the house, pacing up and down the pathway. He knew the CID people that came, an older man and a woman. He rushed over to their car as it pulled up and before they'd even opened their doors he was explaining it: *a case I'm on ... an alleged kidnap but the father – the stepfather – was suspicious ... eighteen-year-old girl ... several blows to the back of the head ... murder weapon ... a few metres away by the looks of it...*

Hello, Tony, I could hear the woman officer say, *still driving that old Ford? How's Geraldine these days?*

Then my uncle scurried inside the house behind them and I didn't see him for a while.

Judy Hurst hit on the back of the head, *several times*. I felt a shiver stirring in my shoulders. She was hit from behind, perhaps when she wasn't expecting it. Then the can of petrol to burn the evidence.

I thought of the man who had come out of the

house. He was dishevelled-looking but then so were most of the people who squatted or rented the houses around there. I remembered his fighting stance, his fists clenched as though he expected trouble from us. Had he killed Judy?

The CID officers came out, my uncle between them chattering away: *my niece works for me ... knew some of the dead girl's friends ... said she knew the girl was here ... came as soon as I knew.*

The woman was lighting up a cigarette and the man was peeling off a pair of thin rubber gloves.

I've seen worse, the man said, *remember that case over the other side of the river? Down by the marina?* The gloves were skin-like and he was having trouble pulling them off.

Don't remind me, the woman said, *I didn't eat for a couple of days.*

We got into two cars to drive down to the police station and give statements. As we moved away I turned and looked back down the street. I saw a battered sign that was pinned to a wall: EMPRESS ROAD. The only other thing I noticed was the white ribbon that was cordoning off the area. It was attached to the lamp-posts and the gate and it hung like macabre bunting in the darkness.

We spent nearly three hours at the police station. I told the whole story and the CID man wrote it all down on a form for me to sign. The woman smoked one cigarette after another. She asked me what A-levels I had done and I told her.

Uncle Tony was in another room.

About nine o'clock he drove me home. It was the first time we had been alone since the find.

In the car he avoided talking about it. He talked about the two CID officers that we'd been with. He'd known them some years before when he was still working in the police force. The man, Derek, had been in college with my uncle and had gone into CID a couple of years before he did. The woman, Heather, had only joined the force a year before my uncle had left. She had been promoted two years in a row and was now senior to his friend who had been around for longer and knew more about the area. It was the way of life, my uncle said, positive discrimination. It made him sick.

When we got to my front door he finally broached the subject.

There was no point in me feeling bad about what had happened. I'd done my best, after all. He'd been right though, when he'd told me to keep out of the investigative side of things. I should have told him the minute anything had come to light. He was the expert, after all.

My mum opened the door and he handed me over to her. It was as if I'd fallen over in the street and been taken home by a kind adult. My mum was all sympathy.

I was to have a couple of days off, my uncle said, to get over the shock. He was going to a security conference on Thursday and I could go back into the office. Until then I should forget all about it.

He was just off to see the Coopers.

The door closed and my mum started talking. I listened to her with one ear. She kept telling me not to be upset or to feel guilty; I'd done my best.

I agreed with her and the conversation finished with some hugs. After half a sandwich I had a shower and went into my bedroom. I sat on the duvet, my hair dripping and my arms and legs hanging damply out of the towel.

Judy Hurst had been zipped up inside a black plastic bag. She would be taken to a mortuary, undressed and then there would be a post-mortem. I knew the procedure. I had watched enough cop shows on the TV.

But if I had told my uncle on Saturday morning that I had seen Judy's brother laughing about her disappearance, Judy Hurst might still be alive. She'd be in trouble no doubt, her stepfather and her mother not speaking to her for days on end.

But she'd be alive.

I'd done my best, but it had not been good enough.

8

Driving

Billy took me for a drive on the Wednesday morning. It was the first time I'd seen him since the previous Friday when we'd seen Paul Hurst and the terrible twins. I remembered the girl who had answered his phone. I hadn't thought about her since Monday. My mind had been taken over by Judy Hurst; first trying to find her and then her death. Now I was obsessed by my part in the events.

I got into the driver's seat and put the seat belt on.

Billy said: "I got you some strawberry Fruitellas and a Milky Way;" as if we were in the middle of a journey and I'd specifically asked for them.

"Thanks," I said, taking the sweets. I wasn't really hungry but I opened the Milky Way and took a bite.

*   *   *

I hadn't been in touch with Billy since finding Judy Hurst's body. I hadn't spoken to anyone. When I'd woken up on Tuesday my mum had already left for work. I'd gone downstairs, made myself a cup of tea and hung aimlessly around the kitchen, lounging against the sink, loitering by the fridge, staring intently at the wall phone.

What had I hoped for? That the phone would ring and it would be my uncle saying that Judy Hurst wasn't really dead, she'd just been in a coma? Once they'd got her to hospital she'd woken up and was now sitting up in her hospital bed, her mum and stepdad on either side, the local paper taking pictures of her miraculous story for the "human interest" section?

I'd gone up to my room and tried to shake off the feelings of defeat and frustration that I felt. I told myself that I had not killed Judy Hurst. I had done everything I could to make sure that she was found. I had acted out of the best of motives in not telling my uncle that I had seen Paul Hurst.

I was not to blame, I told myself.

For a few moments I'd felt strong, as if the effect of those words had stiffened up my muscles, my bones. But later, when I was trying to decide what to wear, my back had turned into elastic and my stomach had folded in on itself. I'd lain down on my bed and pulled the duvet around me, even though I wasn't cold.

I hadn't rung Billy.

I knew he would hear bits and pieces of the story. I should have contacted him and filled him in on the details. If it had been the other way round I'd have expected it from him.

I avoided it though, imagining his sensible face, his grown-up, responsible ways, his quiet way of making me feel like a primary school kid.

When my mum had said he was on the phone on Wednesday I almost made a hand signal to her to say that I was in the bath. In the end I'd taken the receiver.

"I've got the Mini ready. I want to test drive it. Fancy a driving lesson?" he'd said.

I could easily have said no, that I was unwell, still in shock. I didn't though. I took a deep breath, picked out a cotton hat that covered my head, forehead and ears, put my glasses on and waited for him to come.

After I finished the Milky Way I scrunched up the wrapping and rolled it between the palms of my hands until it was a little ball. I started to throw the ball in small arcs from one hand to the other, across the driving wheel, concentrating on it as though it was the most important thing in the world.

"You might as well tell me," I heard Billy say after a couple of minutes.

He was right. I swallowed hard and turned to look at him.

"I messed up, Billy," I said, "and someone's dead because of it."

"Where are we going?" I said, turning the key in the ignition.

"Anywhere you like," he said. "What about out to the airport and back?"

"OK, fasten your seat belts." I put my foot on the clutch, put the car in gear and pressed the accelerator. Then I had to raise the foot I had on the clutch while pressing my other foot down on to the accelerator. At the same time I had to put my indicator on, look over my left shoulder and in my back mirror while moving slowly away from the pavement.

"All clear my way," Billy said and I moved slowly out, my eyes darting from one mirror to another, my head swivelling on my neck, looking behind, then forward, then down at the gears then forward again. I turned the wheel, clicked the indicator on, eased the choke out and took the hand-brake off.

Once on the road it wasn't so bad. All I had to do was go up through the gears, then come down again; stop at lights, move away from lights, keep my distance from other cars and watch out for the two Ps: push-bikes and pedestrians.

"Which way shall we go?" I said, aware that he hadn't spoken much since I'd told him everything that led up to Judy's death.

"Let's go out along the dual carriageway. Then back via the river. That's a good round trip."

The car was a yellow Mini and I'd been with Billy at the auctions a few weeks before when he'd bought it. It had been in an accident and its front had been completely smashed in. Across the top of the windscreen was the remnants of a sticker that said "SAMMY". There may have been another name that went across the top of the passenger seat but it wasn't there any more.

The car had been parked up for some time; the paintwork had a growth of rust, like algae, along its edges. There were blisters of rust dotted here and there and the roof had a great buckle in it.

Billy had been positively ecstatic about it. He'd kept walking around it making notes on a small pad. I could hear him mumbling things like: *respray job, panel beating, new engine*. The more things he'd found wrong with it the happier he'd seemed.

He'd got it for a very low price and then had to pay someone to deliver it to his garage. All the way home in his car he'd had a smile on his face as though someone had just given him a thousand quid.

I'd been talking to him about the new job my uncle had offered me in his detective agency. I'd not been sure whether I should take it or not. I'd been adding up the pros and cons.

I'd been speaking loudly because of the noise of the cassette. I could see Billy's profile out of the corner of my eye.

It was better to be working than not; it was experience of something; I could get another job after it, I'd have references; it meant that money would go into my bank account instead of out of it.

On the other hand, if I committed myself for three months it meant that I'd have to turn down any other job that came up; it was only office work, filing and answering the phone; it was my uncle who I didn't care for much; my mum would have a daily report on my comings and goings.

"What shall I do?" I'd said to Billy. The song on the cassette had just finished and there was just the hum of the engine against the silence of the tape.

"Um?" he'd said.

"Well, tell me," I'd said, turning in my seat to look at him.

"Oh," he'd said, "I'll customize it. It'll be a lot of work, there's no doubt, but I'm sure I could do it. It'll involve a bit of cash outlay but it'll be beautiful when I finish it."

I had my mouth open to say something just as the next song on the cassette blasted out.

"I love this one," Billy had said, leaning over to turn up the volume. I pulled my beret down over my forehead and sank back into my seat.

"By the way," he'd said, loudly, above the roar of the song, "I'd take that job, if I were you, it'll keep you off the streets for a while."

The airport looked deserted. We parked in front of the fence that divided the runways from the fields around. There were two single-seater planes parked at angles on the runway. A mechanic was working on one of the engines. Further along the field there was a bigger plane, maybe a twelve-seater.

We got out of the car. Billy was walking around it, looking at the wheels. I was leaning against the side, my palms flat down on the roof and my chin resting on them.

"So," Billy finally said, "the sum total is, you think you're responsible for Judy Hurst's death?"

Billy often did that, start his sentences with, *the sum total is…* It was as if he'd been doing mental arithmetic with all the information I'd given him, adding this bit and that bit, minused another section, multiplied it all and subtracted the first point I'd made.

"Not exactly…"

"That if you'd not taken that job with Sherlock Holmes, Judy Hurst would still be alive?"

"No…" He made it sound as though I was claiming some glory in it: *my part in the death of kidnap girl; exclusive.*

"You didn't kill her, Pat. Somebody picked up a

65

bloody great spanner and hit her on the back of the head. That somebody wasn't you."

"I know. But if I'd told my uncle about Paul Hurst being in the pub on Friday, the whole thing would have been over at the weekend. They would have found her and she'd be alive."

"Yes, and if Judy and her boyfriend hadn't faked the kidnap she'd still be alive; if Judy's mum had never married Mr Cooper, Judy would still be alive."

"All right. I take the point."

I was quiet for a moment. It was all right for Billy to be so certain about it; he hadn't been there, hadn't seen that grey, drab house and Judy's curled fingers, stiff as concrete by now. I decided to change the subject.

"The car's looking great."

I wasn't lying. It was a vivid sunflower yellow and it looked as though it had just rolled off a conveyor-belt. Billy had changed the tyres and the windows and put a sun-roof in, where the buckle had been.

"How much are you going to sell it for?" I said, but he just shrugged his shoulders and pulled the bonnet up.

That was Billy all over. He loved doing up the cars but once they were finished he lost interest in what was going to happen to them.

He looked at his watch.

"I'll drive back along the river. You can show me the house where you found Judy. OK?"

He got into the driver's seat before I could answer.

We took the long scenic route. Billy went through as many backstreets as he could, slowing down and turning corners, sitting in small queues of traffic, letting the engine hum quietly at traffic lights or pedestrian crossings; then revving it up to a roar before shooting off.

He believed in testing the car properly. He was thorough, a perfectionist; up against him I usually looked slapdash. I sat back and watched the houses pass by, the people on their way to the shops. As we came nearer to the industrial area around the river, I began to feel a creeping panic. I covered it with talk.

"My mum got a phone call from Tony last night. He filled her in on the developments. The police are looking for the man who ran out of the house before we went in."

"Maybe he was breaking in and she just startled him," Billy said.

"Well, I don't know. It turns out that the man has a history of arson. The police think he might have been trying to burn the house down and she just happened on him, frightened him perhaps."

"How did he get into the house?"

"He lived there from time to time. Apparently, some of the squatters pay a basic rent so he may have had a key."

"Um."

Billy turned into Empress Road and I pointed up the street to the house. As we got closer I could see that some shreds of the white ribbon were still attached to the lamp-post. We pulled up a few yards beyond it.

"They identified the man from some prints in the house," I said, looking at the overgrown garden.

"It's neat though," Billy said, turning the engine off.

"What do you mean?" I glanced up at the first-floor window, the last place that I had seen Judy Hurst.

"That Judy was murdered by one of her stepdad's tenants!"

"What?"

"George Cooper is a landlord. He owns lots of the houses round here. I thought you knew. He was in the local paper a while ago for letting sub-standard housing. There was quite a fuss about it."

I hadn't known.

No one had told me and I hadn't bothered to find out. As I said, I was slapdash. I picked up the Fruitellas and started to unwrap the packet.

I looked up at the grey house with its crumbling brickwork.

"Let's get away from here," I said.

9

Paperwork

On my way into the office I bought the local paper. The story was on the front page.

LOCAL BUSINESSMAN'S STEPDAUGHTER FOUND SLAIN.
Body discovered in one of George Cooper's "slum" properties

I folded the paper up, put it in my bag and walked on to the office.

It was my first day back. My uncle had left for Manchester that morning. He'd left me a list of instructions and jobs to do. I was just to mind the office while he was away, answer the phones.

I had no intention of doing anything else. Billy

and I were going to the cinema that evening. It was a way of getting it all off my mind.

I picked up the key for the office from the "Crusty Bake".

The office smelled of stale smoke and I opened the window. I clicked the radio on and filled the kettle. Then I looked at my uncle's list: *telephone, filing, and send out reminders of bills.*

All straightforward stuff; nothing that I could mess up.

I laid the local paper flat out on the desk, put some milk in my tea and sat down to read. Most of the stuff in it I already knew.

The battered body of eighteen-year-old Judy Hurst was discovered in one of the notorious river slums owned by her stepfather, businessman George Cooper.

The gruesome find was made on Monday evening by a private investigator who had been hired to find the Hurst girl.

Judy Hurst, a hairdresser, had been missing from her home for some days when the fatal blows were inflicted. It is understood that the murder scene was sprinkled with petrol.

The police are keen to contact Steven Hardy, a twenty-five-year-old, unemployed man of no fixed address. It is believed that he had previously resided at the house and was thought to be in the area at the time of the murder.

* * *

I folded up the newspaper.

The man's name was Steven Hardy. He hadn't looked twenty-five though, he'd looked younger. And there'd been no mention of the kidnap plot.

I sat back in the chair. It was nine-thirty and the day yawned emptily ahead of me. The jobs my uncle had left me to do were minor; a couple of hours' work. I reprogrammed the radio to a music station and started to work through the files.

I had to glance through the top sheet of each file and see if there was any outstanding money owed. If there was I had to type a pre-prepared letter, gently reminding the client that they hadn't paid their bill. It was the sort of job that could have been done in minutes, if only my uncle had owned a computer.

While I was doing it I had a browse through my uncle's cases. He did a mixture of work. There was an insurance company he worked for that was based in Manchester. He had three on-going investigations for them: a house fire, a back injury and a shop theft. They were similar cases; the insured people had made large claims for damage: the house had been gutted by fire just weeks after the owner had had his final notice from the mortgage company to quit; an anonymous phone call had been received from someone to say that the man with the back injury was faking it; the hi-fi shop that had been broken into had claimed a loss of stock that wouldn't have fitted in a store twice its size.

Then there were the marital files. I counted eight. Five husbands and three wives who hadn't trusted their spouses. The top one was of a local schoolteacher who was sure that her husband was having an affair with a woman who worked in his office. I flicked a few pages back and skimmed over the final report that my uncle had written. He had followed the man on and off for almost two weeks at the wife's instruction and had found nothing, or as he put it, *no foul play*. In the end he had given up trying to catch the man out and had told the wife that her husband was faithful.

She hadn't believed him and had gone elsewhere. And she still hadn't paid her bill, almost six months later. I put the file to one side to type a reminder letter.

The rest of the files were a mixture of security check-ups and casual store detective work. There was also a couple of missing persons but the files were dusty and the pages yellowing. One of them caught my eye; it was of a sixteen-year-old boy who had disappeared three years before. It looked as though my uncle had done a lot of footwork on the case, going to Brighton where the boy had friends, as well as up to Newcastle where the boy's father had gone to live. Nothing seemed to have come of any of it though and the last entry on the file was nine months previously. Down at the bottom of the page, where the expenses were usually added up, there was a line and the words scribbled: "account open-ended".

Then I looked at the name; Mark Johnson. The same surname as the woman in the baker's.

I pursed my lips and closed the file.

My uncle usually handled most of the cases himself but he had a friend who worked in a security firm, Bob Franks, who helped him out with odd things. Now and then, if he was really busy, he called one of his freelances.

I typed the letters and tidied up the files. I sat back in my chair and saw that it was almost eleven o'clock. The time had gone quicker than I had thought it would.

I decided to put the files away and then go for lunch. I thought I might go to the Exchange and have a browse round the shops, one of my favourite activities. I could spend a couple of hours there, have a tea and Danish in one of the posh cafés, and then come back to the office about four and listen to the answer-phone. That way, if anything important came up for my uncle I'd be able to tell him.

I picked up the pile of files and carried them over to the cabinet. When I pulled the drawer out there was one file that had been left in there. I groaned, thinking there might be another letter to type, but then I saw it had "Mr and Mrs Cooper" written on the outside.

I put the other files away – in alphabetical order – and took out the Coopers' file. I sat down in my seat and held it in my hands for a few seconds. I knew I should put it away again, that the case had given me enough aggravation.

I didn't though. I laid it flat on the desk and opened it.

My uncle's files contain a number of documents. There's the initial Data Sheet, where the information on the client is entered and details of the case they want my uncle to follow up. There's the contract the client signs, which outlines the possible cost of the investigation. There's the Client Report which is neatly written or typed and sums up the events in the investigation and explains the resolution or not of the case. In among these formal documents there were always some sheets of notes that my uncle made from time to time in the investigation. He said they were made on the spur of the moment, while on a case or directly after.

I pulled out the Client Report that my uncle was drafting. Attached to it were some pages of rough notes that my uncle had made. At the top of one of them were the words: *Monday 11.30 p.m.* He'd obviously written it as soon as he'd got back from seeing the Coopers. The handwriting was tiny and heavily slanted but I managed to read it: *Coopers already knew when I got there. WPC still with them.*

Mrs Cooper in tears. Mr Cooper lying down upstairs with a headache, probably shock at the girl's death. The WPC went and I sat down and went through what had happened. Told her about Patricia's part in it. She wasn't as angry as I'd thought she'd be. She just shook her head over and over.

He came down after a few minutes in a dressing-gown with a towel around his head; just had a shower, he said.

He says he wants the whole kidnap thing played down. He doesn't want the boyfriend charged by the police. He wants it viewed as a "domestic". Can I help, he says. Can I persuade the police not to pursue the case. Whatever else, it would make his stepdaughter look bad and he didn't want that.

I said I would see what I could do.

Mr and Mrs Cooper wanted the kidnap plot hushed up. I couldn't blame them really.

I put everything back in the file and went off to the Exchange.

10

Lovers

It was in the Exchange that I first saw them.
I'd had my Danish and tea and was walking around looking in the windows of the various shops that I liked. I'd been spending imaginary money on different outfits that would make me look more interesting, more glamorous. I'd been picturing myself on winter beaches, posing in long skirts that were split by the wind, with silk shirts or scarves flying out behind me.

I'd begun to think of Billy and the mysterious woman who'd answered his phone. I made a resolution that I was going to ask him, at the cinema, who she was. Just casually; just say: *oh, by the way, some woman answered your phone the other day, who was it?*

If it was a girlfriend I'd make sure the smile stayed on my face and nod approvingly as he told me about her. I could see in my head how it would be; me with a plastic grin and my head going up and down like a nodding dog in the back of a car.

I'd walked into Smith's and was flicking through the clothes magazines on the rack. I was struck by a dark red dress a model was wearing that had a row of tiny buttons from the neck to the hem; there must have been thirty, maybe forty small pearl buttons on that dress; and not buttonholes but tiny fabric loops.

I didn't bother to look at the print at the bottom of the page which would tell me the cost of the dress. It wasn't important. I wasn't looking to buy; just to give my imagination some stimulus. Me, looking great, wearing something nobody else owned; it was the usual fantasy.

Don't get me wrong, I wasn't dissatisfied with my life, my clothes. I liked my jeans and my DMs, my heavy sweatshirts, my thin blouses and long, loose skirts. I loved my hats and the couple of men's jackets I'd found in the charity shops. I didn't even mind the neat, straight skirt and blouse that my mum had bought me to wear to the office.

But sometimes, when I was alone and had no book or magazine to read, or when I was just about to drop off to sleep at night, I liked to play a kind of make-believe game. It was childish and not something that I'd ever told anyone about, not even Billy.

In this game I imagined myself at rock-bottom.

I'd let my hair go, my skin was yellow, I'd put on weight and none of my clothes fitted. Old friends nudged each other when they saw me and shook their heads. I was walking with my shoulders rounded and my lips had a sulky look to them.

But one day something happened; I saw a man I really liked, or an old friend didn't recognize me. I went home, pulled myself together. I resolved not to go out until I looked better. I dieted. I exercised. I designed and made a beautiful garment.

Then I walked out looking a million dollars. Friends gasped at the transformation.

It was nonsense but it gave me a warm feeling.

The red dress was made of shot silk and was partially see-through. I leant back against the garden magazines in Smith's and began to drift into a daydream.

I was nudged out of it though when I saw them through the window, in the café opposite.

Mrs Cooper and Terry Hicks talking animatedly across a table.

At first I didn't recognize them, out of context, in a different place, with each other. When I saw them it took a couple of seconds to place them. It was Judy Hurst's mother and her boyfriend, talking across a table in a café in the Exchange shopping centre.

There was nothing wrong with that.

I smiled to myself for a moment, realizing that for the previous couple of hours I hadn't thought about the Coopers or their dead daughter. It must have been the first time in days that I hadn't been dwelling on them and the house in Empress Road.

And here they were, in the Exchange, straight in front of me. The dead girl's mum and her boy-friend, in a café, having lunch, talking together.

There was nothing wrong with that.

I put the magazine back in the rack and moved closer to the glass where I could get a better view. I even took my glasses off and polished them with the bottom of my blouse.

They weren't smiling. They were silent for a few moments. Then she began to speak. He seemed to listen for some seconds, then began to shake his head; his ponytail shook from side to side. She raised her arm to gesticulate and it ended up with her pointing her finger at him. Then he was quiet again.

She was angry with him. It wasn't surprising. I was amazed that she was even speaking to him. He didn't cause her daughter's death but he was a party to the "kidnap" and the deception. If Judy hadn't been in that house, maybe she'd be alive.

They got up from the table. I watched them walk out of the café. Mrs Cooper's face was stony and her hands were firmly in her pockets. Terry Hicks was talking quietly, the palms of his hands upturned as if he was trying to make a point.

He was probably trying to make amends; or excuses. I didn't know. It was like watching a silent film with no captions. After a few moments they disappeared into the crowd of shoppers.

So it was only four days since Judy Hurst had been murdered. So Terry Hicks was meeting with Mrs Cooper.

There was nothing wrong with that.

The second time I saw them was in the car park.

I was taking the short cut out of the shopping centre, holding my breath to avoid inhaling the car fumes. I cut through the second floor and across to the emergency stairs. It was only a couple of flights down and then I'd be out, away from the crowds, in the backstreets, behind the shopping centre. I could cut down the alleyway and be at my uncle's office in about five minutes.

An older woman was in front of me, fiddling with her purse. She was about to pull open the door when she lost her grip and her purse and all its contents cascaded to the floor.

"Oh, bother!" she said and looked hopelessly around. Over her arms she was holding three or possibly four plastic carrier bags. Her hands were trapped at her waist. I had no choice. I looked tersely at my watch and said, "I'll help," less than graciously.

The money had rolled off in different directions. I picked up her credit cards first and then a couple of pound coins and some silver that was nearby. She said:

"Thank you, dear. Clumsy? Don't tell my husband, whatever you do."

I had a quick look under the nearby cars for any coins that might have rolled further. There were none. I stood up and put her purse into one of her hands.

"There we are," the woman said, "no harm done!" and went through the doors. I was just about to follow her when I saw something glint over by the wheel of a car.

"Wait," I said and walked over to pick up the coin. The woman hadn't heard me though and it looked as though I was going to have a twenty pence piece for my trouble. I stood up and that's when I saw them sitting in a car across the way.

The car was in a darker area of the car park, away from the daylight. I stood back behind a post just to look at them. They were talking again; Mrs Cooper and Terry Hicks.

There was nothing wrong with that.

But then they started to kiss. She put her hand on his face and sort of pulled his mouth on to hers. It went on for a long time, her head moving from one side to another, his hand grabbing some of her hair.

I held tightly on to the twenty pence piece. It was something I hadn't expected at all.

Mrs Cooper and Terry Hicks were *lovers*.

11

Paul Hurst

I couldn't wait to tell Billy.

I ran all the way from the shopping centre with my bag flying out behind me. My hand was automatically lifting itself up to my head to stop my hat falling off, even though I didn't have one on.

Once in the office I picked up the phone. It rang and rang. Billy was either working on a car or listening to loud music. After about a minute he answered.

"Billy," I said, "Billy, I've just seen—"

"Pat! Did you get my message?" he interrupted.

"No," I said, "but…" I looked down at the answer-phone light and saw that it was blinking slowly at me.

"I can't make tonight. Something's come up. I'm just on my way out of the door."

"But I've just been in the Exchange and seen—"

"I'll be back sometime in the evening. I'll give you a ring at home. I've got to go. Talk to you later."

And he hung up.

I looked at the receiver crossly and then replaced it. I sat down, then stood up. I walked up and down the office, to the window and back. I opened my uncle's office door and went and sat at his desk.

I didn't know what to do. I had to think it through. I turned Tony's angle-poise lamp on and sat back in his chair.

I thought, if I were a real detective I would look for the bottle of Jack Daniels' whiskey in the bottom drawer, pour myself a glass and put my feet up on the desk. If I were a real detective there would be a pink neon light flashing on and off through the venetian blinds. I'd be sitting in a leather swivel chair and my trilby would be resting rakishly on a wooden coat stand that had hooks like curled fingers. The door would be half glass and after a while of sitting in the dark and thinking about life and love, a silhouette would show against it. It would be a beautiful rich woman who wanted me to find her missing husband.

Or missing daughter.

I sat forward and sighed. Mrs Cooper had asked my uncle to find her daughter. Now her daughter was dead and I had seen her, not four days later, in an embrace with her daughter's boyfriend.

Then it hit me. When I'd followed Terry Hicks I'd thought I had seen him kissing his girlfriend, Judy Hurst, in the upstairs window of the house in Empress Road. What if it wasn't, though? What if it was Mrs Cooper I had seen and not Judy at all? Did that mean that Mrs Cooper knew about the kidnap plan? That *she* was a part of it as well?

I stood up and walked back out into my office. I opened the filing cabinet and took out the Coopers' file. I opened it at the first page, the Data Sheet. I scanned the page and then saw what I wanted.

Michelle Cooper; previous name Hurst; maiden name Bowhill.

Her name was Michelle. I hadn't known what it was. My uncle always called her by her title and I hadn't heard Mr Cooper call her anything.

I thought of the first time they came in. In my uncle's office they'd sat as far apart as they possibly could. I put the file down.

The question was, what, if anything, did I do about it?

Did it matter anyway?

If Judy had been murdered by the man, Steven Hardy, then did her mum and her boyfriend's relationship matter? It was in bad taste but did it have any relevance? And if Mrs Cooper knew about the kidnap plan, was that relevant?

I went back to my uncle's desk and got out his address book. I turned to the "P" page for police.

On it were the names of police officers he knew or had contacts with. About half-way down the page was the name Derek Robinson and a couple of names underneath was Heather Warren – the two officers who had taken our statements at the police station.

The phone number was there on the page. In my head there was a voice that said: ring them, leave it to them to sort out. But there was another, more cautious tone; look at the mess you made last time, leave it alone. It's not your business, it's all over now.

I left the file open on the desk while I went and wrote down the messages from the answer-phone. There were five: two from solicitors, one from a security firm and one from a new client. Then there was Billy's message.

"Listen Poirot, I can't make it tonight. A last minute thing's come up. I'll ring you later."

I wrote down the other messages. Then I went back to the Coopers' file to copy out the address I wanted.

I knew it wasn't any of my business but it was in my head like a mental itch.

I turned all the lights off and made sure I double-locked the door on my way out.

Paul Hurst lived with his dad in a small house that skirted the council estate. It was a house that had been looked after. A regular fence around the front garden had been recently creosoted and there were shrubs and plants dotted about. A deep red plant scaled the brick walls almost to the guttering and the roof. The wood around the windows was painted canary yellow and the glass glittered from a recent cleaning.

The houses around it were in different stages of disrepair. The next-door-but-one house had towels across the downstairs windows instead of curtains, and the one on the other side had two rusting motorbikes reclining in the front garden.

I went to the door and knocked. I was taking a chance that he'd be in and that he'd see me at all. I was thinking through all the things I would say to persuade him to talk to me when the door opened suddenly and he was standing there, in jeans and a T-shirt.

"I'm Patsy Kelly," I said boldly, and then held out my hand to shake his. He lifted his hand slowly. I continued, "I found your sister on Monday night. I'm not here officially, but if you could spare me a few moments I'd like to talk to you about her."

His hand hardly clasped mine but he went through the pantomime of shaking it. Then he stood for a few moments. He finally said:

"You're the one who saw us down the pub, last Friday. You're the one who told Georgie Cooper."

My heart sank and I prepared myself to turn

away and walk back down the path and home. I didn't have to though.

"You'd better come in," he said, and turned abruptly away from me. I followed him into the house.

He didn't offer me a cup of tea. He didn't ask me to sit down. I did anyway, taking off my jacket to show that I meant to stay my ground.

"What do you want?" he said.

"Is your dad in?" I said, looking around. The inside of the house was as immaculate as the outside. There were scatter-cushions on the chairs and the smell of air-freshener filled the room. Small statuettes lined the shelf above the fire and a couple of spider plants crept quietly around the corners. On the table in front of me was a vase of carnations, blood red with small white veins.

"No, he's out."

"Why don't you sit down," I said. "I just want to talk about Judy, that's all."

He looked at me with deep suspicion. Gone was the carefree stance that he had had in the pub the previous Friday; the sarcastic comments, the cocky expression. His shoulders seemed rounded and in his casual clothes he looked thin and young.

"I didn't say anything about seeing you and the Bradleys in that pub last Friday. See, I'm not the detective. Look, I'd better start at the beginning."

He sat down while I told him about my job and

what had happened over the weekend. I told him how I'd followed Terry Hicks and what I'd seen. I described finding his sister, as sensitively as I could. I didn't go on to say that I'd seen his mum and Terry Hicks kissing. That was my secret. After it all I said:

"I feel some responsibility for your sister's death. If I had spoken up, said that I'd seen you and thought you might be involved, your sister might be alive. I'm sure you would all have got into a great deal of trouble with George Cooper, but she wouldn't have been there, in that house, when Steven Hardy happened by."

I stopped talking and took a breath.

I was unprepared for what happened next.

Paul Hurst started to cry. His face was impassive for a moment but then it began to colour slowly. His eyes became glassy until he blinked and tears dripped down his cheeks, one after the other, until his face was wet.

"Paul," I said, not knowing what to do.

His shoulders shook and he used the back of his hand to wipe the tears away. His head was shaking imperceptibly and he was breathing shallowly. He picked up one of the scatter-cushions and held it against his face.

I didn't know what to do. Part of me felt sorry for him and part of me was suspicious, unconvinced. I said:

"Why don't I make a cup of tea, Paul." I took the cushion away and put my hand on his shoulder. "Come and show me where everything is."

We drank the tea in silence and he began to speak.

"Judy wasn't supposed to tell me about it. It was only supposed to be her and Terry that knew. But she couldn't keep it to herself. She was like that. Everyone had to know what she was up to."

I almost nodded in agreement, remembering her boasts in school.

"It started off as a joke between her and Terry, she said. I was worried about her. I don't even know Terry Hicks that well; you know what sort of bloke he is. He was years older than her."

I drank my tea without speaking.

"They were going to do it just for a couple of days. And if it didn't work they would come clean; say that it had been a joke. When I saw the twins on Friday, I thought, we all thought, she was going to go home on the Saturday. When my mum rang me on Monday morning and told me that she'd received the hair I was dumbfounded. I didn't know what to do, what to say."

I made a mental note that Paul Hurst didn't seem to know that his mother was probably involved as well.

"I spent all day Monday not knowing what to do. I went to Terry's work. That's where you saw me and him talking. He told me, he assured me that it was all going to end that day. She was going to go home. If only she'd gone an hour earlier."

Paul's voice was beginning to crack again, so I tried to steer the conversation away from Judy's death.

"Why did she do it? Did she actually think he'd pay the money? What if he did? What was she going to do with it? How could she spend it? The police would have been involved."

"I don't know what she thought she was going to do. I know why she did it, though. She hated him – Georgie Cooper. She couldn't stand being in the same room as him."

"Why did she live there? Why didn't she come back and live here?" I raised my hand and gestured.

"Be serious," he said. "Have you been to Cooper's house? Why do you think my mum left here?"

"She hated him but she liked the good life," I said, thinking aloud. I pictured George Cooper pressing the buttons on his mobile phone, his stomach bursting through his silk shirt.

Paul shrugged. The sound of the front door opening made him jump to his feet. A man's voice shouted:

"Paul, I'm back."

"It's my dad," Paul said, blowing his nose loudly. "Don't mention Judy!"

Mr Hurst came into the kitchen. He was a small, round man. He had a heavy jacket on, with a scarf and gloves, even though it was only October and not particularly cold. He looked older, much older than Michelle Cooper. Perhaps that was the other reason why she had left him.

"Hello," I said, "I'm a friend of Paul's. I was just going."

"Don't go on my account," he said. He took his coat off and put it on a hanger.

"No I must; thanks anyway." I felt that I should say something about Judy; sorry for her death or your loss, but I didn't.

At the door Paul was shivering. I said:

"Your dad's taking it well."

"No, you don't understand."

"I mean he seems quite composed. I expect he's hiding his feelings."

"No, look, my dad hasn't spoken to Judy in four years. When Mum left and Judy went with her, my dad said that he was finished with her. As far as he was concerned, she was dead."

"But surely, now that this has happened..." I said, and pictured the pleasant little man I had seen inside the house.

"You don't know my dad. He's never forgiven her. When the police came round to tell us, he said that it was nothing to do with him, that he'd mourned the loss of his daughter four years ago."

"So George Cooper was the only father she had then."

"She didn't see it like that," Paul Hurst's mouth crinkled. "Quite the opposite," and then he closed the door. The interview was over.

On my way home I stopped at a phone box to ring Billy. I was hoping he'd be there so that I could tell him everything that had happened.

The phone rang just three times before it was answered.

"Billy," I said. "Billy, can I come round?"

A soft female voice said, "Hold on, I'll get him for you."

I looked at the phone with sudden rage. That was why Billy couldn't make the pictures. That was the thing that came up suddenly.

"Don't bother," I said to myself and put the phone down.

12

The Investigation

Billy Rogers had a girlfriend and he'd broken an arrangement with me to see her. I was still angry a couple of hours later when I was sitting in the kitchen drinking some tea.

Why hadn't he told me? He could have just said: *the sum total is, I've met someone nice.*

It was no big deal; it wasn't as if he and I had anything going on between us.

I pushed my teacup away and let out a slow sigh.

Patsy Kelly and Billy Rogers; the ideal couple.

Then I let it all slip out of my mind and thought back to my visit to the Hursts'. I remembered things that had been said earlier. Mr Hurst hadn't spoken to his daughter for *four* years. Judy Hurst *hated* her stepfather. I decided to write it all down. I used an old notebook from school. My mum was ironing in the other room. From time to time she shouted something to me. It was a distant and bitty conversation.

"Kid in college the other day gave me an essay about Milton. I gave it back and said it might as well have been about Milton Keynes for all I could make of it."

"Yes," I said, not really taking in what she said.

I wrote down all the things I'd seen in the car park. It read like a wooden police statement: *I was looking at magazines in Smith's and while passing through the second floor of the car park I saw…* I even tried to remember what they were wearing. I decided it might come in useful. I couldn't remember the make or the registration number of the car. I couldn't even remember the colour. In future, I decided, I should bring a small notebook with me. That's why policemen used them, after all.

"I went to Milton Keynes once, you know," I heard from the other room.

"Yes?" I said, wondering why my mum was talking about new towns.

I started a clean page to write about the visit to Paul Hurst's. I wrote down the information he had given me, but I also made some personal conclusions about his dad and his mum. *Mr Hurst considerably older and poorer than George Cooper. Michelle Cooper may have wanted a more exciting, affluent life. Mr Hurst loves his home and seems to be a careful, thorough man* [I'd remembered his scarf and gloves], *decent but unexciting. Refused to speak to Judy after she left home with her mum. Hasn't spoken to his daughter for four years.*

"Your dad had some friends who lived in Milton Keynes. Penny and someone."

"Michael," I said, "Penny and Michael."

The iron was hissing and I turned a page and made a heading: "THINGS TO DO". Underneath, I wrote a list of about six things.

"They had a house in France, I think."

"Um."

Then I looked at the list and put numbers beside the things I wanted to do, indicating which was the most pressing. It took me a couple of crossings-out to decide which one I should attend to first.

I closed the book over and looked at my watch. It was gone eleven o'clock and I was tired. I would start my own investigations in the morning. I had a day in which to find things out before Uncle Tony returned and chained me back to the leg of my desk chair.

"In France the biggest killer is alcohol poisoning, did you know that?"

"No," I said. I was looking at the front of my old school book. At the bottom I had drawn a heart and put mine and Billy's initials in it. Beside it was Billy's handwriting and it said: *you wish*. I pursed

95

my lips. It had been a joke at the time but now I felt cross when I looked at it. I decided that it was time to go to bed.

"The college vice principal got charged with drink-driving, did I tell you?"

"No," I said and sat back, looking at the cover of the book while my mum flitted from one conversation to another like stepping-stones across a river.

I went for a run the next morning. My mum was delighted. She was doing sit-ups on the floor of the front room as I entered in my old green jogging trousers and a huge grey sweatshirt of hers. I also had a brown woolly hat on that I'd found in her drawer. It covered my hair and came right down across my forehead. A bit of dirt smudged on my face and some dog tags and I'd have looked like a commando on active service.

"Good, Patsy," my mum said, lying back down on the floor. In a second her head rose again and curled in close to her stomach. "Thirty-eight," she said, breathlessly.

Why did she do it?

I lifted one leg up and jangled it about as though I was "warming up". Then I lifted the other. I went out of the front door and started my "run" round the streets.

When I got to the office the first thing I did was to

get Tony's address book and look up the number for Derek and Heather, the local CID officers. The question was, which one of them did I ring?

I'd decided to start at the beginning, the murder scene. I needed to know what the police thought. If they were certain about Steven Hardy murdering Judy Hurst, then my worries about her rancorous family probably didn't amount to anything. I had to be careful though; I didn't want my uncle Tony coming back and chewing my head off again.

I decided to ring the woman, Heather. I thought that my uncle was less likely to bump into her and hear about what I had done. She'd seemed nice anyway.

She came to the phone almost immediately.

"Warren, CID."

"Ah, Heather," I said, as though this was the sort of phone call I made a couple of times a week, "Patsy Kelly here. I'm ringing on behalf of Tony Hamer."

I left a brief pause, hoping for some kind of friendly sound, some encouragement, but there was nothing. I rushed on. "I'm trying to wind up the paperwork on the Judy Hurst case. Tony asked me to ring you for any relevant details … forensic … scene of crime…" I was waffling madly, searching my brain for memories of TV cop shows, anything. "Just for our paperwork, you understand."

"Patsy Kelly," I heard her say, "you're his niece, aren't you?"

"Yes," I said, hopeful at the bright sound of her voice.

"What are you doing working for that old fogey? Why aren't you at university getting a degree?"

"Well…" I said, wearily. It was a subject I had discussed with a number of adults. I didn't have to worry though; she just sped on.

"You could have joined the force if you wanted to be a *real* detective. We need people like you, especially women."

"Yes, it's worth a thought," I said. Then, taking a deep breath, "Now about Judy Hurst. I expect you'll have the post-mortem details." I was trying to sound as if I was in a hurry.

"I've got them here, somewhere," she said and I could hear papers being rustled. "So where's the boss then?"

"He's at a conference in Manchester," I said, my pencil poised ready to take down the details.

"Manchester! It's all right for some. And I'll bet it's all tax-deductible."

"We thought the time of death was between two and four," I said, steering back to the conversation. I felt as though I was trying to hold a slippery eel.

"Two and four. Wait a minute, here it is. Judy Hurst died between three and four. Three and four. So she'd been dead for about three hours when you found her."

"Cause of death?" I said, as though it was a

question on a form I had to fill in, like: *type of shampoo?*

"Um … several blows to the back of the head by a heavy blunt object."

"The spanner?" I asked.

"No, not the spanner. The blows weren't as hard as that. It says here, a heavy object impacted with the head some four or five times. Anyhow, that's not what killed her."

"No?" I said, surprised.

"No, once she'd been hit she must have fallen on her face, there's some bruising by the chin and cheekbone to indicate that. But she'd been turned over and left lying on her back. She died by choking on her own vomit."

"Oh, God!" I said, my voice quavering, my confident front crumbling. She didn't seem to notice, she just went on.

"So, no weapon at present. Let me see, petrol sprinkled about the room but not on her, interestingly enough, not a drop on her. A pair of small nylon gloves were found, possibly discarded by Hardy. Hardy's fingerprints on the door handle, the light switch."

I was scribbling it down, saying, "um" and "um" occasionally. Then I said:

"But we didn't get there until about six. Does that mean Hardy murdered her at about three, say, and waited around all afternoon? That he only decided to burn the place at about six and was disturbed by our knocking?"

"It's like this, Patsy. No one can tell what goes through the mind of a disturbed young man. He's got a record for arson; he's spent time in prison because of it. It's one of those random things. Maybe he just wanted to torch the house and happened on Judy. He gets frightened, hits her a few times, then sits in remorse for a couple of hours before he decides to start the fire. Who can say? No one else had any motive or reason for wanting the girl dead and that includes the silly kidnap plot. We've checked the family's alibis; the girl's mother and her stepfather were at home together all afternoon. Cooper's doctor came round and gave him a sedative for migraine about two. The girl's boyfriend, Terry Hicks, was fixing a friend's car – Sharon Bradley's; we've already checked that. The brother Paul and his father were together on his allotment, we've already checked that.

"Apparently, Terry and Judy were going to give up the kidnap nonsense and go round and see the stepfather that evening; to grovel, no doubt. It's a pity they didn't do it at lunch time, when he was there with her. Perhaps this Steven Hardy wanted to burn the place because he had a grudge against Cooper, slum landlord and all that. Or maybe he just wanted a fire and had a key to that particular house. Until we find him we can't fill in the details."

"Of course, that's what Tony thought," I said, writing furiously.

"Tell the old rogue he owes me a couple of drinks for this. And listen, Patsy, seriously, why don't you come down to the station and have a chat with one of our sergeants about joining? A girl like you could go far."

I said all the polite things I could and then rang off.

I read over my notes and sat back shaking my head. I tried to picture it all.

Terry Hicks was there seeing Judy Hurst about two. I knew that. I saw him kissing someone up-stairs a bit earlier. I now thought that person was Michelle Cooper, although I had no evidence.

The point was, if Judy had decided to give up the kidnap ruse, why did she stay in that damp dismal place all afternoon? Why not go somewhere else?

And did Judy know about her mother and Terry Hicks?

Unable to answer any of these questions I began to think about Steven Hardy.

Why would he have a pair of gloves, take them off and leave his fingerprints everywhere? Why turn her body over? To make sure she was dead?

None of it made any sense.

I remembered Steven Hardy appearing out of the front door. He had looked genuinely shocked to see us; as if he hadn't expected us to be there, as if he

101

hadn't heard the knocking on the door. Why did he leave the room half-covered in petrol and not start the fire? If that's what he'd intended to do?

If he had heard us knocking and panicked, why did he not run out of the back of the house, over the back wall?

My exercise book was starting to look dog-eared. I had covered about eight pages with scrawly writing.

Who was I trying to kid? None of the questions would be answered just because I had written them down. In order to find the answers I had to go out and look for Steven Hardy. If he was the murderer, then none of the other things mattered.

Where did I start? What did I do?

My uncle was due back tomorrow. I looked down at the cover of the notebook, at the crooked heart with "WR loves PK" and the words "*you wish*".

I needed help.

Billy was in his garage when I got there. There was no sign of the woman – the disembodied voice that I had heard on the phone, the reason for him standing me up the previous night.

"I need some help," I said, looking straight at him.

The top half of his body was in the mouth of a car, an old brown Ford.

"What happened to the Mini? Sell it?"

"No, a friend's using it," his voice echoed under the bonnet.

"Right." The words stung me and made my temper rise at the same time. I should have demanded to know then – *Who? What's she like?* – but I had other questions to ask that day, things I had to find out that had a greater priority than Billy's love-life.

"I want to find Steven Hardy," I said, "tonight. It's important. I need your help."

He surfaced from the engine. His face and overalls were differing shades of light and dark brown. His forehead was shining from grease. What I noticed though was the new haircut he had, short and styled.

He was looking after his appearance after years of claiming that those things didn't matter.

"OK, Dr Watson, what time shall I pick you up?"

13

Homeless

There were three local places where young homeless people often ended up. There were the houses down by the river, but I was sure that Steven Hardy would stay away from those. Railway Mansions was a possibility; it was an old block of flats that had been boarded up by the council and then taken over by squatters. There was also Jubilee Parade, a small shopping precinct that had been closed down a couple of years previously; large numbers of young people often congregated round there.

I was hoping that Steven Hardy might still be in the area, hidden out by some friends. I was banking on the fact that he wouldn't have the money or the contacts to run away to some other town.

At seven o'clock I was ready, peeking out through the front room window curtains for Billy's car. My mum was out for the evening.

I'd dressed in my oldest clothes and had a woolly hat on.

I'd considered getting into some kind of "disguise", dirtying my hair and face, ripping my jeans and pouring some whisky over my jacket. I'd even got out my make-up bag to put some dark shadow under my eyes so that I'd look ill, hung-over. Then I'd started to look for something to use as a begging tin.

Something had stopped me though.

I'd tut-tutted at myself for a while, thinking about how I'd been drawn in by the stereotype. Me, Patsy Kelly, taken in by the tabloid view of the Homeless. Drunken, sick, dirty, and money-grabbing.

Some homeless people were dirty and some were sick; maybe some were drunk and others out to make as much money as they could. Mostly though, they were just like me or Billy, only they didn't have somewhere to live.

The disguise had been shelved and I'd settled for some make-up.

I'd put on a lot of black mascara and some eyeliner. I'd pencilled in my eyebrows and put rouge on my cheeks. Lastly, I'd spent some time putting dark red – almost maroon – lipstick on. I'd wanted to look different; not like Patsy Kelly, but not like some cardboard cut-out of a homeless person.

I saw Billy's car come into the street. I turned the lights out and, grabbing my rucksack, went out of the front door.

"The police know these places, Pat," Billy said, after I had told him where to go. "If they can't find him what chance have you got?"

"Maybe that's why they can't find him, because they are the police. I'm not. Somebody might talk to me," I said, putting my seat belt on and inhaling a strong smell of aftershave.

Billy was wearing jeans and a buttoned-up shirt. He had loafers on instead of the usual trainers. He was looking smarter, more cared for. I was about to comment on it when he said:

"Did you ring me last night?"

I could have been honest and said I had rung. It would have been a good way to bring the subject up. I didn't though.

"No, I was over at Paul Hurst's."

"Right," he said. He leant over to turn on the cassette-player and his elbow brushed my knee. For some reason I stiffened and moved aside. He didn't seem to notice and as the music filled the car he said, loudly:

"Some pear drops, in the glove compartment."

As if I were a child. As if I had to be looked after and given treats.

*　*　*

When we got to the shopping precinct I took the intercoms out of my rucksack. I'd got them out of Tony's equipment stock. They were brand new; the batteries had been in a box on another shelf.

"I don't like this," Billy said again. His voice had an edge of impatience to it. I knew he didn't really want to be there.

"I know, you've said."

"I could come with you. I don't look like a policeman."

"No," I said. It was true, he didn't, but I was sure that more people would talk to me if I was on my own. I needed Billy around but not actually with me.

"It's dangerous," he said finally, fiddling with the cassette-player. There wasn't much conviction in his voice.

"I don't think so. I'm going to wander round and chat to people. Every twenty minutes or so I'm going to press the transmitter button on the intercom. It will light up the red light at the top of your set. That will be my signal that everything is all right."

"If it's not?" he said. He was getting a newspaper off the back seat and his tone of voice suggested that he was humouring me. I couldn't see his eyes but I imagined he was rolling them, thinking perhaps that I was being ridiculous.

"If there's something wrong I'll call through and speak to you. Or…"

I left a silence for some sort of dramatic effect. Billy rattled his paper.

"…Or if you don't get my signal in, say, over forty minutes you should come looking for me."

"Um…" he said and looked at his watch. He was like a disgruntled parent whose advice hadn't been taken. I got out of the car and walked round the corner to Jubilee Parade.

There were about twelve shops set around a courtyard. They'd all been small shops, the kind that went out of business quickly: florists, hardware, stationery, boutiques. They sold the kind of stuff that you could get in the chain stores, usually cheaper. One by one they'd gone bust, their "CLOSING DOWN SALE" signs curling slowly in their windows, like flags of surrender. The final blow though had been the building of the Exchange shopping centre a quarter of a mile or so away. Dozens of shops on three floors amid a forest of pot plants, glossy escalators and piped muzak. People liked it better.

The Parade had fought back with some arty shops, antiques and stuff, but it hadn't taken. Bit by bit it had been deserted, leaving empty cardboard boxes blowing around like tumbleweed in the courtyard.

The homeless hadn't come at once. They'd drifted in in small groups, at first making do with the doorways and the sheltered walkways. There'd been security notices and artists' impressions of guard dogs but none of the real thing; it had only taken a couple of months for people to break into the shops and start to use the interior of the buildings.

Every now and then the local paper did an exposé on the Parade. How it was a magnet for young runaways. The police came occasionally and threw everybody out, and once the bailiffs had put wooden boards over the shop windows and padlocks on the doors. It hadn't mattered though. Bit by bit they'd returned.

It was a bleak place, somewhere the rest of us avoided. I wouldn't have wanted to live there and I could see, when I walked round the corner and into the courtyard, why Steven Hardy and those like him paid for sub-standard accommodation down by the river. Anything was better than living like that.

There were small knots of people, mostly young, huddled in the interiors of the shops, the wood and glass from the windows gone; some were sitting in the middle of piles of cardboard, some had sleeping bags already rolled out. There was no lighting, just candles here and there, and someone, in the far corner of a shop, had a small oil lamp, the type you buy in camping shops.

It was chilly and there was a feeling of damp in the air. I walked into one of the shop interiors and saw a space by the wall. I put my rucksack down and sat on the cold floor. I was hoping that I could talk to some of the people around me; if it seemed as though I really was there for the night I might not be looked on with suspicion. I put my hand into my bag and let the top of the intercom poke out for a minute. I pressed the call button.

Around me were about twelve people, all in small groups, older than the ones I'd seen from outside. There were three or four women of my mum's age talking quietly. After a couple of minutes of steeling myself I walked over to them and asked them about Steven Hardy. They shook their heads rapidly, saying no, no, definitely not, dear. I smiled anyway, thinking that that was probably their reaction to anything that was asked of them.

On the other side of the women were four men playing cards, a number of beer cans acting as ash-trays beside them. The men were swearing and slapping each other on the shoulder. There were also a couple of ancient men in the far corner; one was wearing a Balaclava and his silver beard was flicking out of the bottom, the other had tiny round glasses on and was looking closely at a crossword in a newspaper. I passed them all by, holding my breath at the pungent smell rising from their bodies.

I went and sat by three younger people who'd had

their backs to me, and asked them if they'd seen Hardy, but they started to say no before I'd even finished my question. They had a skinny dog who was sniffing around, poking its nose under and in between the layers of cardboard and the sleeping bags. I stepped over it as I went back to my space at the wall.

Out through the glassless window I could see people walking along in twos or small groups, going into the other shops. There didn't seem to be any single people. I wondered, for a moment, if I stood out for being on my own; perhaps I should have let Billy come with me after all.

But then I mentally shook my head. I thought of Billy's smart clothes and his mystery girlfriend. I remembered his expression of disdain when I'd told him that I was going "undercover" to find Steven Hardy.

"You've been watching too much telly, Inspector Morse," he'd said.

I'd just ignored him. He hadn't been the one who had seen Judy Hurst, stone-dead on the floor of the house in Empress Road. I kept thinking of Heather Warren's words: *she died by choking on her own vomit*. It made me shiver; somehow it was more gruesome than a quick knock on the head, more messy, more untidy.

I looked at my watch. It was eight-fifteen. I'd need to send Billy another signal in about twelve minutes. I took my rucksack and made a pillow out of it, laying my head down and closing my eyes.

In the dark, I began to notice the cold.

I was warmly dressed, my mum's running thermals on under my jeans and three layers on top. I felt it creep through though and imagined it like dry ice rising up from the concrete, enveloping my legs and feet.

I sat up and hugged my knees. I put my hand into the rucksack and gave the intercom button a jab. It was a minute or two early but I didn't care.

A couple of young women came over and made a place by my side. One of them was about my age, the other much younger.

"All right?" the younger one said, when she'd laid out her sleeping bag.

"Yeah," I said. I was tempted to start talking straight away but I held back; I didn't want to look too desperate for conversation. The older woman took out a packet of cigarettes and I saw, as she turned her face, that she had a scar, like an exclamation mark, at the corner of her eye. It was about three centimetres long and hung straight down to the edge of her mouth. I must have looked at it too intently because I found her glaring straight at me.

"Yeah? What you looking at?" she said angrily.

"Sorry," I said weakly, "I was miles away." It was the best I could do. I quickly looked away and the two of them talked quietly to one another.

I was feeling shaken by her rage. After a while that dissipated and I just felt gloomy. I'd been there nearly an hour and had got nowhere. I lay my head down again and closed my eyes. After what seemed like ages I sat up again; only five minutes had passed though. I was thinking of packing up and going into another shop front when the younger one spoke.

"You're new, aren't you? I haven't seen you before."

The older one kept her head turned away.

"No," I said, "I've been living down by the river, but we got chucked out last week."

"Near where that girl got killed?"

"Yes, down that street. My mate was living in the house. I've been looking for him." I was trying hard to keep the urgency out of my voice.

"Yes?"

"Stevie Hardy. We were living down there, in a squat. When the police chucked us out I went up the West End for a few days. I came back yesterday and I can't find him anywhere."

"Hardy?" the younger girl said. "Isn't that the bloke the police were looking for?"

"Yes," I said, leaning forward.

The older one was waving to someone across the way and the younger one inhaled from her cigarette. I waited for a few seconds, hoping for an answer of some kind. When none came I tried again:

"Only I know he had a couple of mates over here

and…" I left the sentence hanging, hoping she'd pick it up.

"Nope," she said, "I've not seen him. Have you heard anything, Angie?"

The older woman turned back, staring directly at me. She had a penetrating look, as though she knew who I was and why I was there. "Who wants to know?" she said. I tried to look her straight in the face without focusing on the livid scar, red and raw-looking, even in the dim light.

"Who are you anyway?" The words came like small knives from her mouth.

I lost my nerve.

I didn't know how to answer. I looked around and it seemed as though everyone was looking at me. Conversations had stopped and there were sets of eyes turned in my direction. The card players held their hands close to their chests and looked over. The other youngsters turned their heads back to see and the dog had even stopped his snuffling in the debris.

"How do we know you're not the law?" she said, her words louder now.

Whatever story I had in my head suddenly seemed full of holes. It was going to sound fake. I knew it.

I stood up. It was time to back off. I picked my rucksack up. "Oh, stuff you," I said, mustering as much dignity as I could under the circumstances. I turned to the younger one and said: "Look, if you see Stevie, tell him Patsy was looking for him."

And I walked away, out into the far end of the courtyard.

I stood for a few moments, watching the younger kids come in off the streets. They were an unappealing bunch. They looked filthy and dishevelled. Some of them had saucer eyes and chins that hung down. Others were cavorting and laughing; there were loud voices swearing and shouting across the square, names called, hoots of recognition.

What had I hoped for? That these people would warm to me, tell me about Steven Hardy? I was an outsider. I looked about as inconspicuous as Father Christmas.

I'd been a fool to think I could do it.

I turned and started to walk away, back to Billy's car.

14

Steven Hardy

I could see Billy about two hundred metres down the street. He'd got out of the car and was leaning against the door. My spirits were hanging around my knees and I was about to give him a weary wave when I heard the sound of footsteps running behind me. I turned round and saw the younger of the two women who'd been sitting beside me.

She stopped a few metres away and walked the remaining steps, holding her cigarette out as though she was a model for an advertisement.

"Don't mind Angie," she said.

I put my hands in my pockets and kept my shoulders rounded. I wanted her to think that I was still annoyed. I was hoping that Billy would stay where he was.

"What's her problem?" I said, adopting a peeved expression.

"No, it's just that she hates the law. You know, she's had some bad experiences."

I pictured the scar at the woman's eye and wondered if she had got that from the police. Anything was possible.

"She doesn't have to take it out on me," I said, using my foot to kick at a stone on the pavement.

"Right. Look, I don't know if this is any help but one of the old boys heard that your friend Stevie had gone over to the Mansions. He's with Big Alice. She's looking after him. That's what he said."

"Big Alice," I said, pushing the excitement down in my voice.

"Number 32, third floor."

"I'll go over there then."

"Only Angie's all right. She's looked after me for about three months now."

"Um."

"She just don't like people looking at her."

"Because of the scar?" I said, trying to make conversation, glancing over my shoulder to see Billy, still standing in the same position. "How did that happen?"

"A car accident," she said and threw the dog-end of her cigarette on to the ground where it glowed for a few seconds. "Her mum and dad got killed and she got thrown through the windscreen. She's got no one left now, just me. That's why she's a bit funny," she said and turned to walk away.

I watched her until she had turned the corner, my feelings of glee about Steven Hardy's whereabouts collapsing quietly inside my head. Angie's mum and dad killed outright. Just like Billy's.

I turned and walked towards Billy. A gloom had settled around me like a thick fog. When I got to him, Steven Hardy was no longer uppermost in my thoughts.

"How'd you get on?" Billy asked.

All I could think of was the cold and the dark in that shop front; the dirt and the cardboard, the smell, like the inside of an old laundry basket; the slovenly people who looked like the refugees of a war. In the middle of it I remembered Angie's look of malevolence and her scar and her dead mum and dad.

"Did you find out anything?" Billy said, his hand on my arm.

"Yes, I found out a lot," I said, but I couldn't say any more because it felt like there was a big black cloud in my head that was about to burst.

Without saying anything else he put his arms round me.

Railway Mansions were a step up from Jubilee Parade. A lot of the flats had electricity and although the place was crowded it didn't seem as dank and dilapidated as the shops I had just left. Many of the windows were boarded over with wood and one or two of the front doors had been smashed through, but most of the flats were closed up and looked lived in. Some had some glass in the windows and there were even some curtains in evidence.

The wall outside had slogans painted on it: HOMELESS HAVE RIGHTS, SQUATTERS UNITE, and someone had even painted, HAMMERS FOR THE CUP.

Billy and I made our way up the dark stairwell to the third floor, passing numbers of older men and women who were sitting on the stairs. Some were holding bottles to their mouths, some just smoking and staring into space. Billy's expression was one of disgust.

"Why don't these people *do* something?" he said.

"What, like suing someone?" I raised my eyebrows at him. "Maybe they should make a formal complaint."

"All right, all right," he said, taking the stairs two at a time.

As we got near the top there were fewer people to step over, less rubbish strewn about. Up on the third floor the place seemed more cared for. There were no broken windows that I could see and lining the edge of the balcony was a variety of pot plants.

There were one or two people standing chatting

at front doors, bathed in the light that was spilling from the interior of the flats. They looked up as we passed, not overly interested, and continued their conversation when we'd gone by. There was an air of normality about the landing. It was as if we were in a regular estate; I half expected to see milk bottles, washed and ready to be picked up by some cheery milkman.

When we got to number 32 I stood for a minute and felt apprehension; butterflies it's called, but to me it was as though there were small birds flapping about in my stomach.

If Big Alice was there, would she talk to us? Would Steven be there? Would he talk?

Billy was leaning over the balcony looking down at the small numbers of people sitting on the wall along the front of the flats.

I knocked on the door, expecting it to be opened by some hugely fat bag lady, with treble chins and a breathless voice.

After a few moments though, we were faced by a woman of about my mum's age, maybe a bit older. She was tall, about five foot nine or ten, with black and grey peppered hair. She had a kind of boiler suit on and row upon row of beads hanging round her neck. Hanging from her ears she had a pair of metal birds, suspended as though frozen in flight. Through her nostril she had a silver ring.

"What?" she said bad-temperedly. "What?"

"My name's Patsy Kelly, and…" I started. I had decided to drop the undercover stuff and be completely honest with her.

"I don't know who's sent you but I'm full up. I've four kids kipping here, I can't have anyone else. Sorry." She pushed the door over to shut it.

"Alice, I want to see Steven Hardy," I said, putting my foot in the door.

She stopped pushing and pulled the door back. Her eyes flicked across me and on to Billy, whose clean, pressed clothes and neat haircut made him stand out.

"Alice, I know that Steven Hardy is with you." I leant towards her, lowering my voice. "I'm not the police. I've got no connection with them. I found Judy Hurst's body. You ask Steven, ask him to look out of the window at me. He'll tell you because he saw me there."

"Who told you that Steve was here?" she said it quietly, angrily.

"I need to know if he had anything to do with the murder. I won't go to the police, no matter what he tells me. I just have to know to rule some other people out. I need to talk to him."

There was quiet for a minute while she looked back towards Billy.

"Billy's my mate. He's just keeping me company. He's got nothing to do with this. Ask Steven to look out the window at me. If he doesn't want to see me

I'll go away and I won't go to the police. I swear. I'll give you my address so you'll know where to come and find me if I do."

A voice came from inside the flat. Alice looked back for a moment. I couldn't catch what was said. Turning back to me she said: "Stay there." And closed the door.

I stepped back and into Billy. My arms were rigid with tension.

I wondered what I would do if Steven told me he had killed her. Would I keep my word and not go to the police?

"You did well," Billy whispered, clapping me on the shoulder. I looked to the windows hoping the curtain would twitch and Steven Hardy might look out at me. There was no movement though, but after a few seconds I saw a shape at the window. I stood still, holding my breath, feeling as though I was on an identity parade. My hand, hanging down by my side, was clasped by Billy. Only for a second. Then he let it go.

The door opened and Alice stood there.

"You better come in," she said, her lips pursed with annoyance, her eyes scanning the balcony in case we had a whole van full of police hiding round the corner.

Steven Hardy looked completely different. He had had his hair cut and dyed black and there was a small gold ring through his nostril, just like Alice's. If I had seen him on the street I would not have recognized him.

He was sitting on a sleeping bag on the floor in the back room of the flat. He had a giant blue roll-neck jumper on that came up to his chin and covered his hands. Even then he looked cold. Around him were piles of blankets and clothes and a couple of upside-down plastic milk crates. Cardboard boxes had been turned on their sides, like makeshift cupboards. There was a small calor gas fire that had the word "ALICE" scrawled on its side. I could hear the sound of a telly from the other room and the voices of people talking amid the sound of cutlery and crockery.

We stood awkwardly, saying nothing until Alice came in and shut the door.

"Get on with it, then," she said crossly. I wondered if she was ever relaxed, if she ever smiled. She was shaking her head and the birds on her ears were flying frantically around.

I went over and sat beside Steven. Billy leant up against the wall.

"Steve, you were coming out of the house in Empress Road as I was going in. Last Monday. About half-five, six o'clock."

He said nothing. Alice was standing with her hands on her hips as if she was bracing herself for an argument. I tried again.

"Steve, I found Judy Hurst's body, a few minutes after I saw you at the front door. I know the police think that you had something to do with the murder."

He visibly flinched at this, looking quickly at Alice. She knelt down beside him.

"It's all right, Steve. This girl's not from the police. She just wants you to tell her what happened." Alice turned to me and said: "Steve's not a good communicator, see. He's had what you might call a bit of bad luck."

I lowered my voice, aware of Billy behind me.

"When you came out of that house you looked frightened to death, Steve. The police think that you killed Judy. I need to know what happened."

"Not me," he said and looked again at Alice. Alice took his hand, still covered by the jumper and held it.

"Tell me what happened, why you were there."

He was quiet for a moment and then he leant over and whispered in Alice's ear.

"He wants me to tell you," Alice sighed, her shoulders drooping a few inches, the sharp lines on her face becoming rounder, softer.

"Stevie lived in Empress Road from time to time. I lived there for a few months last year, before I got this place. There are dozens of houses down there, mostly owned by Cooper, that are just left empty year after year. We rent some of them and that gives us a way into some of the others. The rent's low, always in cash; probably just backhanders for Cooper; money the taxman never finds out about.

"Steve's got some friends in a squat in west London and sometimes he lives there and sometimes here. Last Monday he was coming back from his mates' after being there for about a month. He went to Empress Road; he's still got a key."

I looked at Steven Hardy. He didn't look as though he had enough sense to get from one side of London to the other. I imagined his key on a bit of string round his neck.

"He gets to the house about twelve…"

"Twelve o'clock," Steven said.

"He goes upstairs to the top floor, to the room he's used in the past, and unrolls his sleeping bag, gets in and has a kip. When he wakes up he hears these voices from downstairs; raised voices, angry voices."

"Yes."

"And the thing is, Steve hates conflict, can't stand it."

"I don't like arguments," he said. He'd raised his knees and was hugging them with his arms.

"So he stays upstairs. For hours he says."

"A long time," Steven added.

"And when he went down he found the girl's body. Then he must have bumped into you."

I sat quiet for a moment, letting the story sink in.

There was nothing surprising at all about it. It was more or less what I'd thought he might say; it all sounded so fragile though. I could see how weak it would look to the police, to Heather Warren, CID.

Alice must have mistaken my quiet for disbelief.

"My God, you don't believe him!" she said.

"I ... I do," I said, looking round at Billy for some support. His face was impassive though. For a moment he really did look like a policeman.

"Show her, Stevie. Go on, show her!"

Steven Hardy looked concerned; then a frown grew on his face.

I looked at Alice, puzzled. Steven Hardy held his arms straight out in front of him. Alice took the sleeves of the sweater and started to fold them back to show Steven's hands. He was still holding them in a fist shape, or at least they were bent up, as if he was holding something tightly.

Alice looked at me and Billy. I didn't understand what was happening.

"See Stevie's hands," she said.

I nodded.

"He can hardly move them. He's had arthritis since childhood; it affects his joints, some worse than others. His hands are bent up like that. He can't move his fingers very far, so he can't pick much up. Pens, money, a fork, a key, but nothing bigger. And he's got no strength in them. He could

126

pick up a paintbrush but he couldn't work it up and down on a wall. You feel them; go on, go on."

I reached over and held Steven's hand. His fingers felt rigid; for a fleeting moment I thought of Judy Hurst's fingers, the first part of her dead body that I had seen. I pushed the fingers slightly. They moved but I could see Steven's mouth tense.

"So he couldn't have killed a fly, let alone some strapping girl."

"Then why not go to the police?" Billy's voice came from behind me, sensible and calm.

"Because people like us don't trust the police," Alice said and got up.

Alice made us a cup of tea and Steven told us everything he remembered.

"I heard three voices, two women and one man. One man, just one man."

"Did you hear what they said?" I looked at Alice. There was an expression of concern on her face; she looked at her watch.

"Did they say anything?" I repeated, my own voice sounding more urgent than I wanted it to.

"No, no," he said, and I crossed my legs and put my head in my hands. Disappointment settled on to my shoulders.

All I'd found out was that there'd been three people present when Judy Hurst was murdered. One of them had been her; the other two, a man and a woman, had been the murderers. Who were they though? That was what I needed to know.

I pulled myself together, finished my tea and stood up.

"Thanks, Steve," I said. Steven Hardy wasn't Judy's killer. That was all I knew. I gave Alice a scrap of paper with my name and phone number on it in case he remembered anything else.

As we went out I could hear Billy talking to Alice:

"The police said he had a background of arson; that he'd been in prison. He doesn't look capable."

"No, he's not. Steve's been in and out of care for years. He was moved to this place, then to some foster parents and then to some other institution. Eventually he snapped. There was a fire. They said he started it but... That's another thing he can't do with his hands, strike matches."

Poor Steve.

I went back to thinking about Empress Road. A man and a woman were there when Judy died. Did they both kill her? Or just one of them?

"And he was sent to prison?" Billy was saying, pushing the point.

Just then I heard a voice calling out from inside the flat. Alice and Billy looked around and I stopped in my tracks. Steven Hardy came hurrying along the balcony towards me, looking pleased with himself.

"I've remembered something he said."

"Good, Steven," I said, going through a show of

interest. I hardly thought it would matter. In my other ear I caught Alice's loud whisper to Billy:

"It was a young offender's institution. *Another* institution," she said.

Steven Hardy reached over and grabbed the sleeve of my jacket.

"He said: 'For God's sake, Michelle.' That's what he said. 'For God's sake, Michelle.'"

I stood, speechless for a moment, his words like a whirlpool in my head.

For God's sake, Michelle. That's what the man had said.

I looked at Steve's face and then over to Billy. Alice was looking warily at us all. I had a sudden urge to dance along the balcony but I didn't. Instead I put my hands on either side of Steven Hardy's face and gave him a noisy kiss.

For God's sake, Michelle. That's what the man had said.

15

Making Plans

We bought some McDonald's and sat in the car eating it. It was eleven–thirty and Billy was going to drop me home when we'd finished.

"Michelle Cooper was there when Judy Hurst was murdered. Can you believe that?" I said. "Her own *mother*?" I had a visual image of Michelle Cooper looking down wickedly at her daughter's body.

"I thought she was with Cooper though, all afternoon."

"Yes, that's what the police said but remember, George Cooper had been given a sedative for a migraine. Maybe he was fast asleep all afternoon and she slipped out. She could have got to Empress Road in minutes in a car and be back before he had even woken up!"

"Maybe Judy got hit by accident," Billy said, trying to find a rational explanation.

"She was hit on the back of the head repeatedly," I said. "That sounds pretty premeditated to me."

"Maybe Michelle didn't do it. Maybe the man with her did."

"The man with her." I repeated his words and then bit into my cheeseburger.

There was quiet for a moment as Billy and I ate our food. The man with her had to be Terry Hicks. That was how it all fitted. Judy Hurst had found out about her mum and Terry Hicks and confronted them with it. Perhaps she had threatened to tell Georgie Cooper. Paul Hurst had implied that Michelle and Judy liked the luxury of living with Georgie Cooper. Maybe Michelle Cooper couldn't face losing all that.

"But would she kill her own daughter?" I said out loud.

"I can't see it," Billy said, "no matter what she'd done."

We finished our food and I brushed away the probabilities conversation and patted myself on the back again.

"I was right though, wasn't I? There was something more to it all. Michelle Cooper's affair with her daughter's boyfriend was significant."

"All right, Inspector Wexford, don't go on," Billy said, patting me on the head, his hand resting on my shoulder when he'd finished.

I packed all the bits of paper and empty ketchup cups into the paper bag and got out of the car to chuck the litter away. I was feeling pleased with myself; then I remembered Steven Hardy's bent fingers. It had helped my investigation but it was something he had to live with every day.

I pulled my coat around me and shivered with the cold. I used my fingers to scratch at my eyes and felt the hard, wiry lashes, still caked with mascara.

I wondered what my mum was doing. It was time to go home.

I got back into the car.

"One problem though," I said, pulling hard on my seat belt.

"Only one?" Billy said, looking at me. "Here, that gets stuck," he said, pulling the belt hard so that it came out suddenly. He leant down to fix it into its slot.

He was only centimetres away from me and I could smell the heavy scent of the aftershave he was wearing. He was concentrating on the belt fastening and his hair was tickling my nose. I had this strong urge to pull him close, to hold him, as he had done for me earlier in the evening. For a brief moment he looked up and his mouth was close enough to touch. I looked him straight in the eye without flinching.

His lips were open and I could feel his warm breath on my face.

I wanted to kiss him.

My insides were swirling with indecision. There was the girl he was seeing, and our friendship, but most of all, most important of all, there was the possibility that it might not be what he wanted. I might kiss him on the mouth and he might say: *Pat, I don't think of you in that way*, or *Pat, I'm involved with someone*.

I pushed myself back in the seat, away from him, a silly giggle escaping from my mouth.

He turned away, and, taking up a cloth, began to wipe the inside of the windscreen.

"One problem, you said." His voice was business-like.

"Yes," I said gloomily, my previous euphoria crumbling, "Terry Hicks. My theory only works if he was there. But the police checked his alibi. He went home sick from work but told the police that he'd been skiving to fix a friend's car. The CID officer who I spoke to told me. It was Sharon Bradley's car. She said he was there all afternoon."

"Maybe she's lying?" Billy said, starting up the car.

"But why should she? You don't think she's involved too? My God, the killers are multiplying."

"Um," he said.

We were quiet driving the short distance to my road. When we arrived, Billy said:

"I think we should go and talk to her."

I made a fist with my hand and bit into it…

"Maybe we can shake her story. I've got some free time in the morning."

"Maybe," I said. "See you about ten?"

I gave him a peck on the cheek, fluffed up his neat haircut and got out of the car.

My mum was still up when I got in. She was sorting out file papers on the floor of the living room. Beside her was a half-empty bottle of wine with a plastic stopper at the top. A long-stemmed crystal glass sat in the fireplace, and on the coffee table was a bag of tortillas.

"Tony rang," she said, looking up from her stuff. "He says he'll be back from Manchester about midday tomorrow depending on the traffic and he'll see you in the office. He sounded a bit peeved, to say the least. Have you been upsetting him?" she asked, raising her eyebrows sardonically.

"No," I said, kneeling down on the carpet beside her.

I wondered what it was he wanted; whether it was something to do with the case. I was hoping to have something really concrete to tell him. At the moment it was still just a list of possibilities. Still, one thing was certain: Michelle Cooper was there when her daughter was killed.

I looked at my mum cross-legged on the carpet, put both my arms around her and gave her a long hug.

16

Sharon Bradley

"What do you know about Terry Hicks?" I said to Billy.

We were sitting in a café across the road from the hairdresser's that Sharon Bradley worked in. She was going to meet us there at one o'clock, her lunch break; just to talk about Judy, I'd said. Billy was reading a newspaper. I was looking out of the window at the shoppers milling by.

"Terry Hicks: good mechanic, not particularly bright, loves vintage cars as I recall…"

"Good-looking though," I said, "good dress sense;" and I added: "if you like that sort of thing."

"Not really one of the lads, at the garage, I mean. Doesn't muck around; is fairly serious. Doesn't say a lot…"

"I wonder why he went for Judy Hurst," I said, remembering her inane chatter and her face glued to the mirror in the girls' toilets. I pushed my fingers through my own hair wondering, for a moment, if I'd remembered to comb it that morning. It was lucky I'd put my San Francisco Giants baseball cap on.

"And why would he get involved with her mother?" I said.

Billy looked up from his paper and raised his eyebrows. It was a gesture that said: *are you serious? Don't you know the answer to that?*

I took a gulp of my tea.

He was right. Men often got involved with older and younger women. Judy Hurst was very attractive. Michelle Cooper was in her mid-thirties. She was good-looking and well-groomed. She was in an unhappy marriage and had money to spend.

But why take her daughter's boyfriend?

I looked at my watch. It was quarter to one. I made myself think about Sharon Bradley and the questions we were going to ask her. We were going to be blunt and lie. I was going to say that I'd seen Terry Hicks walking along a street down near the river at precisely the time that she said he was with her. We were hoping that her story would crumble and she would break the alibi; particularly if we threatened to go to the police before she did.

Before we mentioned that though, we were going

to talk to her about Judy and her mother.

That was the plan.

I finished my tea and looked at my watch again.

Billy was still reading his paper. He'd said he could help me that morning but that he had somewhere to go in the afternoon. I wondered where it was and whether his secret girlfriend was involved. I had to go and see my uncle Tony. I tried not to think what it was he wanted to talk about.

I thought about wanting to kiss Billy. It was nine or ten months since the Christmas kiss. We'd been close friends all that time. Even closer since I'd decided to take a year off before going to university. All my girlfriends – Mo, Sherry, Beth – had gone their separate ways, were living in halls of residence, joining freshers' clubs, holding up the bar in the students' union. Other people in school, that I'd been loosely friendly with, had got jobs and were nowhere to be seen.

Billy and I had spent a lot of time together in the summer and not once had I felt the urge to kiss him or try to push the friendship on to another level.

Why had it changed now?

I knew what people would say (if I told anyone, which I wasn't going to). Patsy's jealous of the new girl. She doesn't like it that her oldest friend is having a romance. Her nose is out of joint.

Was it true?

I looked at Billy's profile and thought of him with

a woman on his arm. I replayed the woman's voice in my head: *he's not here at the moment, can I take a message?* It was a territorial statement that meant: I'm in Billy's house even though he's not here. I have the advantage.

I tutted at myself for thinking in this way. Wasn't that what feminists said men did to women, set them in competition with each other? Here I was, cross at some person I didn't know, because she had a claim on a man that I had strong feelings for.

And then I thought about Michelle Cooper and Judy Hurst. Had they been in competition for Terry Hicks?

"Well, fancy that." Billy's voice interrupted my thoughts.

"Um," I said.

"A classic Morris Minor sold at the auction for seven thousand pounds. Can you believe it?"

I was about to say something back about keeping to the subject or there being more important things at hand when I looked out through the window and saw her.

There, walking along the paved precinct, dressed in an immaculate black trouser suit, was Michelle Cooper.

"Well fancy *that*," I said.

"What?"

"Michelle Cooper out doing her Saturday morning shopping. And she's in mourning." I noted the carefully made-up face and the matching handbag and shoes.

"That's Judy's mum?" Billy said.

"Yes, she's attractive, I know."

"And you wondered why Terry Hicks would get involved with her?"

"All right, all right. There's no need to go on," I said, watching her walk along casually looking in shop windows. She stopped at a cash dispenser and waited in line.

"She doesn't look like she's killed someone," Billy said.

I watched Michelle Cooper with my heart sinking. Billy was right. There should be some sign, some outward clue. Can one human being kill another and then bury that deed deep inside them? If she had killed her daughter, could she apply her eyeliner straight? Could she blow-dry her hair? Or stand idly at her wardrobe, her fingers running along the hangers, and choose which outfit to wear? Wouldn't it sit there, heavy in her chest, like some food that she couldn't digest? Or maybe it would jag at her thoughts, a collection of broken glass shards inside her head.

I watched as she stabbed her number into the machine and then, looking briefly over her shoulder and back, took the money and walked away.

A few seconds later she turned, looked around the precinct, and then went into a shop.

"Look at that!" I said, unable to believe what I'd just seen. "Look at that! She's gone into a travel agent's!"

Just then Sharon Bradley came out of her hairdresser's across the way and started to walk towards us. Inside my chest there was a feeling of glee. I was tapping my feet frantically on the floor. I felt certain I was right. Michelle Cooper was the key to Judy's death.

"I know someone who works there," Billy said casually.

Right then, at that moment, I imagined Michelle Cooper inside purchasing tickets for herself and Terry Hicks; tickets that would take them to some other country, out of reach from the police and away from George Cooper.

"Who?" I said, not really taking in what he'd said.

"A girl. Someone I met a few weeks ago."

"She's probably planning to run away with Hicks," I said. "Find out, from your mate. Find out why she's in there."

"OK," he said, "I'm seeing her later." He looked relieved, as though he'd expected me to be upset at what he'd said. Maybe I was; I had other things to think about though.

When Sharon Bradley came into the café she walked over to our table. She stood for a moment – in pose – with one finger on her lip as if she were thinking some very important thing through. Then, raising her voice only slightly, in the direction of the man behind the counter, she said:

"Just a salad bap today, Les. No butter or mayo. And a bottle of mineral water." She smiled at us (Billy mostly) and said: "A girl's got to watch her weight."

"What nonsense," I could hear the man behind the counter chortling, his voice loud enough for her and the rest of us to hear. "Lovely figure, gorgeous figure."

Sharon rolled her eyes, as if the compliment had been unsolicited, as if these shows of male approval were a daily hazard of life that she had to endure. She sat beside me and opposite Billy.

"How's life with you then, Patsy?" she asked, glancing at me briefly before turning her eyes back to rest on Billy.

"So-so," I said and was about to open my mouth again to speak when she said:

"And Billy? I hear you're in the motor trade these days."

"Um," Billy said.

"Sherri," the man behind the counter shouted. Sharon got up and stepped across to pick up her lunch.

"Sherri?" I said, when she had sat down. "Sherri?"

"It's my new name. It's an adaptation of my birth name."

She looked from me to Billy and back again.

"It suits the clients. I get more bookings. Would you want someone called Sharon doing your hair for twenty quid a cut?"

Point taken. I got up and bought two teas and two large cream slices for me and Billy.

"You know that I was the first to find Judy's body," I said to Sharon.

"Yes, I heard."

"Tell me about the kidnap. I know that you knew about it."

"Um…" Sharon said. She picked up her water and drank from the bottle.

"Whose idea was it? Judy's? Terry's? Or Michelle's?"

"Michelle's? Who told you…"

"Never mind who told me, Sharon. I just know she was involved. Whose idea was it?"

Sharon sat back and looked out of the window. With her fingers she started to toy with a gold chain that was round her neck. It had the word 'Sherri' pressed in gold in the middle.

"Look, it's all over now. What's the point of talking about it? It was one of those horrible things. A random killing or whatever the papers said."

"I need to know!" I said, raising my voice a few octaves.

Sharon visibly flinched and her lips pursed with

annoyance. I sat quiet for a minute, chewing my tongue. I was lost for what to say next. I didn't know how to get her to talk.

"Sherri," I heard Billy's voice, soft and low, "you don't mind if I call you that, do you?"

"No." She shook her head and started to tap her fingers on the table, as though she was playing an invisible piano.

"Look, Sherri, Patsy's been really upset about it all. It's not nice to see a dead body, particularly someone that Patsy knew and liked as much as Judy."

He stopped and they both looked at me. I had to hold my eyebrows down forcefully and fake a sigh.

"She feels responsible, you know, if she'd got there earlier and stuff. She just needs to talk about the whole thing really. It was me who reminded her about you. 'Remember there's your mate Sharon, Patsy. I'm sure she'll throw some light on it.'"

I leant back against the chair as he smooth-talked her, my mouth twisting up to the side. I was seeing a side of Billy I had never seen before. What had happened to the nervous, awkward teenager who always bought the year before's fashionable trainers, or the blushing young man who was only relaxed talking about gear boxes and engines? I also remembered, momentarily, the months of mourning and the period of black despair he had experienced when his parents died.

In front of me, smoothly taking over my investigation, was someone quite different.

"That's all," he was saying. "We just want to know the truth. To put our minds at rest."

Sharon Bradley sighed and clasped her hands on the table. She looked at her watch and then started:

"It was Michelle's idea, the kidnap. She was fed up with Georgie Cooper and wanted some money out of him. See, there was a pre-nuptial agreement of some sort that said if they parted without children then Michelle would just take her clothes, nothing else. Michelle said that he'd tricked her into signing it. She said that he was worth thousands and could afford it.

"So – Judy told me all this – so they decided to pretend that she'd been kidnapped. Judy even let them cut her hair off. She was supposed to lie low, down in Empress Road, for a few days until the money was paid. Then she'd be found wandering aimlessly along a road, taken to a hospital and so on, the money and the kidnapper having disappeared. I wasn't supposed to know any of this, no one was. Only Judy told me some of it and … anyway, that was the plan."

So far, it was more or less what I'd put together myself.

"She told *you*," Billy said, edging her on, keeping her talking.

"Yeah, we were mates, you know…"

"What about Terry Hicks?" I said. "He was involved in the plan."

"Yes. It was Michelle, Judy and Terry. They were the only ones who were involved."

"I can understand Michelle trying to get money out of George Cooper but why would Judy help her? It was illegal. They could have got into lots of trouble." I was trying to draw Sharon round to talking about Judy and her mum, hoping that she'd say something about the competition between them.

"Judy hated Georgie Cooper. She'd hated him for years. See, before Michelle married Cooper, her and Judy were really close, like girlfriends, or sisters. Once she got married that changed. Georgie Cooper was always wanting to leave Judy behind when they went out or on holiday. That's why Judy hated him so much. Anyway, Judy would have done anything for her mum, she adored her."

I couldn't hold back any longer.

"Are you sure, Sharon? What about when she found out about her mum and Terry Hicks? Did she still adore her then?"

Sharon sat back. It was clear that she hadn't expected that. I felt as though I'd just made a good move in chess. I hadn't won, but I was well ahead.

Billy came in then.

"You did know, Sharon, didn't you, about Michelle Cooper and Terry Hicks? What we're wondering is whether Judy knew."

Sharon Bradley sat very still for a moment; then she threw out a fake laugh. She began to shake her head.

"You think you know it all, don't you? Judy and her mum were as close as two people could be."

"But what about Terry Hicks? How could they be close when Judy's own mum was stealing her boyfriend away?"

"You don't understand," Sharon said, exasperated.

"What?" my voice was insistent.

"Terry Hicks was never Judy's boyfriend. He was always Michelle's. Michelle met him while he was doing her car. She started to see him. It was only when it looked serious that she asked Judy to pretend that Terry was her boyfriend. So that Michelle could see him, so that he could be around in the family."

Billy and I looked at each other. Sharon was sliding along the seat, getting ready to go. I suddenly realized that we hadn't asked her about the alibi, even though it didn't seem important any more.

She sat at the edge of the seat and turned back to us.

"Michelle Cooper got whatever she wanted, even if she had to use her own daughter to get it. Judy was fed up with it at the end. She wanted to go out with boys. Terry Hicks was fed up with it as well. That's why Michelle wanted the money, so she could bribe him to stay with her.

"But that's all over now. He's not with her any more. He came round to me last Monday, upset, told me all about it. He's asked me to go out with him, if you must know. I didn't tell the police that. I told them he was fixing my car but he wasn't. He doesn't want Michelle to know about me and him, for a while, until she's got over Judy's death."

And she stood up.

"Just be sure you don't tell anyone that I told you any of this. It's all irrelevant, anyway. Poor Judy's dead now. It all went wrong and she's dead."

I watched her walk out of the café and across the precinct back to the salon.

"Terry Hicks was definitely with her then, at the time of the murder," Billy said, rubbing it in. My perfect theory was in pieces. I looked back out of the window, just as Michelle Cooper emerged from the travel agent's. She was closing the zip on her bag and looking edgy.

I watched her weave among the shoppers and then disappear from sight.

Michelle Cooper hadn't stolen her daughter's boyfriend after all.

"Never mind, Pat," Billy said, counting his money out on to the table.

I looked at him and wondered who it was that he knew in the travel agent's.

17

The Sack

I got to the office at about two. The door was open and my uncle Tony's bags were on the floor but he wasn't there. I had a quick look round to make sure everything was all right. I was feeling gloomy, trying to work out what it might be that he wanted to see me about.

I'd done the files; I'd opened and sorted the mail; I'd noted down all the phone calls and had replied to any that needed it; I'd sorted through all the equipment catalogues and put them in alphabetical order; I'd chucked out all the old newspapers and junk mail; I'd cleaned the sink and tea and coffee things.

For a while I'd even solved the Judy Hurst murder. I wondered where he was. I went into his office and pushed open his window. Leaning out, I looked down to see if he was in the baker's, but I was at the wrong angle. I closed the window and went back into my office.

I did have a few things that I could tell him. Michelle Cooper was the one involved with Terry Hicks, not Judy. Michelle Cooper was there when her daughter was killed. So was a man.

I sat down in my chair with my coat still on.

But it wasn't Terry Hicks.

The door opened and my uncle came in holding a bakery bag. He had a smile on his face which he dropped as soon as he saw me.

"Patricia," was all he said.

He was dressed casually in jogging trousers and trainers that looked as though they'd just been taken out of the box. He had a cotton jacket on that had a small anchor stitched on the breast pocket. I half expected to see a sailor's cap balancing on one of his bags.

There was a strong smell coming from him. It was either a very sweet aftershave or a woman's perfume.

"I've got a quick phone call to make and then I want a word with you, young lady."

I sat back in my seat adopting a sulky look that I hadn't used since my younger years at school. I was about to be told off.

It wouldn't be the first time I had been told off by

my uncle Tony. I remembered any number of occasions when my mum had called him over to reprimand me. Once it had been for smoking and another time for coming in at two in the morning.

If only my mum had known that his words, gruff and angry as they were, had never mattered to me. Whenever I'd done something wrong the biggest emotion I usually experienced was regret and shame at hurting or upsetting her. That was enough to make me change my ways. But we still had to go through the ritual of my uncle being called, me waiting in my room and the lecture that would come; the inevitable comparisons of me with his daughter Sarah, who was marvellous at dress-making and never did anything wrong.

In front of me was the office phone. I leant over and gently picked up the receiver. Putting my hand over the mouthpiece I put it to my ear.

All I could hear was my aunt Geraldine's voice. She kept saying, "Yes dear, yes dear, yes dear", at the beginning, middle and end of his sentences. He was telling her that something had come up at the office and he wasn't going to be home until late. Then he said goodbye and put the phone down as she was still saying, "Yes dear, yes dear". I leaned over and held the receiver in mid-air so that I could replace it at the exact moment he did.

As soon as I dropped it into place it began to ring. I picked it up again, at the same time as my uncle.

He must have forgotten I was there, because I usually took all the incoming calls. I shrugged my shoulders and was about to replace it when I heard Michelle Cooper's voice. I held my breath and listened.

"Mr Hamer?"

My uncle answered in his public servant voice. Michelle Cooper rushed on.

"I hope you can sort out your staff, Mr Hamer. I don't want any of my family upset any more than they already are by this business."

He was going to speak to the person concerned, my uncle said, grovelling.

"I refuse to have my son bothered about these things. Don't you think that we've got enough to worry about?"

Someone was going to get harsh words, he assured her.

"My husband and I are going abroad for a couple of weeks to our villa in Spain. Just to get away from the press and the investigation. We've told the police everything we know. It'll be weeks before they release the body for the funeral."

It was a sensible thing to do, my uncle assured her.

"So, if you'd send your bill to my husband's office, it will be paid in full."

My uncle's voice lifted at this point. Oh, thank you very much, it implied, as though Michelle Cooper was doing him a great favour.

"Remember," she said, "I don't want my son bothered again. He's been through enough."

And the line went dead. No goodbye, no thank you; nothing.

I quickly replaced the phone.

Michelle Cooper's son had been through enough. Paul Hurst and his tears that didn't look quite real. Had he been the one with his mother on that afternoon?

I picked up my bag and tipped it on to the desk. There were several scraps of paper and I unfolded them one after the other. Then I came to it. The list of alibis that Heather Warren had given me. I skimmed them until I came to Paul Hurst's name. He'd been with his father at his allotment. Helping him.

The door opened and I jumped as if I'd just been caught with my hand in a till. My uncle's face was like thunder. I half expected rumbling noises to come when he opened his mouth.

But it was much worse than that.

I was never sure why I'd burst into tears.

It could have been because my uncle had shouted at me, his hand slicing the air to make his points, his finger occasionally coming into contact with my shoulder. Every now and again he'd lapsed into silence and done a circuit of the room, and through the blur of my tears I'd watched him take a brief glance at himself as he passed the mirror, straightening an eyebrow or checking his shave.

He'd only taken me on as a favour to his sister, he'd said. The last thing he'd ever wanted was some over-educated schoolkid cluttering up his office. And now she was upsetting his clients!

And that was after she'd mucked up a case by withholding information. Did he have to remind anyone that the girl's life could perhaps have been saved? Was there anyone who needed reminding of that?

Who had she thought she was?

(Patsy Kelly, Private Investigator, that's who, I'd thought bitterly.)

The tears had come thickly, like liquid plastic, and seemed to hang on the corners of my eyes until I'd pushed them away.

I'd even tried, from time to time, to throw in a few "buts" and tell him what I knew about Michelle Cooper, but the word had just floated for a second and then sunk beneath the verbal torrent that was gushing at me.

All the time, my uncle had kept looking at himself in the mirror, tightening up his belt and doing and undoing the buttons on his jacket.

About ten minutes after he'd started, he'd given me the sack.

Collect your stuff, he'd said, be out of here as quick as you can. There's the key. Lock up before you go. Drop the key into the baker's. I'll ring your mum later this evening.

And with that he'd left.

The door slammed and I was left sitting there, the contents of my bag scattered on the desk, a bit of paper in front of me with the Hurst and Cooper families' alibis.

I put my head in my hands and cried even louder; not because of what Tony, the bully, had said, but because I had messed it all up. I was no nearer knowing the truth now than I had been last weekend when I'd thought we only had a missing girl to look for.

In a dramatic gesture, I grabbed up all the scraps of notes I'd made and shoved them into the bin.

As I left the office the phone began to ring. I left it. It wasn't my problem any more.

I thought of going to Billy's but then remembered that he was going out somewhere; with the travel agent. Even that fact didn't make me feel any more miserable. He would find out that Michelle Cooper had tickets to Spain; to their villa.

In the end I decided to walk around the Exchange. I purposely went to a couple of expensive dress shops and looked for items that I might like to wear. I saw a chiffon skirt and a long silk top. I saw a long mac and some heavy boots. There was even a heavy velvet hat that looked warm and yet elegant.

I bought a cup of tea in the eating hall and tried to weave some of these clothes into a fantasy which might cheer me up. Nothing came though; one by one the garments slipped out of my mind and were replaced by Judy Hurst, in her black leggings and black top, lying on the floor of the kitchen of that damp old house.

I imagined myself standing in that kitchen face to face with Michelle Cooper. My hand would be slicing the air and my finger would be pointing close to her face. I know that you're the murderer, I would say and watch her composure crumble, her good looks become strained, her manner a little more humble.

But it was a dream. I had no evidence against her and she was going away with her husband the next day to their villa in Spain.

If only I knew who had been with her. It wasn't Terry Hicks. Could it have been her son, Paul? But why? Any why would his father cover up for him?

Or could it have been Mr Hurst with Michelle, looking for his daughter whom he hadn't spoken to for years?

Or both of them.

I sat up with excitement. Were all three of them there? Steven Hardy had said he'd heard male and female voices. Perhaps he was mistaken about the number?

Did Michelle Cooper, her son Paul and her first

husband go and see Judy in Empress Road? Did they kill her?

But why?

It was all too much. Unless I knew for sure who'd been with Michelle Cooper, I'd never know who'd killed Judy Hurst or why.

It was a waste of my time thinking about it all.

An hour or so later I was opening my front door when my mum half-ran, half-walked up the hall to meet me.

"There's someone to see you," she said, in a loud whisper.

"Oh," I said.

"Someone a bit odd…" she said, standing in front of me.

"Right." I was puzzled.

"Who are you palling around with these days?" she asked, her teeth clenched with concern.

The living room door opened behind her.

"Hello, Patsy Kelly," a gruff voice said. "I've got something for you, from Stevie Hardy."

It was Big Alice.

18

Big Alice

Big Alice looked out of place in my living room. She was still wearing the boiler suit but she had different jewellery on: small coloured beads that fitted tightly round her neck and hung from her ear. She still had the ring through her nose and parts of her hair had been finely plaited and woven through with small beads. She wore a kind of workman's donkey jacket which had several ornate badges pinned on.

She towered above us and seemed to fill up the tiny room. My mum, in her powder blue leggings and baggy top, had a smile on her face but was fidgeting around, picking up her ornaments from the mantelpiece and putting them back down again.

"Would your friend like a cup of tea?" she said

finally, stepping across to the door, her eyes still moving up and down Alice's clothes, resting eventually on the ring through her nose.

"No," Alice said, "I've not got long. I just want to talk to Patsy here."

Alice turned and looked at my mum, clearly expecting her to leave. Mum stood her ground though and looked at me, as if to say: *who is she?*

"It's all right, Mum, Alice is a friend. She's been helping me … on a case that I've been working on for Uncle Tony."

It was only half a lie and I could see her visibly relax, the mention of Uncle Tony's name giving respectability to Alice. I thought, briefly, of the phone call he was going to make later that evening, to tell my mum that he had sacked me.

I walked across to the door and led my mum out.

"I'd love a cup of tea, Mum, and I'm sure Alice would too." I looked back into the room to see that she had sat on the settee with her legs splayed and her hands behind her head. My mum looked as well and said:

"I'm not sure I like you doing that job, mixing with all sort of people…"

I gritted my teeth and went back into the room.

"Where's Steven?" I said.

"He's gone," Alice said, "you won't see him around."

"Oh."

It was a disappointment. Even though I no longer had anything to do with the case, I had still hoped that Steven Hardy would be available to go to the police and tell them what he had told me.

"He's in south London. With some friends of mine. Police won't find him."

"Oh." I couldn't manage anything else. My chin felt as though it was sitting on my chest.

"Look," Alice leaned across and tapped me on the arm, "there's no way, in a million years, that Stevie's going to go and talk to the law."

The door opened and my mum came in carrying a small tray with two mugs of tea on it. There was a plate with some Nice biscuits.

"Help yourself," she said, looking warily at Alice's large feet and legs that were filling the carpet.

Alice went silent and watched as my mum backed out of the room.

"Here," she said, as soon as the door was shut, "I haven't got time for tea; I was due over at the Shelter project ten minutes ago. I found this in Stevie's bag when I was helping him pack. He stole it, I guess."

She handed me a brown paper bag. Inside it there was something heavy and metallic.

"He says he picked it up, on that afternoon in Empress Road. He said it was there on the floor, in the corner of the room that the girl was lying in. He wanted to throw it away but I thought you might like it."

She let her words hang there and I opened the bag and the object slid out on to my lap.

"It looks important to me," she said.

When I saw what it was several lights started to flash inside my head. I picked it up and held it to my ear. Then I held it out and looked over it, as though it was a precious antique and I was looking for markings.

It was a mobile phone.

It had red buttons like a series of dots and at the top was a viewer which had gone blank. The battery cover at the back had gone and I could see the gold and black of the battery that was still there.

It was heavy in my hand. At the top corner was the aerial. I pulled it out and pushed it back in.

Along the top rim were some dark stains, some caked blood. I made sure I didn't touch it with my fingers.

"Steve found this in Empress Road?" I said.

"I've got to go," Alice said, standing up, her tea untouched. "You can tell the police whatever you like. They won't find Stevie. Oh, you should also have this, I guess." She threw a key at me and left.

"Thanks for the tea," she shouted down the hall.

The front door slammed and she was gone.

The mobile phone had been found in Empress

Road. There was blood on it; very probably Judy Hurst's blood. At last I knew who was with Michelle Cooper, even though it didn't make any sense.

Why should Michelle Cooper join together with her husband – someone that she couldn't stand – to kill someone that she loved?

I picked up one of the biscuits and dunked it in my tea.

The door opened and my mum came in.

"Was that your friend leaving?"

"Yes," I said, putting the mobile back into the paper bag along with the key.

"By the way," Mum said, picking up the tray with the cups, "Billy rang just before your friend came. He left a message. I wrote it down on the pad by the phone."

"Thanks," I said, looking at my watch. It was just gone six-thirty. I'd need to get the mobile phone to the police. It would be better though if I gave it to Uncle Tony first. It might make him less angry with me.

On the pad beside the phone was the message: *Nobody called Cooper came into the travel agent's at that time. A woman with red hair and a black trouser suit came in to pick up two tickets to Sydney in the name of Parker.*

"Mum," I said, "what does this mean? Is this all he said?"

"Yes, more or less. He said he spoke to his friend who works in the travel agency and she told him that … what I've written down."

"Sydney," I said, "two tickets."

"What does it mean?" my mum said.

"I'm not sure," I said, but I was. I was sure that Michelle and Georgie Cooper were going to make a run for it. "Did he say when? I mean, when the tickets were for?"

"No, that's all he said, I think. I'm sure that's it."

I dialled Billy's number but there was no answer. I paced up and down the hall, letting the phone ring thirty times. I could hear the clinking of the cups being washed in the kitchen. They were going to go to Sydney. It could be any time. It could be that night. Or the next day.

I dialled my aunt Geraldine, hoping that Tony would be back. He wasn't. He'd rung her an hour or so before saying he wouldn't be back until late. I left a message for him to ring me as soon as he got in. Aunt Geraldine was still saying, "yes dear, yes dear", as I replaced the receiver.

I got out my notebook and found Heather Warren's number. I got through quickly but she wasn't on duty, wasn't due in again until Monday lunch time. They asked me if anyone else could be of help. I said no.

My mum was standing beside me looking puzzled. I said:

"It's OK, Mum, I just need to get a message to Tony and he's not in. It's nothing important. Look, if Billy or Uncle Tony rings, tell them I'm meeting a friend down at Empress Road. They'll know who you mean." I was deliberately trying to lighten my voice so that my mum wouldn't be upset or worried.

I left her standing by the phone as I took the stairs two at a time.

I had some things to get together and an important phone call to make.

19

Empress Road

The phone box was on a corner near Empress Road. I went in and dialled the Coopers' number.

"Yes?" A woman's voice answered.

"Mrs Cooper?" I said, trying hard to keep my voice from quivering.

"Speaking," she said; businesslike, clipped.

"Mrs Cooper, my name is Patsy Kelly, Tony Hamer's assistant. There are some new developments in the case. He asked me to ring you and pass on the message. Is Mr Cooper available?"

"What do you mean: 'new developments'?" she said, her voice lower, as though she was in a room surrounded by a group of people.

"One or two vital clues have come to light that tell us who was in the house at the time your daughter was murdered." I spoke quickly, not knowing when my nerve would give way.

" 'Clues'? What do you mean: 'clues'? I only spoke to Mr Hamer this afternoon…"

"Since then; the clues were discovered since then. My uncle said it's very important that you and Mr Cooper –" I held my breath for a moment to muster enough courage to go on – "especially Mr Cooper, meet him down at the house in Empress Road at about nine o'clock…"

I was about to go on but a male voice interrupted my flow.

"What is this?"

It was George Cooper, his tone demanding.

"Nine o'clock. Empress Road. We'll be there," I said and put the phone down.

In the silence of the phone box I clenched and unclenched my hands to get the tension out of my arms and shoulders. I looked at my watch. It was eight-thirty. I had half an hour to get things ready.

While I'd been changing my clothes and getting my stuff together, I'd worked out what I thought had happened to Judy Hurst.

My mum had been getting ready to go out and every now and then she'd come into my room and said something:

"You won't be out too late?"

"No," I'd said, "I'm just going to meet a friend."

"You're not doing anything dangerous, are you?"

"No."

"I'm not sure that taking that job was such a good idea…"

"Um…" I hadn't answered. Sometimes it was better to let my mum talk things out by herself. I heard her voice recede as she went into the bathroom.

Michelle Cooper had become fed up with Georgie Cooper but she couldn't divorce him because of the pre-nuptial agreement. Judy Hurst loved her mum and hated Georgie Cooper. She was prepared to cover up for her mum by pretending that she was the one who was going out with Terry Hicks.

Judy wanted her mum to leave Georgie Cooper. That's why she was prepared to go through with the kidnap, so that she and her mum could get some money out of Cooper.

But the kidnap hadn't worked. George Cooper had seen Judy walking along the road when she was supposed to be incarcerated.

Then he'd hired my uncle Tony.

Even when the curly red hair came through the post, George Cooper hadn't been moved.

So Michelle and Judy decided to think of some other way to get money out of George. They had hatched some sort of blackmail plot. Maybe Michelle knew some details of dodgy business dealings that her husband had been involved in, something to do with the slum properties he owned.

She and Judy decided to confront him at the house in Empress Road.

There could have been a hell of a row, I thought. In a temper, George Cooper might have grabbed anything to hand, his mobile, and gone for Michelle. But Judy, stricken by the thought of anything happening to her mum, had got in the way and taken the blows.

Michelle Cooper hadn't gone to the police because she hadn't wanted the rest to come out. Or maybe, I thought, George Cooper had at last agreed to pay her enough money.

It wasn't much of a return for the loss of a daughter.

There were unanswered things though: why did George Cooper leave the mobile there for someone to find? What did the petrol have to do with it?

By the time I'd packed my duffel bag and got changed, my mum was lacing up her boots and mumbling something about *speaking to Uncle Tony about Patsy's role in the agency*.

I'd given her a quick kiss and left.

It was crisp and cold and I could see numbers of dressed-up people ready to go out for the evening.

Billy's house was dark as I put the note through his letterbox. I hoped he would come home soon and find it; then meet me at Empress Road.

I wondered what he was doing at that very

moment; walking along a street, hand-in-hand with the travel agent?

I felt a heavy sadness picturing this.

Billy and me.

What had I hoped for? That we'd go on being best friends for the rest of our lives? That we wouldn't need other people? Or maybe that the kiss would happen again sometime and then it would be all hearts and flowers and engagement rings.

And now he had a girlfriend who worked in a travel agent's and places to go on a Saturday night. Probably he'd be going on lots of cheap holidays as well. I shrugged my shoulders and quickened my step to Empress Road.

In my bag was a tape-recorder, a mobile phone and a piece of paper with a story written on it.

I needed to keep my mind on what was ahead.

I'd put on jeans and a heavy sweater. I had my DMs on and a quilted jacket, not what you'd call fashionable, but it was warm and the heaviness of it gave me a feeling of security.

It wasn't how I felt inside though.

I got to number 150. There was no sign of the police investigations but the windows, upstairs and down, had been boarded over. I took the key out of my pocket. The house was in total darkness. It was only a week ago that Judy Hurst had been living there. I pushed the front door open and reached in and clicked the hall light switch on. Nothing happened. I shouted out:

"Anyone home? It's me, Patsy Kelly." And waited there on the step.

There was no answer and the hallway yawned ahead of me, black and deep. I went to step inside but a feeling of unease stopped me. I looked back out into the road. The streetlights were glowing and there were a couple of people walking along further up talking animatedly to each other. The street had a feeling of normality to it; I could even hear, in the distance, the chimes of an ice cream van.

Looking back, the hallway gaped at me, like an underground tunnel.

For a moment I felt like a little girl again, afraid to get out of bed in the middle of the night, terrified of what might be hiding in the sooty blackness.

I stepped back, out of the doorway, on to the path.

Was I doing the right thing? Why not ring the police? Or wait for Billy to come?

It was twenty to nine though. The Coopers might arrive at any minute. It was no time to be indecisive.

I got my mum's torch out of my bag, took a deep breath and went into the house.

In front of me was a long triangle of light and I moved slowly forward. I could see nothing except what was shown up in the beam from my torch. The rest was a kind of inky black, as if someone had taken a thick felt tip and coloured it in.

I called out a couple more times.

"Hello, hello. Pat Kelly here."

But there was nothing and the darkness lay heavily on my shoulders as I moved down the hall towards the kitchen.

I stopped for a second thinking I'd heard something but when I listened it was just a laugh from up the street. I relaxed and moved forward, remembering, for a moment, the night I'd been standing at the cellar door with my uncle Tony, looking everywhere for the missing girl.

I pictured Judy's hand on the floor, her fingers curled as if she were beckoning to someone. I stood, in that gloomy hallway, and remembered her eyes open, like those of a dead fish, staring up at nothing in particular.

I could feel my courage dissolving into the blackness around me. I turned quickly and looked into the heavy darkness and then back into the yellow beam from my torch. I gripped the torch tightly, as if holding on to it would keep my resolve intact. I took two or three giant steps and then I was at the kitchen door. I turned the handle quickly and pushed against the door. I put my hand in and clicked the light switch on.

The light came on, in flashes, as it had done that night; blinding at first then dark, then another flash before it was properly on.

I turned off the torch and leant back against the

door, closing my eyes with relief. That was supposed to have been the easiest bit. Coming into the house, setting up the tape-recorder, waiting for the Coopers.

I opened my eyes and looked casually round the room.

I stopped when I got to the place where Judy had been lying. There on the floor, like a child's drawing, was the chalk outline of Judy's dead body; one arm outstretched, the head at an angle, one leg doubled up.

I had no shock left inside me; I just looked at it, in a detached way, as if it was a drawing someone had done and asked my opinion of. There were sections that had been smudged, but most of it was intact; a ghostly shape that would lie there as long as the chalk lasted.

I walked into the room, over to the table. There was still a faint smell from the petrol, although the container had gone and the liquid itself had been mopped up. The windows had been boarded up, although the curtains still hung lifelessly and faded at each side. I looked at my watch. It was five to nine, time I started to set things up.

It wouldn't be long before the Coopers arrived.

20

Happy Families

They came at about ten past nine.

I heard the door open and then a voice:

"Mr Hamer? Mr Hamer?"

I said nothing, just sat still, behind the kitchen table. I looked down to my right, at the kitchen cupboard where I'd put my tape-recorder. I could see the red light on. It was a new battery and I felt confident that it would last twenty or thirty minutes.

It was the only thing I felt confident about though.

As their footsteps came down the small hall towards me, I realized how fragile my plan was.

I was hoping, banking, on the fact that Billy would get my note and arrive, like the cavalry, to back me up. He had said that he wasn't going to be out all evening. In my head I was willing him to walk through his front door, bend over and pick up the note.

For the time being though I was most definitely on my own with Mr and Mrs Cooper.

"Patsy Kelly?" Mrs Cooper's face appeared at the door. She looked as though she had seen something nasty. She walked into the small room, followed by her husband.

They didn't look much different from the day they'd first come into my uncle's office. He had a leather jacket and jeans on. His hair was sticking up a bit at the back, as though he'd been lying down. He had a fashionable shirt on and his earring was still glinting in his ear.

She was more casually dressed, in jeans and a short jacket. Her hair was in a ponytail, meant to look as though it had been hastily swept back, away from her eyes. It had been carefully done though, the three or four escaping curls framing her face. I wondered if it had been like that when I called or whether she'd done it after.

"Where's Hamer?" George Cooper demanded, his voice booming.

"He's having some trouble with his car. He says he'll be here as soon as he can," I said. "He asked me to start as soon as you got here."

They were both irritated and were looking round

the room. Michelle Cooper's eyes came to the corner where Judy had been killed and she flinched when she saw the chalk outline of her daughter's body.

George Cooper, taking deep breaths and looking crossly at his watch, also saw the chalk outline. It made him huff with annoyance. He looked back to me and said:

"What is this? What's Hamer up to? He's not even working on the case any more. The police have sorted it out."

"Please sit down," I said. "I'll explain."

Both of them moved reluctantly towards the chairs, Michelle Cooper getting a packet of cigarettes out of her bag, George Cooper putting his hands into his trouser pockets and then taking them out again, still missing his mobile phone. They sat a metre or so apart, neither of them looking at the other.

I started talking straight away, my words covering up my nervousness.

"Because my uncle was unhappy with some of the facts of the case he asked me to continue with the investigation. During the last few days I've uncovered a number of factors that convince me that Steven Hardy did not kill your daughter. I have his statement here," I said, lifting up the piece of paper I'd brought with me.

"What's this got to do with us?" Michelle Cooper said, her cigarette still unlit.

"Perhaps you'd like to read the boy's statement," I handed the piece of paper over to them. "I'd also like you to look at this." I picked up my plastic carrier bag and took out the mobile phone. "It was found in this room, minutes after the murder. My uncle said that he felt a duty to inform you of these things before he went to the police; you being his clients. He said it would give you time to inform your solicitor."

I left it on the table and got up to walk out of the room.

"I'll just go to the corner and ring my uncle to see what's happened to him."

Neither Michelle nor George Cooper spoke as I left the room and walked along the hallway, my fingers crossed that the tape-recorder was working, that the microphone was loud enough to pick up their voices.

I went out into the street and sat for a moment on the wall.

Give them time to talk on their own.

I imagined their conversation, low and angry.

You left the damn phone here; the boy heard you calling my name; they've got his statement. They can place us here at the time of the murder. We can't get out of it now. We've been caught.

I even hoped they might start to blame each other:

If you had never started this thing. If you had been

more reasonable about money; you were the one who killed her, not me. But it wasn't her I was aiming for, was it? They'll never charge me with murder.

And all of it would be on tape.

They would go home, ring their solicitor and proceed to the police station. When they got there, I would be waiting with the tape; their confessions.

All I had to do was keep out of sight and let them leave in their own time; then I would go back into the house and retrieve the tape.

It was just a matter of waiting; then it would be all over.

I'd been in the front garden for about nine minutes when I heard the scream. It came from inside the house.

I ran through the dark hall and flung the kitchen door open. Inside, George Cooper was holding his wife by the throat up against one of the walls.

"Here she is!" he said gleefully. "Your partner in crime!"

"No, no." Michelle Cooper croaked the words out.

My instinct was to turn and run; to leave them to fight it out, to call the police and let them come, but my eye was momentarily distracted. Over by the cupboard I could see my tape-recorder on the floor, the tape out of it, crushed as though someone had stamped on it.

"You'd thought you'd have one last go, didn't you," George Cooper was screaming into his wife's face, and she was staring at him, her eyes popping out of her head, her lips moving, but no sound coming out.

His voice vibrated through my chest and his expression was one of fury. I had no courage left and on legs of putty I turned to go. I reached out for the handle of the door but before I got it I felt a hand grab my hair and yank it backwards.

My head was pulled around and I saw Michelle Cooper stumbling away from her husband, holding her throat with both hands, spluttering a cough or two.

George Cooper led me across the room by my hair until I was half-standing, half-kneeling over the cassette-recorder and the mangled tape that was on the floor.

"This her idea, was it? Get Georgie on tape and we'll be able to get money out of him?"

I tried to speak but no words came; I even tried shaking my head but it only made him pull my hair harder.

"For God's sake, George," I could hear Michelle Cooper saying, her voice hoarse, "this isn't anything to do with me."

He let my hair go and I stumbled forward on top of the broken cassette-recorder, my mouth touching the smashed tape. My head felt as though I'd been scalped and I was afraid to reach up and touch my hair. I could hear slapping and Michelle Cooper crying. I closed my eyes in absolute fright and pulled my knees up under me.

If I had been a real detective I would have had a gun secreted somewhere. I would have stood up and held it tightly in both hands, my arms outstretched, pointing it straight at Cooper's chest. I could have said something like: *The game's up, it's all over, the chips are down, the chicken's come home to roost.* Instead I cowered on the floor, a lump in my throat the size of a fist, my eyes tightly shut and my hands over my ears.

After a few seconds the slapping stopped and I could only hear Michelle Cooper sobbing and the sound of George Cooper's footsteps up and down the floor.

"I didn't plan this, George. She did. She's been pestering Paul for information. I rang her boss this afternoon to warn her off."

I opened my eyes and looked round. George Cooper was pacing the floor, his eyes moving rapidly to the right and left.

"Sit up, you," he said, and I got up and turned one of the kitchen chairs the right way up.

"Let's have the truth."

"I…" The words wouldn't come out. He walked over to within a couple of centimetres of me and his voice boomed:

"The *truth*!"

"I set this up. I know that it was you and her who killed Judy; not Steven Hardy…" The end of my sentence withered; my voice was hardly audible. "My uncle's on his way here now," I added, almost in a whisper.

Michelle Cooper began to move out of the corner and walk towards us. I could see blood at the corner of her mouth and one side of her face was livid red from the slaps.

"She knows, George."

"Shut up."

"I think Judy tried to blackmail you and…" I said, keeping the conversation going, afraid of what he might do if it stopped.

"Oh, for God's sake. You tell her, Michelle, you tell her the truth," Georgie Cooper laughed, his eyes rolling.

"Why don't we just go?"

"No, I want her to hear it. We'll be gone in a couple of hours; out of the country." He began to walk up and down again. "I want someone to hear what really happened."

Michelle Cooper looked at her husband and then at me. Then she turned and leant her face into the wall.

"The kidnap wasn't working. I'd tried everything, even cut my Judy's hair off and he wouldn't give in."

"She thought I was stupid," he said.

"I would have just left him but he wasn't going to give me a penny. Me and Judy would have had to live in some crummy flat somewhere; some awful place with nothing to live on."

"Poor Michelle." George Cooper was smiling sarcastically.

"We didn't know what to do. It wasn't safe to go on with the kidnap... We just didn't know..."

"I don't understand," I said. I didn't know where any of this was leading.

"She doesn't understand, my darling Michelle, young Patsy here doesn't understand. Let me explain. You see, young Patsy, it wasn't supposed to be my stepdaughter who died that afternoon, was it, my darling? It was supposed to be me."

I looked at him in surprise. He was nodding his head frantically.

"Michelle came home about two o'clock. I'd had a raging headache. My doctor had just given me a sedative, told me to sleep it off. She said, Judy's just rung. She wants us to pick her up. She's come to her senses. She's been staying in one of your houses and she wants you to come and get her.

"I struggled up, stood under the shower to wake myself, drank black coffee. We got here about three-thirty. The door was open and we went in – me first as I remember, my darling." He looked over at Michelle but she was looking down at the floor.

"I walked into the kitchen and bang, that was it –

the lights went out; see here, on my head."

He bent over and parted his hair on the top. There was a scab there.

"Young Judy, my stepdaughter, hit me on the head, tried to kill me. Not that I knew it was her at the time though."

He stopped and walked over to Michelle.

"My lovely wife's idea, you see."

He kissed Michelle on the forehead. She turned away, a look of disgust on her face.

"Look at it from my perspective, Ms Kelly. I'm lying on the floor after having been downed by a blow from a whacking great spanner. I come to, my vision blurred, the pain in my head like a hammer pounding at me. I'm even still dazed by the effects of the sedative. There, a few metres away from me, I see the back of someone who appears to be sprinkling petrol around the place.

"I panic. I stumble up. I grab something – I thought at the time it was the spanner – and hit out as hard as I can.

"Then the person falls and I turn the body over. It's my little stepdaughter and behind me is her mother who promptly becomes hysterical.

"We get out, me and the lovely Michelle. We run. I'm still dazed, don't know what I've got with me, don't exactly know what I hit her with. Michelle there is inconsolable. Took her all of half an hour before she repaired her make-up."

I'd been wrong. Suddenly it didn't matter. I wanted to get out of that room.

"My uncle will be here soon," I said weakly.

"I don't think so, Ms Kelly." George Cooper turned to Michelle. "Go out to the car and get the rope."

Michelle Cooper went without a word.

"What are you going to do?" I said, fear in my voice.

He looked at me for a minute, as though he was genuinely thinking about it.

"Don't worry, Ms Kelly. I'm not a mass-murderer. I'm not going to hurt you. I'm just going to detain you for a while. Meanwhile me and the lovely Michelle will make a new start together."

"You're staying with her, after she tried to kill you?"

"We're stuck together now, she and I. You don't understand. This way she'll never leave me. Wherever we end up, she'll be tied to me; we'll always be together…"

He was still walking up and down, talking gently as if to himself.

I was still seated, but in my mind I was out of the door, through the dark hall and into the street. The breeze was hitting my face and I was on my way to the police.

It was only gradually that I began to notice the smoke.

The air seemed to get thicker. George Cooper was mumbling softly:

"She'll have to stay with me now…"

Then I had to cough a couple of times. In the back of my head I could hear a vague sound like the distant crack of a whip. I looked at the wooden door and imagined having the courage to jump up and pull it open. If Michelle was coming down the hall with the rope I could push her out of the way. I could be out of the house within seconds.

I stood up quietly; George Cooper had his back to me, was looking closely at the back of the mobile phone.

I took a step forward. I began to feel hotter and notice a definite noise from the hall. I saw around the door wisps of smoke threading through the cracks.

"Oh, God," I said, not caring that George Cooper was there.

I pulled open the door and there, through the darkness of the hall, was a dull orange ball of light, the edges of it broken by climbing flames. There was no smoke that I could see in the hall but as it entered the kitchen it rolled like a black mist and curled up towards the ceiling.

"We've got to get out of here," I said, rooted to the spot.

Then I slammed the door and turned to look at George Cooper. His face looked sick and he put his hand over his mouth. He looked at me and then at the boarded-up windows.

I walked past him to the back door and pulled at it. It didn't move.

"We had it all nailed up to stop anyone getting in here," he said hopelessly.

The noise of the fire was increasing and streams of smoke were pouring through the cracks in and around the door.

I heard a laugh and looked round. George Cooper said:

"She's got the last word, my Michelle. The last word."

21

Escape

I pushed against the back door as hard as I could but it wouldn't budge.

"There's no point, I've had it boarded up good and proper," George Cooper said. He was sitting at the kitchen table, his dead mobile in one hand. The other hand he had over his mouth and nose. He had given up. He was just waiting for the fire.

"Help me," I said, but he just shook his head and looked down at his lap.

The room was becoming grey with fumes and I kept holding my breath for as long as I could and then coughing violently when I was forced to inhale.

In the back of my head I thought I heard the sounds of a siren.

I stopped stock-still and listened. There were a

few seconds of heavy silence and I was forced to look at the smoke, gathering up near the ceiling like thin clouds. Maybe I hadn't heard the siren at all. The heat from the fire was pushing into the room, forcing its way inside my clothes, under my hair. I put my hand up to my forehead in an effort to wipe away sweat but there was none. I was just heating up, cooking slowly.

The siren had gone. It had been for some other fire; some ambulance racing to a hospital; a police car chasing a joyrider.

We were on our own.

I felt my knees buckle and sank on to the floor. I let the side of my face lie on the wooden boards. A draught of air hit my skin tantalizingly. I looked round and saw a gap at the bottom of the back door, a centimetre or so between the ground and the wood. There was only blackness through it but I could feel the clear, cold air like the blast from a freezer when it's opened. I sucked the air in and that's when I heard the siren again.

"There's a fire engine," I said, kneeling up. At the same time I could hear a voice, someone calling my name from out the back of the house. I went as close to the door as I could.

"*Patsy, Patsy*," I could hear my name being called from far off. It sounded like Billy. I wanted it to be Billy.

"*Billy*," I shouted but immediately started to

cough, the smoke curling down my throat, poking at my lungs.

The siren sounded as though it was only metres away, but I was feeling weak. George Cooper was lying over the kitchen table. It might have been only minutes before they got to us but I knew that in that time we could both be dead.

I looked down at the door, at the gap underneath where the air was coming in. Then I remembered a film I'd seen on the telly years before. I looked around the room and saw the curtains still hanging on the windows. I got a chair and with a jerk pulled them off. I turned on the tap and pushed them under the gushing water.

"George, move," I said, "*move*."

I pulled him off his chair and he came falteringly, not knowing what I was doing. He fell on the floor at my feet and I pushed his body across to the door, his head nearest the gap at the bottom. The smoke was rising and filling the top of the room. It was only when I stood up fully that I inhaled some of it. When I ducked down the air was still breathable.

I pulled one of the curtains out of the sink, sopping wet, and threw it over his head and shoulders. Then I took the other and put it over my head. I took a last look at the room; it was grey and steamy. The door was still in place but seemed to be vibrating; for a split second it looked as though it was straining against the fire, as though it, more trapped than we were, was putting up a last fight against the ravaging flames. I closed my eyes and lay down on the ground beside George Cooper, the wet curtain covering my head and shoulders. I moved my mouth as close as I could to the gap, taking great gulps of air and holding the wet fabric close to my skin.

I waited.

It was weeks and months and years that I waited. It was everything ahead of me, the rest of my life that I lay through in those seconds. The wet cloth over my head seemed to be drying and I could still hear Billy's voice, only centimetres away through the wall.

There was no movement from George Cooper and I began to feel my breath becoming shallow, panicky. Behind me, at the far end of the room, the sound of the fire was rising; like booming waves crashing against rocks. It was filling my ears and I clutched at the cloth in terror.

Then the door exploded inwards; I felt it tear from its hinges and I thought that was the end.

But it was liquid that came rushing into the room, not heat and flames. It was a jet of ice cold water that cannoned into our midst, throwing us against the wall, soaking through our clothes, the already wet curtains, going up my nose and into my eyes.

When I struggled out from under the cloth they were standing there like spacemen. Yellow hats, black suits, oxygen masks; in their hands they had hoses that looked like giant rayguns.

I felt like a tiny child again.

I did nothing.

I let them pick me up and carry me out and I just kept saying: *don't tell my mum, she'll be worried.*

Out in the street, amid the yards of hose and collection of engines and police cars, I could see Billy. Behind the ambulances I was sure that my uncle Tony's car was parked.

I looked around, through all the people, behind the cars and from face to face.

There was no Michelle Cooper. She had gone.

22

Hammered

It was a week later and Billy and I were in his kitchen.

On the table in front of me, amid the spanners and oily rags, was the local newspaper with the headline: SLUM LANDLORD AND WIFE HAMMERED BY LOCAL P.I. Underneath it said:

Just a week after the battered body of Judy Hurst was found, her stepfather George Cooper has been arrested and charged with her murder. Michelle Cooper, the dead girl's mother, has disappeared and is being sought by the police in connection with fraud and attempted murder charges.

Judy Hurst, an eighteen-year-old hairdresser, was

found dead in the kitchen of 150 Empress Road. Her stepfather, who owned the property, was rescued from a fire in the same house by an undercover agent of "Anthony Hamer Investigations Inc." Mr Hamer was reported as saying: "My operatives are highly trained and professional. We were aware that the case wasn't adding up and it was for that reason that I continued to follow it up. I work closely with the police on these matters and the whole thing has had a satisfactory conclusion."

Mr Hamer is now helping the police to trace Michelle Cooper, who, it is thought, may have fled abroad and may be using a fake passport under the name of Parker.

Billy was washing his hands with some liquid soap, humming to himself.

"Can you believe it," I said, "my uncle's taking all the credit for the investigation!"

"I can," he said. "Listen, Miss Marple, at least you've got your job back."

"But I nearly got killed."

"But you didn't."

I sat silently for a minute. Nothing had gone quite the way I'd planned it. I wasn't getting nearly enough praise or sympathy for what had happened. My mum had been furious with me all week for putting myself in such a position. My uncle had acted as though he'd known all along that Michelle and George Cooper were the murderers. Billy was just carrying on as normal, as though it had been a ladies' toilet I'd been locked in, not a burning house.

The only person who had shown any real appreciation was Heather Warren, the CID officer who my uncle didn't like. She'd sent me an application form for the Metropolitan Police with a note that said: *we need women like you!!*

What had I hoped for?

That my uncle Tony would grovel, beg me to take my job back? That Billy would declare his undying love for me?

Billy was looking into the mirror and combing his hair. His knees were slightly bent and I could see, from the angle at which I was sitting, that he was looking hard at his own reflection, baring his teeth and raising his eyebrows.

It was a new side of Billy that had grown over the past weeks. It had come with the soft female voice of the travel agent, although I'd not heard her voice since it had all happened.

Was he still seeing her? I didn't know.

We had been together a lot, to the hospital and back, going over what had happened. He had held my hand, hugged me a few times, but there had been no kisses.

Once or twice during those hugs I had wanted to put my hand behind his head and pull him towards me.

"What's the film called?" I asked, drinking down the remains of my tea.

"Here," Billy picked up the local paper and read: "'*Cold-Blooded Murder:* a story of incest, death and cover-up in a prominent family; cert 18.'"

He looked at me with a mischievous smile.

"Just what I fancy," I said, putting on my glasses, "a bit of escapism."

End of the Line

Contents

1

The Railway Children

They found the second body in the old disused track down by the industrial estate.

Like the first, she was fifteen and had been strangled.

It was Christmas Eve and Billy and I had been walking along by the river when the police cars had started going by; first one, then another, then two or three more. There was a sense of determination about the way they passed us, not speeding but fast enough to create a whoosh of air, and we stopped to watch them, the policeman in the last one less calm than the others, shouting something at the driver.

The road was eerily silent as well, an absence of sirens, just the sound of the wheels on the ground and a couple of kids across the way playing football; *pass it, pass it*, they shouted.

"That's typical," Billy had said, "when you're waiting for one they never come and then there's five of them together."

"OK," I'd said, "that's an original joke."

We followed the direction they'd been heading and saw them parked at odd angles just outside the old factory estate. Officers were going in and coming out and talking into their radios. They were shouting to each other and reversing their cars up the road to make room for a small unmarked van that had quietly crept down the street. A few minutes later we saw two men carry a long wooden box out of the back of it.

A policeman came towards us, pulling at the collar of his shirt as though it was too tight, and said:

"Off you go, be off home now. There's nothing here for you to see."

Billy whispered "Morgan's Hump" and I followed him off round the corner and up an incline.

We stood on the humpback bridge that passed over the railway sidings, unused now for many years.

Some of the lines were still in place, giant weeds growing up through the tracks. Many of the sleepers were missing, stolen probably, and there were two old carriages which sat, slowly crumbling, at each side of the yard. One line went straight into a long building and it was there that the police were.

"It's a body," I said, stating the obvious.

"On Christmas Eve," Billy said, under his breath, as if that made it more sad. Maybe it did, for the family; unopened presents and a decorated tree that would sit incongruously in the corner beside the cards of sympathy lined up on the mantelpiece.

We stood in silence for a while and watched, some kids and shoppers joining us. One man was carrying a huge Christmas tree under his arm and a number of heavy carrier bags. He let the tree rest against the side of the bridge while he stood and looked at the movements in and out of the siding.

An unmarked car slid along the side of a track. All the policemen turned and looked at it.

"I wonder who that is," Billy said.

The man with the tree and the bags of presents said:

"Well, it's not Father Christmas, that's for sure."

My uncle Tony had closed the agency earlier that day. He'd bought me a small present that he said wasn't my *real* Christmas present; he and my aunt Geraldine would bring that when they came round for Christmas dinner.

I couldn't wait.

I opened the small present while he was standing there. It was a Parker pen.

"It's an office present," he said, adjusting the knot of a new tie he had bought. "My thanks for the good work you've done here, especially since … since…"

He meant since the Judy Hurst case but he didn't say it. I'd tried to find the murderer of a girl that I'd known at school. I'd almost been badly hurt in the process. Since then my uncle had kept his eye on me and I hadn't done anything more strenuous than answering two phones at once.

He'd promised to let me help him on a case though, after I'd made a complete recovery. I'd reminded him of it a number of times and he'd nodded seriously, as though he regretted what he'd said.

"Tony, about that case; the one I'm going to help with."

I left the sentence in mid-air, and watched as he combed his hair in the mirror. He cupped his hands and breathed into them. Then he took out a packet of mints from his pocket and absent-mindedly offered me one.

"The case, Tony. The one you said I could help with."

My words were like an echo and he looked momentarily annoyed.

"Your mum doesn't want you to get involved in that side of the business. Look what happened last time."

"But we did agree," I kept my voice quiet, calm. In my hand I rolled the Parker pen back and forward as though it were a cigar, "that I wasn't just going to work here as a clerk. You promised you'd teach me some of the skills of an investigative agency. That way, you said, I was less likely to get into any trouble!"

"Did I say that exactly?" Tony was packing up his bag, ready to lock up the office.

"Yes, more or less," I said. It had been more like: *we'll see, we'll see*; that famous adult phrase that meant *no, but I don't want an argument right now*.

Tony looked at his watch.

"Are you meeting Aunt Geraldine?" I asked.

"Yes," he said, looking irritated. She was taking him shopping and I knew he didn't want to go. He had planned to meet some of his ex-colleagues from the local police station for a pre-Christmas drink.

He looked at his watch and sighed.

"After Christmas, I'm looking into this insurance claim. A Mr Black who is suing the company he worked for because of a back injury. He says he can't work again, etc., etc. My job is to follow him for a couple of days and see if I can get a photo of him bending over. The company have had some kind of anonymous tip-off that he's faking it. Some nice friend he's got."

I listened to every word, trying to see what there was for me. I'd imagined being allowed to help in an important investigation; after all, I'd not done so badly in the Judy Hurst case. I'd pictured myself with a trench coat billowing over my DMs, dark glasses, maybe even a Trilby. I had one in my wardrobe at home...

"So what we'll do is this. You can come with me while I follow him on the first day and then on the second day you can follow him yourself. It'll be a good chance for you to get to know how to use a camera and surveillance techniques."

He picked up his bag and zipped it shut. He said: "See you about twelve, Christmas day."

He stood for a minute uncertainly, then he turned and went out of the door. I'd thought, for an awful moment, that he'd been waiting for me to give him a goodbye kiss. That he'd regressed some dozen or so years in our relationship to the time when the inevitable words came from my mum's mouth: *Give your uncle Tony a kiss now, there's a good girl.*

I was going to follow someone to try and catch them bending over. It was hardly big time. I felt as though I'd just had some scraps thrown at me and I didn't like it.

I turned off the lights in the office, even the little plastic Christmas tree. I closed the door and looked for a moment at the boldly painted sign: ANTHONY HAMER INVESTIGATIONS INC.

I turned the key, making sure that I had double-locked it, and went out into the street.

They found the third body the day after Boxing Day. It was in a station house that had been closed a couple of years before. Not enough people using the train, a waste of public money, British Rail said.

Like the other two, she was fifteen and had been strangled.

It was all over the national papers. They coined the phrase, THE RAILWAY CHILDREN, and everybody started to talk about the Railway Killer.

"It's a serial killer," my mum's friend Sheila said. "Apparently he leaves the scene of crime exactly the same every time. Strangles them with a piece of climbing rope."

"Honestly, Sheila!" my mum said.

Sheila had recently started working at my mum's college and she had a morbid interest in matters to do with death or murder. She was always reading books about crime or death: *Unsolved Murders of the Nineteenth Century*, or *The Mind of the Killer*, or some such stuff.

"I don't want to think about those awful details," my mum said.

"Do you think your brother, Tony, the detective, might get the case?"

"I don't think so," my mum said, casting a stern eye in my direction, a kind of warning look, as though I might go out and try and find the killer myself. "The case will be top priority with the police. My Tony only follows up things that the police have given up on, or personal matters. He mostly works for insurance companies."

"What about Patsy?"

"Certainly not. Patsy is just working as a clerk, to

give herself some pocket money for when she goes to university next year."

I said nothing. Sheila looked disappointed. She bit into a mince tart and my mum continued:

"I just hope the police catch him, before he does it to anyone else."

Sheila nodded her head but her eyes were staring into the distance, probably imagining the Railway Killer stalking the tracks; his victims soon into double figures. I thought, for a moment, I saw the ghost of a smile on her lips.

A couple of days later I took a drive with Billy. I hadn't seen him since Christmas Day when he'd had dinner with us. It was something he'd done for the previous couple of years, ever since his parents had died.

We were best friends, Billy and I, a bit more than that sometimes. He'd been busy before Christmas though and I hadn't seen much of him. Over Christmas we'd pulled a few crackers and eaten a lot of chocolates. He'd bought me a hat for my collection; a dark brown boater, with a mustard sash on it. It was even in a proper hat box. I'd given him a couple of kisses, one on each cheek. I'd only paused between them for a micro-second, the idea that I should kiss him on the lips only there fleetingly. Then it was gone and I'd stood back and tried the hat on again.

I'd given him a new shirt and a book about vintage cars.

He came round for me at about eight. I got into his latest car and closed the door. I had to pull hard on the handle because the catch was broken.

"That door's definitely coming off tomorrow," Billy said, "and I'm respraying next week. Metallic grey, you reckon? Maybe," he said; then gave me a quick smile before moving off up the road.

Whenever Billy and I met we didn't bother with chit-chat. We often just picked up the conversation where we'd left it the previous time. We'd known each other too long for niceties.

"Where are we going?" I asked, glad to be away from the house. The mince tarts and the turkey now brought on a mild nausea and the glitter of the tree seemed tiresome and garish.

"A bit of a drive? Then a drink?"

We'd been going for a couple of miles when the police cars started to pass us. Billy had turned the music up loudly so we didn't hear them at first. It was me who saw their blue lights blinking frantically behind us, moving rapidly alongside us, then in front. We watched them speed off ahead, the flashing lights becoming smaller, like blue bulbs on a distant Christmas tree. Then they disappeared.

When we got back to my house my mum had the news on.

"They've found a fourth body," she said. "Near

the carriage bays, down at the railway works."

Four bodies.

In ten days.

2

Surveillance

" *Serial killers*." My uncle Tony said the words sarcastically. "They weren't called *serial killers* in my day. That's an American invention."

We were sitting in his car watching a terraced house a hundred or so metres down the street. Mr Black had not come out yet. We'd been there over an hour. On the back seat was a lightweight camera with a zoom lens.

"There was none of this morbid public interest either. You found a couple of bodies, you went on with the investigation, you caught the killer. There were none of these greasy journalists skulking around. Now every Tom, Dick and Harry thinks they can investigate," he said, his voice dropping. "What they don't realize is that detective work is mostly boring, mundane stuff. It's not all car chases and glamorous women..."

I wondered, for a moment, if any of it were car chases and glamorous women. I thought of my uncle's car. A five-year-old Ford that didn't always start; stretch tartan covers and a toy tortoise on the dashboard that was really an undercover air-freshener. I took a sideways look at my uncle; forty-five years old, ex-policeman, family man, immaculately dressed every day, mostly by my aunt Geraldine. I couldn't see many glamorous women in his life.

"Here he is," Tony's voice broke into my thoughts.

A man came out of the door and walked, slowly, to his garden gate and out into the street.

"Come on," Tony said, and we got out of the car. "We'll walk separately to start off. You in front for ten minutes or so, then you drop back and I'll take over."

I pulled my woolly hat over my ears and walked on. Up ahead, Mr Black was walking steadily. He went to the newsagent's and bought a paper; then to the library and chose some books. After that he went to the café where he sat over four cups of something and read his paper and part of one of his books. I had a cup of tea and sat for as long as I could without being noticed. Then I went out and my uncle went in and did the same.

I stood in a shop doorway across the road and waited for them to come out. I was starving but I couldn't go and get any food in case they both moved and I missed them. I was cold as well, my toes like hard pebbles at the tip of my boots.

I saw a headline in a newspaper hoarding across the street: RAILWAY CHILDREN: SCHOOL LINK?

It had been over a week since the fourth body had been discovered. All railway land, used and unused, was being patrolled, guarded, locked up. The dead girls had been named: Mary Williams, Kate Hargreaves, Sarah Roberts and Lucy Jefferson. They were bright achievers, high-flyers; the kind of kids that ended up at university.

Each day the newspapers had printed their pictures. Small, square school photographs that showed the top part of their uniforms; a shirt, a tie, a cardigan or jumper. Pale skin and no make-up; toothy smiles, a glint of fun in their eyes, their friends no doubt larking about behind the photographer.

It was one of the reasons why my mum would never buy any of the school photos that I brought home, year after year. She said they made her shiver, they reminded her of dead children.

There was movement in the shop. Mr Black was getting up and walking out. I joined my uncle and we followed him together, as though we were a father and daughter, out for a walk on a January afternoon. The camera was still over my uncle's shoulder, covered partly by a woolly scarf that he had hanging there.

Mr Black went back into his house and we sat and waited.

"I'll give it to about three-thirty. If he doesn't come out again, we'll call it a day."

My uncle was looking at a magazine, *Sailing Today*. Every now and then I could hear him mumbling "um, um," in agreement with something that he was reading. I put my head back on to the headrest and kept my eyes on the terraced house where Mr Black lived. After a while I felt my eyelids drooping and I had to make myself sit up in case I fell asleep.

I looked at my watch; there was still another hour to go. My stomach had stopped rumbling, but now felt as though it had caved in. More than anything, I wanted to get out of the car and go home.

What had I hoped for? To be part of an important investigation? Like the hunt for the murderer of the Railway Children?

In the distance I heard a train chugging by and wondered how the police were following up the case. I thought about Heather Warren, the CID officer who'd helped me with the Judy Hurst case; she had advised me to join the police, had said that that was where I should go if I wanted to be a *real* detective. Was she in charge of the investigation?

The fourth body had been found near the railway works, where the carriages used to be refurbished and cleaned up. Lucy Jefferson, fifteen, in her last year of secondary school. She'd been found fully dressed with a piece of climbing rope around her neck.

I tried to picture what had happened. Had she been walking along, approached by this man and drawn into a conversation with him? Had he asked her for directions somewhere? Perhaps said he was from out of town. *I'll show you the way*, she might have said. And then, while walking past railway land, had he overpowered her, pulled her back into some undergrowth?

I felt as though I was going to shiver but I didn't. Then I heard a sound; a low growling noise, rhythmic and slow. I looked round.

My uncle Tony's head had fallen to the side and his face was flat against the driver's window, his mouth open. His eyes were closed and his magazine had fallen on to his lap.

He had been so engrossed in the case he had fallen asleep.

Back at the office Tony gave me my instructions for the next day.

"Mr Black is due at the insurer's at eleven, so at least there'll be no hanging around his street. I want you to wait outside from about twelve onwards. You'll see him come out and then you should start to follow him. Give it a couple of hours. Here's the camera. It's an automatic, very expensive. You just point it. It adjusts itself and then, if you press this twice, very quickly, it will photograph half a dozen shots in quick succession."

I took the camera. It felt solid and important in my hand.

"Remember," my uncle said, "if you think he's seen you, just come back. It's no big deal. I have a feeling anyway that Mr Black is genuine. It's no skin off my nose. I still get paid."

When I got home, I put the camera by the side of my bed. I sorted out the clothes I was going to wear. A long coat with a hood; some heavy tights and a long pleated skirt. A close-fitting felt hat and a long scarf.

Somehow, the tedium of the afternoon had disappeared and I was feeling a jittery excitement about the next day. I was to be on my own; trusted with the camera. It was a bit like being allowed to walk home from school by myself for the first time.

It wasn't as though I was being given a case of my own, but it was a start.

3

Smile Please

In the end I wore some trousers and a zip-up jacket. I had a woolly beret on that I managed to pull down over my ears. It was still bitterly cold though and I stamped my feet and hugged my hands as I stood waiting for Mr Black to come out of the insurance offices.

In my shoulder bag I had the camera carefully cushioned and ready to be pulled out at a moment's notice in case Mr Black bent over. I also had a cheese and tomato sandwich that I'd slung together just before leaving home.

Mr Black emerged from the building at about twelve. He drew a sigh as he stood outside the main doors, and then took a look up and down the street. I was only a few metres away from him and I was able to see him up close for the first time. He was about fifty. His hair was thin and he had a small beard, just on the centre of his chin. He had glasses on and I noticed that the left arm had been fixed to the main frame with some black tape. He spent a minute delving into a deep pocket of his coat, then pulled out a handkerchief and loudly blew his nose.

I suddenly felt sorry for him.

I looked back into the foyer of the insurance company's offices. It was a forest of small pot plants and leather seats. On the reception desk was a huge bowl of flowers: lilies, roses, chrysanths, freesias; all the expensive, out of season, blooms.

My uncle had said that Mr Black had strained his back while moving some office furniture. He was making a hefty claim for injury and loss of earnings.

I wondered what a "hefty claim" meant. Tens of thousands? A few thousand?

Mr Black walked off towards the shops and I followed about twenty metres behind. I didn't feel particularly heroic. Some little man was trying to get a few thousand out of a huge company; here I was surreptitiously following him, for an amount that the company probably spent on its foyer pot plants every year.

It was David against Goliath.

Mr Black went into the same café that he had used the previous day. I took my beret off, put my glasses on, and followed him in. I bought a doughnut and a cup of tea and sat in the far corner. I got out a book and laid it open on the table.

He didn't notice me: he didn't even flick his eyes in my direction. He seemed preoccupied. After a while he got some small change out of his pocket and started to count it out on the table. I was beginning to feel such sympathy for him that I considered paying for his lunch myself.

I looked at my watch, it was one-twenty. A woman and a small child came into the café and Mr Black immediately stood up. The woman walked across to him, manoeuvring a pushchair in between the tables. He reached out and took the child, a small boy of about two or three.

"Hello, Dad," I could hear her saying, "another cup?"

"No, love, I've just this minute got this one."

Mr Black sat the small boy on his lap and started to talk to him using a lower, more gentle, voice.

"*Where've you been then? To the shops? Have you got some shopping with Mummy?*"

The little boy reached across him towards the salt and pepper pot on the table and said:

"*Ganggad, Ganggad. Bin the sops, Ganggad.*"

I looked at my book and wondered how long the family lunch would go on. I sneaked one half of my sandwich out of my bag and stole bites from it, wary of the woman behind the counter noticing me. I needn't have worried though. She was gazing out through the window of the shop into the streets beyond, her fingers toying with a chain that was round her neck. Her lips were mouthing words from a song that I could barely hear from a tiny transistor radio on the counter.

Mr Black's daughter left at about two o'clock. Before she went she took out a bag and unpacked it on to the table. There was a plastic cup, a packet of baby wipes, tissues, and some food stuff that I couldn't quite make out.

"Are you sure you'll be all right?" she said, before she went.

" 'Course I will. I'm only going to walk him down the park. *Won't we, my boy?*" Mr Black said, holding up a biscuit for his grandson.

The park was a small, square courtyard in the middle of a shopping precinct. It was like a tiny school playground with swings, climbing frames and a sandpit. There were benches round the side and I took a newspaper out of my bag and sat down to read. After a minute of the biting cold I took out a brown woolly scarf and wrapped it around my neck until it came up almost as far as my nose.

I wondered how long Mr Black would keep the child out in that weather.

I looked around. There were about half a dozen shops that were still open; two or three others that had been boarded up. Near me was a shop called

Ray's Car Spares that took up two shopfronts. Next to it was an Asian shop that had wooden boxes of fruit and vegetables outside and a sign that said: *videos for rent or sale*. An Asian woman came out of the doorway and scooped up some vegetables into a bag. Her sari blew romantically back in the wind and revealed her bare arms and midriff. I felt colder just looking at her.

I looked round at Mr Black. He was sitting on the edge of the sandpit while his grandson was playing. Now and then I could hear his voice: *Now we don't put that in our mouths, do we, son?*

Behind him, sitting on a bench, was the only other person in the tiny park. A teenage girl who was sitting staring into space, her hands in her pockets, chewing slowly.

I turned back and looked at the dry cleaner's that boasted "two hour service" and "expert alterations". The windows looked steamed up and a woman with a grey overall was looking out. I hoped she wasn't noticing me. The Chinese take-away next door had a notice that said "fish and chips, fresh every day" and I actually began to taste the salt and vinegar in my mouth. A packet of hot chips and a ketchup sachet would warm me up nicely. I even began to reach into my bag for the money.

A cry broke into my thoughts though and when I turned round Mr Black's grandson had fallen over. The little boy's mouth was wide open and a pitiful wail came out. The voice was fierce and full of temper and he seemed to be blaming his grandad, the sand, the air, even his own limbs, for the fall.

My first instinct was to get up and go over to help, but then I remembered why I was there. I watched for a minute as Mr Black stood helplessly looking at his grandson.

Then he bent over.

Everything in my head said no but I still got the camera out of my bag and positioned it. Click, it sounded; click, click, click, click, click, it continued to take shots automatically. Holding the camera and letting it take its own photos, one after the other, it didn't really seem as if it was me. I had just started the process off.

Mr Black had stood up by this time and his grandchild was seated in his pushchair.

I quickly stuffed the camera back into my shoulder bag and he turned to face me. His face was riven with pain, his mouth in a grimace and his teeth clenched. I watched with anguish inside my chest. I went to get the camera out again, but it was too late. He turned back, took hold of the pushchair and walked off.

I had missed a chance to photograph his pain. All I had got was him bending over. Exactly what the insurance company wanted.

I looked hopelessly round the tiny park. The only person who was there was the teenager that I had seen earlier. Her head was down though and she seemed to be digging at something on the bench beside her. She hadn't even noticed that the child had fallen over.

I shook my head; then I remembered that I hadn't helped either. I had been too busy doing my job.

I zipped up my bag and walked off towards the High Street.

By the time I'd got to PHOTOKWIK I'd decided what to do. The film had to be developed because there were other things on it that my uncle needed. I would pick up the snaps in the morning on my way to work and destroy the ones of Mr Black. I could say that I'd just taken a few practice ones at home and that I hadn't had to take any of Mr Black because he hadn't bent over.

That would be the end of that.

Feeling pleased with myself I gave the film to Larry, the man in the shop, and went home. My mum's friend Sheila was there drinking tea.

"Guess what," she said, "they've caught the Railway Killer. In the act!"

"Yes?" I said, still disgruntled about the afternoon, not really in the mood for one of Sheila's macabre conversations.

"Quickest police work I've ever seen," she said, "it'll probably be on the local news."

She turned the telly on and there, on the screen,

was Heather Warren, the policewoman that I had got to know on the Judy Hurst case. She was outside the local police station surrounded by reporters.

"Detective Inspector Warren, can you tell us about the latest developments in the 'Railway Children' case?"

Heather Warren was looking down at a piece of paper.

"I have a statement to read out," she said, and then coughed briefly.

"A man was arrested at approximately two-thirty this afternoon in the vicinity of the East London train depot. That man is now helping us with our enquiries. Any further developments we will share with you, if and when they occur."

A cacophony of voices erupted from the reporters but Heather Warren, looking away from the camera, said, "That will be all, gentlemen," and walked off into the police station.

Two-thirty.

Heather Warren had been arresting the Railway Killer at exactly the same time that I was photo-graphing poor Mr Black.

"What do you think of that!" Sheila said, looking from me to my mum, obviously wanting to talk about the murderer and his victims.

"I'm going upstairs," I said moodily.

4

Caught!

I left home early and went straight to PHOTO-KWIK.

My mum had been for her morning run and I'd left her sitting, still in her jogging trousers and sweatshirt, watching Breakfast TV. I'd had to say goodbye twice because she was so immersed in the revelations about the Railway Killer. If her friend Sheila had been there she would have distanced herself and pretended she wasn't interested.

I got to the lab just after eight. It didn't open to the public until eight-thirty but Larry had said it was all right for me to come early. A young dark-haired man in a white coat came out of the swing doors. He was carrying a pile of envelopes and when he saw me he looked momentarily annoyed.

"We're not open yet," he said, dumping the envelopes on to the counter.

"Where's Larry?" I said, rather more brusquely than I meant to.

"Out collecting some supplies. Who's asking?" he said adopting a tiny smile and then letting it drop.

"I'm here from Tony Hamer's," I said, avoiding his direct look. "I'm picking up some film Larry said he'd have done for me." I was looking at my watch, trying to give the impression that I had a busy schedule. In fact I had very little to do that morning; some filing and some phoning around for payment. I wanted the photos though, in my hand. I needed to get rid of the ones of Mr Black; then I could relax.

"And you are?" he asked unruffled.

"Patsy – Pat Kelly. I work with Mr Hamer. These photographs – it really is quite an urgent job. I'm sure Larry has done them. He wouldn't forget a job for us." I was drumming my fingers on the counter top, aware of the young man's penetrating stare.

"Brian," he said. "Brian Martin, at your service."

"Right," I said. "Brian, any chance of looking for the photos? Just as a favour?" That's when I gave him a smile.

"That's nice," he said. "You've got a nice smile."

I gasped at this display of cheek. I stood in silence for a moment and looked him over. He had black hair and dark eyes. He was a bit taller than me and quite chunky. Underneath the white coat he had a dark T-shirt on with some writing that I couldn't read.

"Don't patronize me," I said dismissively. "Whether you like my smile or not I'd like you to go and look for the photos that Larry has put by for me. Otherwise, my company will be looking for some other photographic facility to use." My hand was trembling and my throat was dry but I kept my stare directly at him.

He didn't flinch. He smiled and said, "Certainly. Please take a seat and I'll see what I can do."

He disappeared behind the door and I sat down. The cheek of it! To be leered at so obviously; *to my face!*

I waited, fuming, for what seemed like hours. Only five minutes had passed though and I looked mournfully at the swing doors. They stood still, no tremor of movement that might suggest footsteps coming this way. The young man, Brian, had gone away with no intention of coming back. Perhaps I shouldn't have been so supercilious with him. Maybe I should have just continued smiling and got my photos by being nice to him.

I would just have to sit and wait. I picked up my bag and pulled my newspaper out and started to read.

The capture of the Railway Killer was all over the front page.

The police got a lucky break yesterday when a local resident spotted a man loitering around the East London train depot. After a quick phone call had been made to the emergency services, police raced to the scene just off Regency Road. A police helicopter was called, but in the event was not needed.

The man was apprehended while moving around the carriage bays. When the police found him he reportedly fled and ran along the tracks towards central London. He was chased and caught by officers and then informed of his rights.

The man has been named as 48-year-old Leslie Knight from Essex, a retired railway ticket inspector. Former colleagues are said to be "deeply shocked" by the arrest.

At a press conference late last night, the detective in charge of the investigation, Heather Warren, said that the man had been found with certain suspicious articles on his person, which, in the present circumstances — four dead teenagers — needed to be explained. It is believed that among these items was a length of climbing rope.

Mr Knight is due to appear at East London magistrates court this morning. It is expected that he will be held on remand until all investigations are completed.

*The funerals of two of the victims, Mary Williams and
Kate Hargreaves, are due to take place this week. The
families will be relieved that the investigation has borne
fruit so quickly. The bodies of the other two victims,
Sarah Roberts and Lucy Jefferson, have not yet been
released.*

The noise of footsteps made me look up. The young
man, Brian, had returned. He was not sullen as I'd
expected him to be. He was flushed, quite jovial.

"Here we are!" he said. "Finally found them in
Larry's tray. He had done them."

"Great," I said, giving him a real smile, and was
momentarily flustered when his fingers touched
mine as he was handing over the photos.

"So you're a private investigator, are you?" he
said, giving me the invoice to sign.

"Yes, sort of," I said. He was leaning on the
counter, nodding as though he wanted me to go on.
I was keen to look at the photos though. "I must be
off; thanks for finding the photos." I turned away.

"I'll tell you what – " I could hear his voice as I
went out of the shop doors – "you can follow me any
time…"

I repressed an urge to turn round and give him a
mouthful. I tucked the photos away and headed
back to the office.

*　　*　　*

As soon as I got to the office I sat down at my desk and sorted through the pictures.

Most of them were Tony's. There were several of a burnt-out shop and a couple of two men talking in a park. I wondered which case it was. There was even a photo of Geraldine, Tony's wife. It looked like the first photo in the reel, so perhaps Tony had been trying out the film.

The photo showed my aunt Geraldine in her kitchen, standing beside her Aga cooker. She had an apron on and in her hand was a spatula. She was pointing it at the person behind the camera and she had a half-moon smile on her face. At the bottom of the photo was the time and date that the shot had been taken: 11.49 a.m. 01.01. New Year's Day. Maybe something Tony had said to her had made her laugh. I tried to imagine my uncle Tony being witty or humorous. It didn't work. It was a bit like when I was a kid trying to imagine my mum and dad in a passionate embrace.

I put those photos to the side and laid out the six that I had taken of Mr Black. I sat down in my chair, my coat still on, and looked over my handiwork.

I'm not sure exactly what I had expected. Probably something that looked like a series of stills from a film. A slow-motion scene from the park. Mr Black looking at his grandson lying on the ground; two or three of Mr Black in the course of bending down; Mr Black scooping up his grandson and then Mr Black standing upright again.

The photos were quite different though. Firstly, they were all at a peculiar angle. They showed a slanted world and the top corner of Mr Black's back. I must have been holding the camera crookedly. Not only that but two of the photos didn't show Mr Black at all. He had ducked below the lens at that point and all I'd captured was a shot of the sullen teenager who'd been sitting on the park bench behind him. The most depressing thing was that none of the photos showed any identifiable bit of Mr Black. It could have been anybody.

I sat back, annoyed. I had wanted to throw the photos away anyway but it would have been gratifying if they had at least come out properly; if I had been able to manage the camera more efficiently.

Not only could I not identify Mr Black, but I had even missed him out. I picked up the two photos that he had dropped out of. I had a lovely view of the teenager sitting on the bench. She had her hands in her pocket and her legs splayed and was staring straight ahead, as though she was looking at something to the right of me. Her expression was one of boredom and I could even remember her slowly chewing gum and not even noticing when Mr Black's grandson started to cry.

At the bottom of the photo was the time and the date: 2.32 p.m. 10.01.

The exact time that the serial killer was caught.

It was just as well that Heather Warren did her job a bit more competently than I'd done mine.

I had a last look at the kiddies' park, the top of Mr Black's shoulder and the sullen teenager staring moodily at the world. She looked about thirteen. 2.32. Half past two, she should have been in school. Then I cut the negatives away from the others and put them, along with the photos, into the sink, and set light to the lot.

They curled and blackened and magically seemed to disappear, leaving a residue of what looked like black petals lying in the sink. I gathered them up and pushed them down to the bottom of the bin, underneath the tea bags and the empty biscuit packets.

I finished my tea and resolved to learn how to use the camera properly. Then I got out the forms and began to write out my report.

When I got home that evening and turned on the telly, I saw Heather Warren's face again. She was in the middle of a crowd of reporters. I could see two or three furry mikes being thrust at her and at first I didn't quite catch what the question was. The answer was clear though.

"The body of a fifteen-year-old white girl was found this afternoon. It was in one of the cargo bays in the Holding Warehouses, just adjacent to the

Regent's Road depot. The area hadn't been searched yesterday because there appeared to be no need. When the suspect was apprehended it was strongly believed that a further crime had been prevented. At that time we had no way of knowing that a fifth murder had in fact happened, perhaps only minutes before.

"Naturally, my officers are devastated by this find." Heather Warren turned abruptly away from the cameras even though there was a chorus of cries.

They had found a fifth body.

Five girls he had killed. The fifth one only minutes before Leslie Knight had been caught.

I picked up the remote and pressed the button. The picture died and I sat there for some minutes, feeling flat and aimless.

5

A Familiar Face

My mum was out with her friend Sheila so I watched the ten o'clock news on my own.

It was the same depressing story. During a routine operation two rail workers had stumbled on the body of a fifteen-year-old in a warehouse in a yard along the way from the Regency Road depot. The killer, widely assumed to be Leslie Knight, had done his work and was moving *away* from the scene of the crime; not *towards* it, as had been earlier thought.

Leslie Knight, having already been charged with the other murders, would now have to go back to the magistrates court to be charged with this fifth one.

The picture of the dead girl flashed on to the screen. It was another school photo, taken recently. She had a dark uniform on and her shoulder-length hair blended into her sweater. She was smiling, but only just, her lips upturned at each corner; no teeth, no dimples.

She looked familiar; but then school photographs often made me think of my own school and all the kids I knew then. She was pale with dark hair, not unlike any dozen or so girls whose pictures I had stored at the very edges of my memory.

Her name was Helen Driscoll and she had come from The Valentines, an estate bordering on a local park. "Estate" was the wrong word; it conjured up images of row upon row of identical houses punctuated by tower blocks and waste ground. It made me think of burnt-out cars and graffiti; un-employed teenagers parading with their outlawed pit-bulls.

The Valentines was a *private* estate of a couple of dozen big houses. It was a turning off a side road that bordered the park. The road was gravel and had several "NO ENTRY" signs posted along it. I'd been with Billy when he'd delivered a car that he had sold to a couple who lived down there. It was a small yellow mini that Billy had bought as a wreck and then painstakingly done up. The couple had wanted it as a surprise birthday present for their daughter. When we'd given it over to them the mother had rushed into her house and come out with a giant blue ribbon that she'd promptly tied round the car, as though it was a huge parcel.

Helen Driscoll had lived in one of those big houses.

And now she was dead.

The newscaster was reading the rest of the news, so I clicked the set off.

The house was strangely quiet without my mum being there. I looked around the room and saw her books and papers all over the dining-room table. Over by the door was a pair of her running shoes and draped around a chair was a jacket that she had worn to work that day but not got round to hanging up.

I suddenly felt very alone and wondered what my dad was doing.

He and my mum had lived apart for years. I saw him regularly but he often moved around the country with his job. I knew that he'd been in Birmingham for the last couple of weeks and I was tempted to ring him on his mobile. I even walked casually out to the phone in the hall and let my fingers drum lightly around the buttons.

What would I say though? *Hi, Dad, I'm feeling a bit depressed about these murders…*

Just then the phone rang and made me jump. I picked it up and said: "Hello?"

"That was quick," a male voice said.

"Yes?"

"It's me, Brian Martin. From PHOTOKWIK, remember?"

I stood with my forehead wrinkled up and let the name go through my head a few times. Brian Martin, Brian Martin.

"I'm sorry," I said. The word PHOTOKWIK flashed on and off like a neon inside my head. Brian Martin: the kid with the poor chat-up line.

"I'm the helpful young man who found your photos this morning."

"Right. Brian, how are you?" It was a stupid thing to say but it just came out.

"Good, good," he said, as if it had been weeks since he'd seen me. "We got off to a bad start this morning, Patsy. I was wondering if we couldn't get to know each other a bit, say go out for a drink, or a meal, or both?"

I wasn't sure I liked the way he'd put himself on immediate first-name terms with me.

"Where did you get my phone number?"

"Tony Hamer gave it to me," he said.

Thanks a lot.

"It's a nice idea," I said, "but I'm really busy at the moment." I could hear the key scraping on the lock and looking round saw my mum come through the door. She gave me a silent wave and went into the living room.

"Is this the brush-off, Patsy?" he asked.

The brush-off. Where did he get his dialogue from; an old film?

"I really must go."

"Patsy," he said, "don't turn me down!"

His familiarity with my name was beginning to annoy me.

"Goodbye, Brian," I said, returning the address.

I put the phone down quickly and leant on it for a minute, as though I wasn't quite sure that the voice had really been cut off.

"Who was that?" I could hear my mum's voice from the front room.

"Some kid," I said, not elaborating.

"Billy?"

"No, just some kid who I met today."

"Where?"

"In this photo lab Tony uses. He's just someone I met, nothing important."

I went into the living room. My mum was lying on the ground. Then she started her sit-ups.

"He?" she said and exhaled quickly. I couldn't see her face. I knew that her eyebrows were raised.

"Never mind, it's nobody."

"Are you going out with him?" she said in between breaths.

"No, I'm not," I said, laughing.

"I could lend you that silk top of mine." I could hear her voice as I went up the stairs, and I rolled my eyes.

After I'd got changed into my night clothes I sat on a chair and looked in the mirror for a while. At the right-hand corner my mum had stuck a sprig of mistletoe. It made me think of silly Brian and his terrible chat-up line. *You've got a nice smile*, he'd said.

I had an ordinary face, not unpleasant to look at,

but not the sort of face that sticks out in a crowd. My eyes were quite big and I had an average nose and uniform lips. Any description of me would sound like that of dozens of other girls of my age. I was five foot six and my weight wavered a few pounds here and there but mostly stayed around nine stone. Sometimes I could get my jeans done up and sometimes I couldn't.

My hair was longish; at least I was always growing it, but it seemed to have stopped at my shoulders. All in all, I was a bit of a shop dummy with glasses on. The only way I ever stood out was if I dressed myself up, made up my face or wore one of my many hats.

Billy always commented if I got dressed up: *I like that top*, or, *your hair looks good like that*. The previous week, when we'd been window-shopping in the Exchange, he'd said: *you'd look brilliant in that dress*, pointing at some long chiffon number in an expensive French shop window.

I'd felt a fizz in my chest when he'd said it, as though I'd actually been wearing the dress there and then and he'd been standing back, looking me up and down. For minutes afterwards I'd felt a mild shiver around my shoulders and couldn't look straight at him. I'd felt *embarrassed* to look at him.

Sitting there, in front of my mirror, I pictured Billy's face and remembered the time he had kissed me under the mistletoe, over a year before. It had been a long kiss and we'd jumped apart when my mum had come through the front door. My lips had been wet and I'd wiped them with the ends of my fingers. Or maybe I'd just put my hand there to hide the kiss, as though I'd imagined that it was showing, that my mum would come up and see it there on my mouth.

We'd never mentioned that kiss.

We'd been friends since childhood, Billy and I, much closer after his parents had got killed. He lived alone in his parents' house and we saw each other three or four times a week, sometimes more. We'd always been close but inexplicably, every now and then, I felt a compelling urge to touch him, or hug him or even, once or twice, to kiss him. I never did though; nothing had ever happened between us again.

Smiling at my thoughts, I took the mistletoe down from the mirror and dropped it into the bin. Then I went to bed.

The dead girl's picture was on the front page of the national newspaper the next morning. The headline was: POLICE MISS BODY IN SEARCH. Then, underneath: *Dead teenager not found for twenty-four hours; fifth victim. Questions raised in the House.*

The story went on but I couldn't take my eyes off the picture of the girl.

It was the same shot that they had shown on the telly the night before but it was larger and I sat and looked at it for minutes, while my mum chattered on about her students and their essays that were due in.

Then it dawned on me.

I knew the girl. I knew her face, had seen her recently.

I sat back and thought through my actions over the previous few days.

I stopped when I remembered following Mr Black. I was sitting in the playground, taking photos of him. Then I was sitting in the office looking through the photos. They had been all crooked and I had missed Mr Black out of two of them. I had caught the moody teenager. The one who had been sitting on the bench while Mr Black had played with his grandchild.

She had been sitting staring straight ahead and I had caught her in two of my photos.

The dead girl, Helen Driscoll, was the girl that I had seen in the park. The one that I had photographed.

6

Ashes to Ashes

I went straight round to PHOTOKWIK.

On my way I kept picturing the girl's face, trying to re-create it in detail in my head. While I was waiting for the lights to change I closed my eyes for a few moments and saw her, legs stretched, lying back against the bench, her hands in her pockets, staring straight past me. She had a sullen expression, bored, as if she knew everything.

But I had thrown the photos away.

Two photos; both taken when Mr Black had bent down to pick up his grandchild. I had her there, on film, looking in the direction of the camera.

At 2.32. Thirty-two minutes past two.

The Railway Killer, Leslie Knight, had been captured at two-thirty.

I had Helen Driscoll still alive, on photo, at two thirty-two.

I dashed across the road and ran up the High Street before turning into PHOTOKWIK. The first person I saw was the kid who'd phoned me: Brian.

"We must stop meeting like this," he said, grinning.

"Is Larry in?" I said, ignoring him.

"Larry!" he shouted. "A certain young detective to see you."

I glared at him and he added, "Patsy Kelly here, wants a word."

Larry appeared through the swing doors and smiled when he saw me.

"Now then, what can I do for you? Some pictures, is it? Another rush job?"

"Larry," I puffed, "you know that film I gave you the other day, the one I wanted done quickly?"

"Certainly do? Is there something wrong with them? One or two a bit wonky?"

"No, it's just…"

Larry was often difficult to talk to. He was always asking questions and then answering them himself, before you got a chance to speak.

"I was wondering whether or not the developing machine…"

"The Kodak Deluxe," Larry said proudly.

"The Deluxe; whether it kept copies of what it developed?"

"You want copies of the negs? I can do copies for you."

"No, I wondered if the machine kept copies…"

I was losing my thread. Larry was looking at me with raised eyebrows. Brian was shuffling papers but I could tell that he was listening.

"Thing is, I lost the photos. My uncle will be furious. That's why I wondered if the machine kept copies."

"How did you lose them?" Larry said. "Fell out of your pocket? Oh, dear, no, the Deluxe doesn't keep a master-roll, Patsy. Are you sure you've lost them? They might be in your bedroom. My daughter's bedroom is a real state…"

I stood and let Larry babble on about the bedrooms of teenage girls and realized that the photos were gone.

The pictures I had of Helen Driscoll alive at the time that the serial killer was arrested were in the bottom of my uncle's office bin, under the tea bags and bits of sandwiches.

They were a pile of black ashes.

Billy took the common-sense approach.

"You don't know it was the same girl. You saw the face on the telly and *then* in the papers this morning. That's why it was familiar. Then you just thought back to the last teenager you'd seen. You've convinced yourself of something that isn't true."

I didn't answer him. I gulped down the tea he had made me and watched as he continued to iron. A small weekend bag was on the table, already half full.

"When are you going away?" I asked, changing the subject.

He looked at his watch.

"About five."

"It's very sudden, isn't it?" I said sulkily. Billy had made a last minute decision to visit his mum's sister who lived in Norfolk.

"That's true, but I've got no work on at the moment. She rang me before Christmas, asked me to come and I just put her off again. She lives on her own. The truth is," he said, "she's the only family I've got left. It seems silly not to keep in touch."

"Yes, I suppose so," I said, slightly miffed. I had got used to the fact that we were Billy's only family.

He was quiet for a moment and my mind wandered back to the teenager on the bench. When I concentrated I could see her whole face. It was as if my memory was like a camera and could zoom in to her features. She was sulky-looking, a kind of pout around her lips; she'd looked small, a young teenager. I pictured the school photograph; the smile had seemed forced, as if someone had insisted that she cheer up and she had obliged with the absolute minimum. Her hair had been shorter in the photograph as well. I was sure it was her. Certain.

"Why don't you come with me?" Billy said.

"Where?"

"To Norfolk. It's only for a few days. You'd like my aunt. We could do some sight-seeing. It'd be cold, but it could be fun."

Billy was right. It did sound like fun. I suddenly saw myself walking along a beach, the wind blowing my coat back, the spray of the sea in an arc behind me.

"I don't know," I said, feeling a tiny fist of excitement opening up in my chest. It wouldn't take me long to throw a few things in a suitcase. Two or three hats was all I would need.

"What about work?" I said vaguely, already tucking it away in the unimportant tray. The Helen Driscoll thing; I could write it all out and send it to Heather Warren; she could either look into it or dismiss it.

Then Billy said:

"Tony'll let you go! It's not as if you're doing anything important!"

He said it lightly, not meaning to hurt my feelings, but it hit me like a blow.

You're not doing anything important.

I looked at his cheerful face, his half-packed bag. I tried very hard to stop my feelings showing through but there must have been a crack in my composure because Billy, realizing what he'd said, put the iron down and came over.

"Oh, dear," he said. "I've said the wrong thing."

He squatted down on the floor beside my chair with his arm loosely around my shoulder.

"No," I said, self-pity welling up in my throat, "I suppose what I do isn't very important."

"Patsy," he said in a low voice, and his hand touched the skin at the back of my neck, "it was just a thoughtless thing to say. I didn't mean— "

"Yes, you did…" I turned round to him, my knees almost in his chest. "The day before yesterday I followed some poor old man around to catch him bending over. Yesterday, I harassed half a dozen people for money they owe my uncle; oh, and don't forget all the filing I did and the four cups of tea I made for Tony."

I stopped then and let the rest play on in my head. Billy rested his arms on my knees, drew a huge sigh and laid his head down. I felt his weight on my legs and didn't know what to do or say.

Nothing I did was very important. I was an office clerk who thought she was something better.

I lifted my hand nervously and put it on the back of Billy's head. A trip to Norfolk would be good for both of us. I let my fingers move in and out of his hair and found, after a few seconds, that I was holding my breath.

The iron hissed and broke the silence and Billy sat up.

"Well, Patricia, are you coming or not?" he said,

using my full name for once. For a fleeting moment I thought of Brian Martin and his clever chatter.

"Why not?" I said and stood up, my knees feeling strangely cold since Billy had leant off them. "I'll go and see Tony, then pack a few things in a bag. You could pick me up, about four-ish."

I don't know why I went back to the park where I had seen Helen Driscoll. I told myself it was just to confirm my story for Heather Warren, to find the exact bench, to copy the spelling of the precinct's name. It was on the way back to the office from Billy's house, give or take a few streets.

Whatever my reasons were, I ended up sitting on the bench that I had seen the girl sit on.

You're not doing anything important. Billy's words kept buzzing round my ears, threatening to sting me.

Why ever had I taken this job? Why hadn't I gone straight to university like my friends? A year off, I'd wanted. It had sounded good when I'd said it; as if I'd had some important project in my mind which I could do in the year. All summer long I'd felt excited. It had been a way of leaving college and still having that university place in my back pocket for the following year.

A job with my uncle's detective agency had sounded different. When I'd become involved with the Judy Hurst case I had felt important, even though I'd nearly been killed. Now, though, it was back to being Miss Office Clerk, Miss Teasmade, Miss Filing Clerk, Miss Fed-Up.

I sat for a few moments allowing myself to wallow in the injustice of my unimportant job and mundane life. Then I looked at my watch and shook myself. I got a small pad out of my bag and copied down the name of the precinct: Lister Square. I described the positioning of the bench by noting down the shop it was opposite: Majestic Dry Cleaners.

I put the pad away and just before I got up to leave I adopted the position that I remembered the girl was sitting in. I lazed back on the bench and let my legs lie casually apart. I put my hands in my pockets. I felt an inclination to let my head lean back against something but there was nothing behind me. The girl must have held up her head rigidly for it to sit like that. It was odd. For the rest of her to look so relaxed and yet for her head to be so tense. Had it been Helen Driscoll? Was I absolutely sure?

I let my hands fall out of my pocket and found my fingers playing with an indent in the wood. I glanced down and saw some lettering.

I sat forward and zipped up my jacket. The Asian lady was out in her sari again although this time she had a padded coat over the top. She shouted at a small child who was walking along past the car shop. I wondered if Mr Black had been here since that day with his grandchild.

I found myself staring down again at the lettering that someone had dug into the bench. There were several sets of initials and then, further along, in an area which no one had used, was a new set: HD 101.

I sat very still looking at it. It didn't mean anything, I kept telling myself. HD. Lots of people had those initials. Even if it was Helen Driscoll, she could have gone there at any time and carved her initials. 101. One hundred and one, 101, the tenth of the first. The tenth of January.

And then I remembered. When Mr Black had struggled up with his grandchild, the teenager had been digging away at the bench, ignoring what was happening.

It had been Helen Driscoll, carving her initials in the bench.

I was sure now and nobody, not even Billy, was going to change my mind.

7

A Career in the Police

I went straight back to the office and made a phone call.

"Patsy," Heather Warren said, after I'd finally been connected to her extension, "sorry about the difficulties in getting through. You don't know how awful the press have been over these Railway Murders. How are you?"

"Fine," I said, my voice trembling slightly. "Have I rung at a really difficult time?"

"It's always a difficult time! How's old Tony these days, although don't tell him I said he was 'old'. You know how touchy these menopausal men can be!"

My uncle had worked with Heather when he'd been in CID. She wasn't one of his favourite people.

"I was wondering," I said, getting straight to the point, "whether I could take you up on your offer about having a look around the station. I'm finding my role here a bit limited; only don't tell Tony I said that."

"Of course not," she said and I could hear the pleasure in her voice. "You thinking of joining up then? About time you made a positive career move."

"I'm thinking about it," I said.

"You could spend a day with me, maybe week after next – "

"I was really wondering," I butted in, "if I could come this week, maybe tomorrow. I wouldn't have to stay with you, I know how busy you are, I could just shadow some junior officer. It might even be a more realistic experience for me." I was speaking rapidly, hoping she wouldn't butt in and put me off. She started to say something a couple of times, but then became more quiet as I went on.

"Good idea, Patsy. You're right, of course; a day with me wouldn't be at all representational of what a young officer could expect. It would be much more sensible for you to go with one of my juniors. Let me fix it up for – "

"Tomorrow?" I said. "Tony's out all day in court so he wouldn't know about it. I don't want to hurt his feelings."

"Tomorrow?" She sounded unsure. I could hear the sound of paper being ruffled, as though she was looking something up. "At a push I could probably manage tomorrow. About ten; see you then." The line went dead and I felt a moment of exhilaration.

A day in the station would give me access to details about the Railway Murders. I was hoping that in my totally innocent way I could ask some questions about the case: the *exact* time that Leslie Knight was picked up, the *precise* time of Helen's death.

I sat back, my heart thumping with tension. I looked at my watch.

It was going on for three o'clock. Billy would be at my house in about an hour to take me off to Norfolk. I needed to get home to explain to him why I couldn't go. Doing it on the phone would be no good at all.

There was no one in when I got home. I put on the central heating as well as the kitchen light. Even that early it seemed to be greying over, the sky looking heavier, the clouds dense and solid.

I took off my glasses to clean them and thought about what I would say to Billy. I knew I wasn't going to tell him that I was staying behind for Helen Driscoll. He might think it was because of what he had said to me, that I wasn't doing anything *important*.

The doorbell rang and I went to answer it.

"Your car awaits," Billy said when I opened the door.

"I can't go," I said, taking him by the sleeve and pulling him into the hallway.

"Why not?" he said, looking concerned for a moment. He changed his expression when I didn't answer. "Is it because of this girl at the precinct?"

"No, no," I lied.

Just then the phone rang and he took a step backwards towards the front door. I left it ringing and followed him, grabbing his arm.

"Tony needs me in the office. He's in court all day tomorrow and a new client's coming in. He's going to let me do the initial interview. It will be good experience for me." I was making it up as I went along.

Billy looked straight at me, then he softened.

The phone had stopped ringing and the answerphone had come on.

We're not available to come to the phone at the moment, my mum's teacher's voice sounded in the hall.

"It's good experience for me, Billy. I'll never get anywhere in this job if I don't throw myself into it." I was beginning to believe it myself.

Please leave a message and we'll get back to you, my mum's voice continued.

Billy was smiling. "All right, Pat, a girl's got to do what a girl's got to do!" He leant over and gave me a peck on the cheek. I closed my eyes for the minisecond that it took and was just about to speak when

I heard a familiar voice leaving a message on the answer-phone.

"Listen, Miss Patsy Kelly, I know you really want to go out with me and that you're just playing hard to get. Why don't we take in a film tonight…"

The smile fell off Billy's face and for a brief moment he flinched as if he'd been hit by something.

Embarrassed and flustered I turned and took three giant steps down the hallway to pick up the phone.

"Brian, will you get off this phone and stop harassing me," I said.

"I love it when you're angry," was his reply.

I slammed down the phone and turned around, my mouth open ready to explain. Billy had gone though and the front door was swinging open in the darkening afternoon. I ran out, down the pathway, only to see his car disappearing up the street.

I went back into my hallway and glared at the phone, not sure what had just happened, exactly why Billy had gone off in such an abrupt way.

At least that's what I told myself.

8

CID

The next morning I went into the office and noted down a couple of messages from the answer-phone. I ruffled the files around and left an open one on my desk. I left one of my drawers hanging open and put a note on top of my work: *Just popped out for a while – Patsy.*

I was banking on the fact that Tony would be in court all day. If for some reason he came into the office he would see the note and assume that I'd be back shortly.

Before leaving I looked at the phone with some agitation, wondering whether or not to ring Billy at his aunt's. I decided against it.

If Billy or my uncle had seen me that morning they

would have been much surprised. I had adopted my young career girl disguise. Even my mum's face had dropped when she'd seen me slipping out of the front door.

I'd put my mum's heated rollers all over my head and my hair had bounced out and made a soft halo of curls around my face. I'd got out my make-up bag and sat for a while deciding which face to put on.

A lot of time I don't bother with make-up. I have no objections to it in principle but it can be time-consuming and it means you have to be careful all day not to scratch your nose or rub your eyelids. It also means, once you've applied it, that you have to check from time to time that it is all still there, in place, otherwise you look a bit daft, especially if you have only one bright blue eyelid or one cheek rouged and the other not.

When I did wear it though, I liked to decide on a look.

Getting ready to go to the police station I had decided to go for pastel colours, nothing too threatening. I'd put some light blue on my eyelids and some grey mascara. I'd put on some pale beige foundation and used a spot stick to cover up one or two red areas. I didn't use blusher and I'd put on some very pale pink lipstick.

I'd put on my glasses to see what it looked like.

I'd looked in my mum's wardrobe and found a close-fitting dress that she hadn't worn for a while.

It was shorter than the things I wore but I'd put on some opaque tights so that my legs didn't feel so exposed. I'd put a suit jacket on top of it and found a small scarf in one of my drawers that I made into a sort of cravat.

I'd found some tiny pearl earrings and sprayed some of my mum's scent around my neck.

I'd decided against a hat. It was a mark of eccentricity and I didn't want to appear odd at the station. I'd put some things into a small handbag and taken a look at myself in the mirror.

I'd looked like someone's secretary. The dress, somewhat tighter on me than on my mum, restricted my stride and meant that I had to take shorter steps. I'd smiled at myself. I definitely looked sweet, nice, easy-going: Miss Perfect WPC.

My mum, who'd been talking on the phone, had looked at me in amazement as I'd come down the stairs.

"It's all right," I'd said in a loud whisper, "I'm working deep undercover."

I was taken straight to the CID suite. Heather Warren was in a meeting when I arrived but a young man in jeans and a suit jacket got me a mug of tea. He gave it to me abruptly and some of it sloshed over the side and on to the desk and my leg.

"I'm Des," he said. "You'll be shadowing me today."

I smiled but he didn't. I put the tea on the desk and got out some tissues to wipe up the mess. Des hadn't noticed and was intent on looking through some papers. A woman cleaner appeared at my shoulder.

"Here, dear," she said, mopping up the mess with a J-cloth. She picked up my sopping tissues and dropped them into a large black plastic bag that she had. Then she continued on up the room, emptying ashtrays and wiping surfaces.

The "suite" was a long area with three glassed-off rooms along the side. One side of it was lined with windows and there was still spray snow stuck along them and the remains of a "Merry Christmas". There were about ten desks and a number of filing cabinets. A number of Christmas cards were still stuck to the filing cabinets and I could see a half-full bottle of red wine standing, corkless, on top of one of them. Along the back wall was a line of computer terminals, each of them with someone sitting in front. The walls were covered with several maps and there was a large white board in the corner that had writing all over it.

"Working as a *private detective*, Miss Kelly," Des said, smiling and nodding at his papers.

"Patsy, please," I said, less friendly this time. Des wasn't ecstatic about having me with him.

Just then I heard a voice.

"Patsy!" It was Heather Warren. She came

striding across the room, numerous people moving out of her way, one or two hastily stubbing cigarettes out on to ashtrays. "You're looking well, Patsy!" she said, an unlit cigarette between her fingers. "Des and Stevie will look after you today. I'm very busy this morning but I'll probably see you later this afternoon."

She didn't wait for me to answer but turned away and in a loud voice said: "People!"

The sounds in the office lessened.

"Plan for today as follows: meeting in ten minutes in the conference room for update on the Leslie Knight case; apart from that, there's the burglaries on the Selby Estate, Tricia – you, Terry and Leon follow that up; the fake welfare workers have been active again over in Archer Street; Peter – you and Mac follow that up..."

Heather went on but I was thinking about the meeting in ten minutes in the conference room on the Leslie Knight case. I was hoping – praying – that Des Murray was part of that team.

He wasn't.

"Des – you and Stevie, and Patsy, of course," she smiled, "go down to the Harley youth centre and see if you can find out any more about who's bringing drugs into the place."

Then she walked back up the room and disappeared into an office.

A couple of people let out sighs, as though they'd

been holding their breaths all the while she'd been speaking.

"Are you coming then?" Des Murray was rattling his car keys. I looked round the office with frustration. Some people were tucking important-looking files under their arms and getting ready for the meeting in the conference room. I was on my way to a youth centre to find out about drugs.

It hadn't been part of my plan.

Outside, it was a bright winter's day, the sun glittering against a blue sky, bouncing off windows and dazzling us when we looked around. The wind whizzed around though, lifting the ends of my coat and pulling my hair all to one side. It had an icy edge and I felt goose-pimples rise on my arms.

In the car I made the best of it. I didn't have much choice. Des silently chain-smoked and Stevie, a woman of about thirty, ate constantly: cough sweets, chocolate bars, cakes, chewing gum. She also chatted to me the whole way. She'd known my uncle – well, briefly – at least she'd seen him around. She'd wanted to do A-levels but the teachers didn't like her; at least, one male teacher picked on her all the time. She'd considered going private; at least a friend of hers knew someone who worked Security in a big department store. They paid good money but there wasn't the job security. She had boyfriends, not many of them serious because they couldn't take her job; at least they didn't like the fact that she had to work closely with so many men.

We both looked at Des Murray when she said this; he had just inhaled a lungful of cigarette smoke and was looking peaceful and sublime. His hands were on the steering wheel and I noticed a heavy gold ring on his finger. It glinted confidently in the sunlight.

We went to the youth centre but it was all locked up. A note pinned to the door said that the youth worker was off sick.

"What shall we do?" Stevie said. "Go round his house?"

"No," Des said, "let's take a walk through the flats."

As we walked through the flats the wind sliced past us, blasting at us head-on round the corners. We were heading for a small sweetshop that had bars over the windows and an entryphone at the door. On the brick wall underneath someone had sprayed "Fort Knox" in untidy lettering.

Des went up to the door. "I need some fags," he said and after speaking into the wall he was allowed in.

Stevie said: "Don't mind Des, he's just annoyed at being taken off the Railway Murders."

"For me?" I said perplexed.

"No. Now that they've got Leslie Knight, it's

being trimmed down. Half a dozen detectives were reassigned yesterday. Des was one of them."

The door of the shop opened and Des came out with the flicker of a smile on his face.

"Let's go and see old Florrie Roberts," he said.

"Florrie?" Stevie said. "Florrie's at it again? After what the magistrate said?"

"She probably believes that her great age will protect her from prison. Maybe not this time."

"An old-age pensioner is dealing drugs?" I said incredulously.

"Maybe," Des said, lighting a cigarette. "Some grannies just knit jumpers for their grandchildren; Florrie looks after a few pills."

As we went up the stairs Stevie nudged me. "Keep away from the old girl," she said, "she's got a nasty pinch."

I sat in the front seat with Des; Florrie and Stevie sat in the back. On the floor at my feet were several small bags of tablets. Florrie's white hair was permed into tight curls. She had drop-pearl earrings on and a red T-shirt that said "Majorca" across the front.

Des had found the drugs in an ornamental tea pot.

"She leaves them there every time. No imagination," he said.

"I'm saying *nothing*," was all Florrie had said.

*　　*　　*

It took until after lunch time to process Florrie, and I was allowed to have a walk around on my own. I had a visitor's badge on and I had a quick look at the interview rooms, the cells, the communications area, the offices, the canteen, everywhere.

After a while I came on the conference room which had a "NO ENTRY" sign on the door. I took a quick look around to make sure no one saw me and went in. The room was empty and I closed the door quietly behind me.

The far wall was covered with photos, maps and writing. The words "OPERATION ROSE" were written in block letters at the top of a white board. I walked closer and saw, with shock, that the photos were all of the dead bodies of the murdered girls. My eye jumped from one to another, not really looking at faces, but at the dark marks on the necks of the girls, the open mouths, the tip of the tongues. They were unrecognizable from their school photographs.

I looked away to quell a sensation of nausea.

There was an overhead projector and several files piled on the table. There was a computer monitor with words typed on half the screen. It probably meant that someone had been working in there and would be back any minute. I had to be quick. My hand shaking, I took my notepad out of my handbag and, holding my breath, I looked through the files;

just underneath "KATE HARGREAVES" was "HELEN DRISCOLL".

I looked round again, my heart noticeably thumping, and opened the file.

I didn't read what was there, I just copied everything I saw. I would read it later. My hand scribbled down every detail that I could see. The first page done, I turned over and jotted down stuff from another sheet. I looked up at the white board. At the top corner, written in giant blue lettering, were the words: "LESLIE KNIGHT CAUGHT 2.30, 10TH JAN!!!" They were ringed with red and stood out delightedly. Around them were odd phrases and words that I jotted down. A voice from outside the door made me stop and put my notepad away. It was time to go. I took a last look around and for the first time my eye was caught by small photographs of roses pinned down the edge of the board. I glanced at them for a second, then turned and walked quickly out of the room.

As I closed the door and walked away a WPC passed me with a mug of steaming coffee. She went into the conference room and I stopped and leant against the wall to catch my breath. I felt as if I'd just done a half-hour run.

Des Murray was still in the midst of paperwork. Stevie was in the toilets. I joined her there in front of a mirror. She was painting a dark line across each eyelid. I got some bits of my own make-up out and tried to look as if I was concerned about my face. I tutted loudly and got out my eye-shadow.

"This stuff's always coming off," I said.

"I know," she answered.

"What's 'Operation Rose'?" I asked, squirting a dollop of foundation on to my finger and dotting it over my cheeks.

"That's the code name for the Leslie Knight case. It's a bit confidential really, but now that he's caught I don't suppose it matters."

"Oh, the one Des got taken off," I said, as though that was the only interest the case could have for me. "He's really fed up about it, isn't he?"

"I should say. He's been a real pain ever since. I can understand it really. You work with a case, go through all the hard bits, looking at the bodies, telling the mums and dads, house-to-house enquiries and then, when they get someone or it starts going right, when there might be some *satisfaction* in it, you get pulled off. It's not fair."

"The rose then; that's just a name, something someone thought up?"

"No, no, it's to do with the roses that we found on the bodies."

"Roses?" I said, my pink lipstick in mid-air.

"Yes, well, it's confidential too, but it'll come out in a couple of days, I'm sure. The police always try to keep some detail back from the press. It's to stop people confessing to the crime. You wouldn't believe how many people want to confess to a murder!"

"What did they keep back?" I said, a grumbling sense of unease growing inside me. I scooped up my make-up and shoved it back into my bag.

"On each of the bodies there was a rose. He strangled them with rope, then left a rose, a single rose, lying on their chests."

"On all of them? Even Helen Driscoll?" I said, feeling my case crumble before my eyes.

"On each of them. How perverted can you get? He kills them, then leaves a rose. Weird bloke." Stevie was patting her lips with a tissue.

A rose was left on Helen Driscoll's chest. It must mean that she had been killed by Leslie Knight; just like the other girls.

9

A Rose by Any Other Colour

I let Stevie's words sink in while I ate my lunch. We were in an unmarked car at the end of the High Road, parked opposite a cash-dispensing machine. We were on the look-out for a group of muggers who worked round the area.

All the time, in my head, there was an argument going on. Helen Driscoll was killed by the same man who had killed the other girls. He had left a rose on their bodies and he left a rose on hers. But Leslie Knight was caught by the police at 2.30 p.m. I had seen Helen Driscoll *alive* at 2.32 p.m.

Des was smoking in the passenger seat and Stevie was talking about police work being a good job, provided you didn't expect to have a private life. She kept giving examples and then saying: *isn't that right, Des?*, to which he answered a few words. He even had a stab at a joke. Once or twice he commented on women who passed by the car.

I decided to try and take advantage of Des's lighter mood. I kept my voice casual, as if I were just chatting, passing the time of day.

"You were involved in the Railway Killer investigation, weren't you, Des?"

"Um…" he answered.

"My mum's friend is obsessed with that case," I said. "I'd love to be able to tell her a few things about it."

"Confidential," Des said, not wasting any words.

"Oh, go on, Des. Everything will be out in a few days anyway," Stevie said, giving Des a push on the arm.

Des looked around reluctantly, only the suggestion of a smile on his lips.

"It'll be good for the kid to go home and tell her mum's mate a few unknown details," Stevie said. I bristled inwardly at being called a kid but said nothing.

"You tell her then."

"No, you," Stevie said, nudging him.

They were like a pair of silly boys in school. I almost expected Stevie to give Des a half nelson…

"What do you want to know?" Des said in a bored voice, but I noticed that, for once, there wasn't a cigarette in his mouth.

"Well," I said, "why did he do it? How did he do it?"

"Oh, you don't want to know much then," Des said, throwing a smile sideways at Stevie.

"He was a ticket collector, wasn't he?" I asked, deliberately getting it wrong, hoping to get Des started.

"No, no; Leslie Knight was a ticket *inspector* for British Rail. He worked on the Liverpool Street line. Three of the victims used the train to go to school, posh schools, up in the city. Another used the train recently to go up to a London museum, and the last one, the Driscoll girl, had a friend in Bethnal Green whom she'd visited at least twice recently." He spoke in a sing-song voice, as though he'd learnt it all off by heart. "We think that Knight asked to see their passes or some other form of identification, a travel card or whatever. He probably took a note of their names and addresses and then approached the girls when they were out somewhere, tricking them into his van.

"There are traces of fibre from the clothes of three of the girls in the back of his van. The second and the fifth one haven't yet made a match."

I was trying to look impressed; inside my head there was frantic activity going on, repeating and memorizing the things he was saying, trying to listen hard to make sure I didn't miss anything.

"So there were no fibres for the Driscoll girl," I said.

"No."

"Weird bloke," I said, as though that was my only interest in the story, as though it was a bit of gossip for me. "Fancy leaving roses."

Des looked at Stevie.

"I was just chatting to her. It'll be all over the papers soon," she said shrugging her shoulders.

"You've told her everything already!"

"Roses," I kept on. "I wonder what colour they were?"

"Yellow and red," Des said.

"Yellow and red?"

"Yeah, he was changing his colour just as we caught him. He left a yellow one on the Driscoll girl's body."

A yellow rose. A *yellow rose* was left on Helen, not a red one.

Just then Des opened the car door and got out and slammed it. He walked a few metres and went into a paper shop. I said:

"Imagine what the press would make of the roses."

"It'll be in all the papers tomorrow, probably. Now that the case is sewn up. It won't be the only thing the press has got to talk about," she said. "Soon they'll know about John Martin's son and the Driscoll girl."

"John Martin?"

"He's a uniformed inspector. Been around for donkey's years. His son apparently went to the same school as the Driscoll girl and he went out with her for a few months. It finished a while ago. Don't tell Des I told you that."

I said nothing as Des got back into the car.

I felt weighted down with all the information I'd been given in the previous few minutes.

"Here," Des said and threw a bar of chocolate into the back seat and one at Stevie.

"Thanks," I said and we sat in silence for a few minutes. Then Des said:

"There's nothing happening here, Stevie. Let's go back to base."

We got back to the station at about two o'clock. I went straight into the loos and jotted down everything that Des and Stevie had said – as much of it as I could remember. Just as I came out of the cubicle, Heather Warren walked into the toilets.

"Patsy!" she said. "How's your day been?"

"Great," I said. "Des and Stevie have been really nice."

"Good. Stevie's a good policewoman," Heather said. I noticed she said nothing about Des.

"Yes," I said, closing my bag. I was keen to go back to the office. I wanted to be alone so that I could sort out all the things I had heard.

"Tell you what," she said, "why don't you finish off your day with me? I've just got one more visit to make and then I'll drop you back to Tony's office. It should only take about an hour."

"I don't know," I said, looking at my watch. I needed to be alone. To think it all through.

"It could be interesting, if a bit morbid. I need to go and close the scene of crime where the last murdered girl was found, Helen Driscoll. It might be good for you to see what it's like."

I almost swallowed my tongue with surprise.

"I'll get my coat," I said.

We drove to the scene of crime in the back of a dark unmarked car. As we got closer I felt my tension level rising; it was as though she was taking me to see Helen Driscoll's actual body, rather than just the place she'd been found. As we reached the gate of the old yard I saw flowers stacked up along the pavement. Dozens of tiny bouquets left presumably by members of the public. Beside them was a sign: *KEEP OUT, POLICE INVESTIGATION.* Someone had even draped a child's teddy bear over that. As we went into the yard there were metres of white ribbon strung up between the buildings, and a single policeman was standing outside a door that was closed.

The yard was criss-crossed with railway tracks, mostly sunk into the concrete, so we just drove across. When we parked I got out of the car and looked around.

It was an area about the size of a football pitch,

mostly open with a couple of buildings along the side. There were some small wooden sheds over by the entrance and a van that had its wheels removed. There was something painted on the side of the van, a name, stylized, in chunky lettering: JACKO.

"This way, Patsy," Heather said, striding ahead. She stopped for a few seconds and talked to the policeman who was standing guard.

Then we walked through the door into the dark interior of the warehouse. There was no lighting, although a portable lamp on a stand had been erected. Heather turned it on and it suddenly looked as though we were inside a small theatre. As if some actors were going to come on and start a play.

On the ground, half on top of some sacking, was the outline of Helen Driscoll's body. It was a strong white line drawn carefully, the way that kids do sometimes when they're drawing outlines of their hand.

"Oh," was all I said.

I'd seen a dead body once before. It had been pale and doll-like. The girl had been lying still, her eyes open; like a model for an artist. My breath had caught in my throat and my limbs had gone weak and jelly-like.

There was no body this time but I still felt uneasy. The dark corners of the warehouse seemed sinister and the bright light harsh and unreal. For a brief moment I got flashes in my head; pictures that I'd seen of the dead girls lying flat on their backs, no breath left inside them, their mouths open as if in a silent cry.

"She was a tiny girl, you know," Heather said. "She was only five foot one. I'm sure she couldn't have put up much of a fight. We found her almost twenty-four hours after we caught him."

"Really," I said, dragging my eyes away from the white-line drawing on the floor.

"He must have killed her and then walked out of here and on to the road. His van was parked there, about a hundred metres down. For some reason he didn't go away. That's one thing I don't understand. Why didn't he just go home? He'd done it the other times. No, he wandered off towards the Regent's Road depot."

"That was where he was caught."

"Only minutes later! That's what's so frustrating. He never said a word. Just sat silently in the back of the police car when metres away, two minutes' walk away, was the dead girl."

Heather picked up a torch and shone it into the far corners of the warehouse. The beam of light caught two eyes looking at us. Then they disappeared.

"Rats," Heather said.

"Oh."

"She lay here for twenty-four hours before anyone found her."

I felt as though I was going to shiver and tensed myself. Twenty-four hours in that dark, cold, rat-infested place.

"When was she killed? I mean, what time exactly. You caught him at two-thirty, I think."

"Yes, we did. We chased him up the railway tracks. We were lucky that a train wasn't coming the other way."

Heather clicked off the light switch and the warehouse was black again.

Walking out she said, "Forensics say that she'd been lying there from twenty-four to twenty-six hours."

"Can't they be exact?" I said, trying to sound interested in the science of forensics.

"Not really. They can sometimes, but in this case the overnight temperature was below freezing so it's not possible to give a precise time. They think it was probably between, say, one o'clock and two-thirty."

We walked out into the daylight and I found myself inhaling as much air as I could.

"I've just got a couple of things to arrange with the constable, Patsy, then we'll go." Heather walked across to the PC and within seconds he was smiling at something she said.

I walked through the yard to the gate and looked at the border of cut flowers that sat on the pavement; reds and yellows, blues and whites. Some were dying, had been there for days but some were new, perhaps only laid there that morning.

It was a touching sight. People who had never known Helen Driscoll feeling grief at the manner of her death. The flowers placed closely together looked like a giant garland. It was almost festive; there was nothing funereal about it.

I bent down to look at a new bunch that had been placed on top of some dying blooms. There may have been more than thirty assorted flowers inside the cellophane. Also inside it was a small card.

I glanced at some of the other bouquets. They too had cards. People had written messages on them like: *with sympathy; so young; to sweet Helen; we won't forget you.*

The small card inside the new bouquet had a more personal message on it though: *Helen, you should have got to know me better.* I wasn't sure what it meant. I could see Heather, in the car, coming towards me, so I said it over and over in my head.

When I got into the car Heather said:

"Do you think it's been worth it; today, I mean? Have you learned something?"

"Yes," I said, my notebook and my head full of details. "I've learned more than I thought I would."

10

Decisions

Heather dropped me back at the office. As soon as I got in the door I wrote down the message from the bouquet of flowers: *Helen, you should have got to know me better.* I didn't want to forget the wording.

There was no sign that Tony had been there. I put the kettle on and looked at my notebook. It was full of scribbled sentences, words that I'd underlined or circled. I read all of it over three or four times and then sat back to think.

There were a number of possibilities, the main one being that the girl I had seen was not Helen Driscoll. All sorts of things pointed in that direction. Helen Driscoll had been killed in the same way as the other victims of Leslie Knight, strangled with a piece of climbing rope. There was a rose left on her body, just the same as the others. She was fifteen (even if she hadn't looked it) and was still at school, exactly the same as the others.

But I was sure I had seen her *alive* at the time that Leslie Knight was picked up. If I were right it must mean that someone else murdered her and tried to make it look like she was another victim of the serial killer.

I looked at my notes that I'd copied from her file. She had lived with her mother and father, Elizabeth and Peter Driscoll. She had one brother, Joe, who was about a year younger. Her family were quite well off and she went to the local secondary school. She was an ordinary girl, not unlike the other victims.

There were some important differences though. The other girls were all "high-fliers". Helen Driscoll was not; in fact it said in the notes that she "*had been a problem in school and had recently taken to truanting regularly*". The other girls, Des had said, had all been using the railway for school or educational matters. That might have meant that they were in school uniform. Helen Driscoll, though, had used the train to see a friend who lived in Bethnal Green, so presumably she had been wearing her own clothes, not uniform.

The dead girls all had red roses left on their bodies. Helen Driscoll's rose was yellow.

The alleged killer, Leslie Knight, killed Helen Driscoll, but instead of then going home, he'd stalked another railway yard to make another killing. This was completely out of step with the previous murders where he had made just one killing.

There were none of Helen Driscoll's clothes fibres in Leslie Knight's van (although they hadn't found any of Kate Hargreaves' fibres either).

The kettle had boiled and clicked itself off. I sat and looked at it and began to think of a possible explanation.

What if someone had the motive and desire to kill Helen Driscoll. The newspapers were full of the gory details about the serial killer and the Railway Murders. Why not make the murder look like that? Then she would have been just one of the victims of a killer who would perhaps never be caught and even if he was, wouldn't be believed.

But no member of the public knew about the roses.

So, whoever it was had to have some link to someone who worked in the police station, someone with access to confidential information.

I remembered Stevie's words: *soon they'll be talking about Inspector Martin's son and the Driscoll girl.*

Helen Driscoll had gone out with a boy for a few months whose father was a police inspector. What was I thinking? That the boy and his father plotted to murder Helen Driscoll and covered it up by making it look like one of the serial killer's murders?

Why would they do it?

My suspicions were getting out of hand. It was ridiculous. I needed to talk to Billy so that he could calm me down, straighten the whole thing out.

I sat back in my chair and looked at the phone, wondering whether or not to ring him. I got out my diary and looked up the Norfolk number in the back. Something stopped me though. I got up and made a cup of tea instead.

The trouble with Billy was that he was just too sensible, he would never take chances. I'd known him since secondary school and he was the kind of kid who wore the complete uniform day after day. All his exercise books were covered and his home-work done.

He wasn't a boffin or a goody-goody, it was just that he liked to do things properly. He was good at knowing our rights as pupils and anyone who had had the rough edge of some teacher's tongue went and shared it with Billy. When I first knew him he was always talking about suing people. If a computer game went wrong or a bus conductor shoved us off the bus he would shout: *I'll sue you; I could sue him, you know!*

He calmed down over the years but he was always

arguing with the teachers, or disputing some adult rule.

Billy was an only child and so was I. It was the thing we had in common, no siblings. We sort of drifted together, long-time friends. He was the person I always went to if I was upset or annoyed with anyone. He was good at talking me out of things; a proposed fight with a big girl in the year above who'd said I'd been talking about her behind her back; a plan to play a practical joke on a new teacher; a scheme to write the irregular French verbs all down my right leg so that I wouldn't get poor marks in a test.

Don't do it, Patsy, he'd say, and most of the time, I took his advice.

Sometimes I didn't though, like the time my friends Sherry and Beth and I told our parents that we were staying at each other's houses for the night, when in fact we stayed out all night, at a club until about three o'clock, then an all-night café, then a walk through Hyde Park at dawn.

The sheer daring and naughtiness of it had thrilled me and even though we'd ended up dog-tired with wrinkled clothes I'd not regretted it. It had been an *adventure*. There had been an element of *danger* involved.

That was something Billy could never under-stand. When I'd told him about it afterwards his forehead had wrinkled and he'd shaken his head like a wise old man who simply didn't understand the younger generation.

We'd always known that Billy had been born with the common-sense of a thirty-year-old. He just didn't take chances.

And I did. That was the difference between us.

I dialled the Norfolk number and let it ring a few times, then just as I heard the phone being answered I put the receiver back down, cutting the line dead.

If I spoke to Billy about Helen Driscoll he would put me off taking the case any further. I needed to make a decision about whether to pursue the investigation, as I had done with the Judy Hurst murder, and I had to make that decision on my own.

It wasn't even as simple as that. Even if I wanted to follow up the case I couldn't think of a way to move forward without being able to talk to the girl's family, her friends, her boyfriend, Inspector Martin's son. How could I? I wasn't a police officer and I wasn't officially investigating the case.

Why should anybody talk to me?

I heard footsteps on the stairs outside and saw my uncle come into the office.

"Hi," I said lightly, closing my notebook and pushing it into my bag.

"My God, Patricia, what've you done to yourself? You look lovely," Tony said.

I'd forgotten about my career girl disguise, my bouncy hair and short dress.

"I wish you'd dress like that more often," he said, taking his overcoat off and hanging it up on the hook.

"Um…" I said. He went into his office and closed the door. A second or so later the intercom came on:

"Patricia, can you get me the Missing Persons' file and a nice cup of tea."

I let the water reheat and thought back to the day I'd seen Helen Driscoll lounging on the bench in the park, looking steadfastly at something in front of her, digging out her initials on the bench that she was sitting on. I closed my eyes for a minute and tried to visualize her. I could see her shape and the colour of her hair and for a mini-second I focused on her face. It was Helen Driscoll, I was sure; as sure as I could be.

The picture in my head began to fade though and all at once it was gone. I tried hard for a few moments to reconstruct it but it was blurred and featureless.

I was losing the memory of that scene. Soon I wouldn't be able to visualize her at all.

I got the Missing Persons' file and took it and the tea through to my uncle.

"Thanks," he said. He'd taken off his suit jacket and was sitting with his shirt–sleeves rolled up. He looked as if he was too hot.

"I bumped into an admirer of yours today," he said.

"Really?" I said. "Who?"

"Young Brian, from the developers."

"You mean PHOTOKWIK."

"He seems smitten by you."

"Don't be silly," I said, pulling the hem of my mum's skirt down. My uncle was always using old-fashioned words like "smitten". He once asked me if Billy and I were "courting".

"You could do worse," he said, "he's a nice young lad. He's got a good job. His family are…"

"Tony, I'm not interested in him, or his family. He's not my type," I said, my cheeks heating up. The last thing I needed was Tony trying to fix me up with a boyfriend from a nice family.

"His dad's a police inspector. I thought you were considering police work."

"Really?" I said, trying to sound interested.

"Nice man. He and I collaborated on a number of cases," Tony said. "I can remember a house-breaking case that we worked on for weeks…"

And then it came to me.

Brian at PHOTOKWIK's dad was a police inspector. Further back, somewhere on the edges of my memory, were his words the first time I met him: *Brian Martin, at your service.*

"They used to shift their stuff at car-boot sales," Tony was reminiscing.

Inspector Martin was Brian's dad. He was Brian Martin's dad!

I waited, bursting with agitation, while my uncle continued his story.

"We posed as punters, he and I, browsing round the boot sales."

"Actually, Tony," I said, breaking into his story, "I said I'd give Mum a ring a while ago, so I ought to get on with it."

"Sure," he said, waving me out with his hand. Closing the door I could hear him talking quietly to himself: *Car-boot sales, whatever next...*

Brian Martin was too old to have been Helen Driscoll's boyfriend. There was one other explanation. I dialled the number of PHOTOKWIK. He answered straight away.

"Hi, Brian," I said, "it's Patsy Kelly."

"Pat," he said, immediately irking me by shortening my name. I kept my composure and continued:

"Brian, I'm really sorry I was a bit short the other day; your phone call came at a bad time for me."

"That's all right – " he started to speak.

"Hey, my uncle Tony was telling me about your dad working with him when he was a policeman. What a small world!" I rushed on, not giving him a chance to speak. "It's terrible about the Railway Murders though. I'll bet your brother's upset, you know, about his ex being one of the victims." I had my fingers crossed; I was willing him to answer the way I wanted him to.

"A bit, I suppose," he said, "but it's been over between them for a while."

"Awful business." I was almost jumping up and down in my chair. "Listen Brian, I wanted to take you up on that offer you made, for a meal or a drink. What about tonight?"

"Yes, OK. Where?"

"Why don't I meet you at that pizza place over the road from the shop. Say about seven. We can have a chat."

"OK, see you then."

I put the phone down and looked around. My uncle was standing at the door of his office smirking at me.

"In my day, it was the men who asked the women out. Call me old-fashioned but I liked it that way."

11

Dating

I sat in the pizza parlour and had a drink while I waited for Brian Martin to arrive. I had some very mild misgivings about being there on the basis of a date.

I had no choice though. He was the only link I had with Helen Driscoll.

I'd also discarded my pretty girl disguise. I'd nestled into my jeans and put a giant silk shirt on top. I'd unpeeled the tights and found a warm pair of wool socks and my DMs. I had my heavy overcoat on and a tight, floppy-brimmed velvet hat that my mum had found in a car-boot sale.

I'd given my face a good wash too and put a couple of thick black lines on my eyes and some maroon lipstick. I looked a bit Gothic. It suited my purposes. I didn't want to appear too inviting for Brian Martin.

He came just after seven. I waved to him as he walked in the door.

"Hi," he said. "I'm not late, am I?"

"No," I said. "Have a seat."

"You look a million dollars," he said, and I cringed.

"Thanks," I said, making a mental note to avoid the Gothic look in all future visits to PHOTO-KWIK.

He sat opposite me and for a minute neither of us said anything.

I suddenly felt very awkward and embarrassed to be there. He picked up the menu and started to read it intently.

"Let me see…" he said, as though he was considering his choices. "I'll have Italian sausage pizza, garlic bread, a salad and a drink."

"Same for me," I said, giving him a jolly smile.

I wasn't prepared for what happened next. He reached across the table and took one of my hands into his and held it tightly.

"I was really pleased when you rang me, Pat. I really like you."

"Oh," I said, feeling my hand squeezed hard.

The waitress came and he let my hand go. I pulled it back across the table and kept it safe in my lap. We ordered our meal and then Brian leaned across the table and said, in a low voice, "I love the hat."

"Thanks. I was in the police station today, where your dad works." I decided to plunge straight in. I didn't know how long I was going to be able to put up with his interest in me. It might be that I shortly got an attack of food-poisoning or remembered an important appointment.

"What for?" he said, his hands clasped on the table, his eyes searching my face. I had my hands firmly in my lap and I avoided his direct look.

"I was shadowing a CID officer. I'm thinking of joining the force. It seemed a good idea to get a feel of what the job might be like."

"A WPC? My mum was a policewoman."

"Really?" I sat forward, looking interested, hoping to steer him slowly round to police business.

It was a mistake. He leant forward too and, ignoring my question completely, gave me a light peck on the lips.

I held my eyes closed for a moment after the kiss. When I opened them he was looking delighted with himself.

"Yes, she met my dad while they were in Hendon, training." He was moving around in his seat looking excited. He was like a kid who had just got a new toy. It was still in the box and he just couldn't wait to get it out. I was sitting still but inside I was squirming. I just hoped that there was no one around who knew me.

"Didn't you want to be a policeman?" I asked,

taking a sip from my drink.

"No thanks. Roger, my brother, it's more in his line."

"He wants to be a policeman?"

"Ever since he was a little boy. Whenever my dad came home from work Roger wanted to know where his hat was, where his truncheon was. In the end my mum and dad bought him a kiddie's policeman outfit."

His smile had disappeared and he was fiddling with one of his rings.

"Lots of kids dress up," I said, thinking for a moment of myself in a nurse's uniform, a cowgirl's outfit, a Spiderman suit.

"It wasn't just that. He was obsessed with it, my brother, even as a small child. He's still as keen as ever. Spent three years in the army cadets, works out down at the gym, is always talking to my dad about what's going on. He's got it all worked out. He's not like a normal fifteen-year-old kid. It's like a vocation with him."

There was a trace of bitterness in his voice.

"What about you?" I said, disconcerted by his sudden change in mood.

"Me? No, I'm not good at taking orders. That and exams. No, working in casual jobs suits me fine. I've had a lifetime of the police force. I don't want anything to do with it. Now, shall we talk about something else?"

His smile returned and I thought, for the first time, that he wasn't bad-looking; if only he'd stop all the silly clichéd chatter. He reached over again and put his hand on top of mine. I left it there. At least there was a table between us.

When the meal came he chatted about his great love: football.

"I've been supporting West Ham since I was nine."

"Um," I said, fitting a triangle of pizza into my mouth. Football held about as much interest for me as a Latin test paper.

"I've got a season ticket and I go to away matches. You should come to one. You'd enjoy it," he said. He meant it too.

I knew a lot of boys from school who were passionately interested in football. I'd even been out with a couple; an Arsenal supporter and a fanatical Liverpool fan. They talked on and on about this goal or that free kick, about defensive play or the long ball game. They never seemed to notice the glazed, faraway look that settled on my face, the loss of concentration, the stifled yawns.

"Important game, next week," Brian said and I tried to raise my eyebrows to show enthusiasm. "Cup tie. How's your food? Mine's good; garlic bread could have had more garlic though."

"Good," I said.

"The trouble with the Hammers," he went on,

"is they don't spend enough money on players and they depend on the long ball game."

I counted the squares on the tablecloth while he talked on. Occasionally I said, "Um" and nodded.

At least Billy wasn't interested in football. With him it was cars and their parts; the quality of a respray job, the joys of power-assisted steering, the safety features of a Mercedes.

Inexplicably, I felt a pang of guilt thinking of Billy in Norfolk, still annoyed with me for not going with him. What would he say if he could see me there, sitting across the table from Brian Martin like a nodding dog?

Eventually, after what seemed like ninety minutes, he said: "That's enough about me. Let's talk about you."

"There's not much to tell," I said, shrugging my shoulders. I told him a few things and then it went quiet. I glanced at the clock and decided to try and pull Brian back to the topic of conversation that I wanted to talk about.

"Did you know Helen Driscoll?" I said. "The dead girl."

"Not really," Brian said. "I saw her with Roger a few times. I said hello to her once or twice, but I didn't know her."

"What an awful thing to happen. Had your brother been deeply involved with her?"

"He'd gone out with her for a few months. But

she was a bit odd. Anyway, why the interest? It's a bit of a depressing subject."

"Only I spent some time today with the detectives on the case. It's made me curious, you know."

He sat looking at me for a moment. I didn't know whether he was going to oblige me and talk about Helen or whether he was going to kick off on some other subject.

I did the most awful thing. I put my hand across the table and gave his hand a squeeze. As I was doing it a voice inside my head kept shouting at me: *that's going too far; that's not fair.*

"You don't mind talking about it, do you?" I looked him straight in the face, solid eye contact. He really did have rather nice eyes.

"Not at all, *Detective* Kelly," he said and my teeth grated at his feeble attempt at wit. "I need another drink though; how about you?"

When the waitress had brought our drinks he started to tell me about his brother Roger.

"Roger's this really organized, kind of grown-up kid. All his life he's been dead serious. He was completely sold by all the policeman stuff; my dad's radio, his handcuffs, his notebook. He was always asking our mum to take him down the station to see our dad in his uniform, on the front desk or patrolling the streets."

Brian smiled for a second, as though he was

remembering some fond memory.

"My dad was pleased as pie, you know, that his son looked up to him so much. I was never very good at those kinds of things. I got in trouble at the Cubs and couldn't tie knots in the Scouts."

"When did he meet Helen Driscoll?" I asked, steering him back to the subject.

"She was in his year at school and she lived close to us. I don't like to speak ill of the dead, but she was a strange girl."

"Strange?"

"Yes. Moody. Arguing with Roger or her parents. She'd burst into a temper any time, Roger told me. I wasn't surprised when he gave her the push. I wasn't even surprised when she started harassing him. It seemed in character."

"Harassing him?"

"Yes, my dad actually went round to her house, *in uniform*, to warn her off. This was all a while ago. She used to follow Roger and Suzy, his new girl-friend, around. Sometimes she'd shout at them from across the road, saying awful things about Roger. I really thought, at the time, she was a bit unstable. He was a fool to get involved with her in the first place. I'll tell you what, I know it's a bad thing to say, but I'll bet he breathed a sigh of relief when he heard she was dead. Especially since he's started talking about getting engaged. Can you believe it? He's fifteen and he's thinking about marriage! Me, I'm not going to get married until I'm about thirty. Unless I meet the right girl, that is."

He looked straight at me and I felt a ball of panic in my throat.

"Shall we have a sweet?" I said quickly.

It was late when we left the restaurant. He drove me to my street. I knew, on the way, that it would be awkward when he stopped the car, that he would want to kiss me.

I thought, at one point, that it was time to be honest with him: *Look Brian, I like you more than I thought I would, but not in that way. Couldn't we just be friends?*

I kept letting the words play over and over in my head as the car slowed down and the engine hummed to a stop. I was about to open my mouth and say it when he turned across me and put his lips gently on mine.

That was the time to push him away. It wouldn't have been hard. He was near to me but not resting on me. His mouth, open on mine, was barely touching me, yet I felt his hot breath, close and warm. Instead I put my hand up to the back of his head and touched his hair and he kissed me harder.

In the back of my head an excuse was forming: I was tired, I was lonely. I felt grateful towards him. I even quite liked him.

He pulled back and smiled at me. It was a

dangerous moment; he was bound to make some inane comment which would spoil the kiss.

He didn't though. He said: "Come round my house, tomorrow lunch time. My mum and dad will be out. Roger and Suzy will be there. You could meet them."

He scribbled something on a small notepad. "Here's my address."

"OK," I said. I got out of the car.

"See you soon, Patsy Kelly," he said and drove off.

"Yes," I said. I looked at his address: *6 Orchard Drive*. It was round the corner from The Valentines Estate.

12

The Family

Even though it was bitterly cold I decided to walk through The Valentines Estate to get to Brian Martin's house. I went round the edge of the park and turned off the road and past the sign that said: *PRIVATE ROAD RESIDENTS ONLY.* I was only a few metres from the traffic but it seemed quieter. The streets were lined with trees and shrubs and the further I walked the more hushed it became.

The road itself felt different. It took me a minute to work out why. There were no markings; no broken white line down the middle, no yellow lines at the sides. The street lights were smaller, more old-fashioned. There were no cars parked on the road itself, just sleek expensive saloons and hatchbacks sitting side by side in the driveways. Billy would have been interested in exactly what make and type. To me they just suggested wealth; that and the detached, brick-built, solid, two and three storey houses that stood behind them.

I got out my notebook. In among the scribblings I had made from the police station was Helen's address: 8 Park Drive, The Valentines. I walked on, further away from the traffic, into the trees and shrubs. At one point I could no longer see the end of the road and it felt as though I was in the middle of the countryside.

I stood outside number eight. It was almost opposite the house that Billy and I had delivered the yellow Mini to some months before. The down-stairs curtains were still drawn, even though it was past midday. There were no cars in the drive. It looked deserted. I walked on a few metres and stood at a lamp-post, looking at the house. The windows were small and wooden and the glass was leaded. I wondered which one was Helen's bedroom.

How I would have liked to get into her room and look through her stuff; to rummage through her wardrobe, dressing table, maybe a bedside chest of drawers; to sort through her schoolbag and pencil case, a rucksack, a shoulder bag; to dip into the pockets of her clothes, her coats, jackets, jeans; to read the things she had written, her books, her diary maybe, some letters.

I mentally stamped my foot with the frustration

of it; if I were a police detective I would have access to such things. I would be able to talk to all her family and friends, to call at the neighbours, to go to her school, to really find out about her, what she was like and whether she had made any enemies.

Instead I was sidelined. It was like running a race with my feet tied together.

Just then I heard a front door slam. I looked round and saw a young girl come out of the house across the way and walk towards the yellow Mini. I walked quickly across.

"Hello," I said, rubbing my gloved hands together. "How's the car going?"

The girl looked at me quizzically.

"My friend and I delivered your car. In fact it belonged to my friend. He sold it to your mum and dad."

"Oh," she said, looking fondly at the Mini. I noticed then how the paintwork was like a mirror. It had been well looked after. "It's brilliant," she said.

"My friend's a car enthusiast. He buys cars and does them up. He spent weeks on this. I thought he might keep it, he worked so hard on it."

"I'm really pleased with it," she said, still looking at me a little strangely.

"Only I was just coming round to pay my respects to Mrs Driscoll and I noticed it here. She doesn't seem to be at home though."

"You know them?" the girl said warily.

"Yes, my mother and Elizabeth are friends," I said, remembering the name from my notes. "I've been out of the country since Christmas." My mind was racing just slightly ahead of my voice trying to put a story together. "Skiing. I got back yesterday and she told me about it. Awful business."

"Yes," the girl said, relaxing somewhat, "it's upset everyone. The whole family went away because of the press harassment. They were everywhere for days."

"Awful," I said sincerely. "As if the parents haven't been upset enough."

"Her brother had a fight with one of them; smashed his camera."

"Really?" I said, searching for his name inside my head. Eventually it came. "Poor Joe, he must be devastated."

"He was, apparently. It just goes to show you that even adopted brothers and sisters can be close."

"Yes," I said. *Adopted*. It hadn't said anything about that in Helen's file.

"I must go," she said and got into the car. I watched her pull away.

Helen's brother was adopted. I shrugged my shoulders. I had no way of knowing whether that information had any bearing on the case. I just filed it away in the miscellany part of my brain and hoped it would come in useful later.

Brian had the door open as I walked up his pathway.

He had a wide smile on his face, a look of delight that I had arrived, as if he had half expected me not to come. I felt a flood of sympathy for him and resolved to be straight with him, not lead him on any further.

He introduced me to his brother.

"Roger, this is Patsy. She and you should have something in common. She wants to join the police."

"Yes?" Roger said, coming towards me.

Roger Martin was taller than his brother, although clearly younger. He was muscular as well, his shoulders broad. He gave me a firm handshake; a surprisingly confident thing for someone so young to do.

"This is Suzy," he said and pointed to a small blonde girl who was sitting on a chair. She smiled at me but said nothing.

There was an awkward quiet moment when nobody spoke. All sorts of small talk went through my head but it was dwarfed by the real questions that I wanted to ask Roger.

Eventually Suzy said: "Is it still as cold?"

"Yes," I said, moving towards the fire.

"Just as well I made some soup then," Brian said.

"Yes," Roger said, rolling his eyes towards Suzy. Suzy smiled at him and then looked mischievously at me.

"Brian's a really good cook, did he tell you?"

"No," I said, genuinely surprised.

Brian walked round behind me and put his arm loosely round my shoulder. It was a possessive gesture and I felt embarrassed for him. He was clearly building up his hopes on me. It was going to be harder on him when I had to let him down.

"Winter vegetables with Stilton cheese," he said and walked away into the kitchen. I suddenly felt hungry.

Roger dominated the conversation around the table.

"You take the police," he said, "they get the blame for everything. If they're too hard, they get stamped on. If they let people off with a caution, they get pilloried. They can't win!"

Brian was much quieter than he had been the previous evening. He kept cutting up bread and offering the plate of croutons. I ate my soup greedily. I noticed that Roger and Suzy just sipped at theirs, avoided the croutons, and gave each other little secret looks.

"The police force needs women, there's no doubt about that. It has to be said though that women, no matter how bright they are, are simply not as strong as men."

"But – " I said, my mouth full of soup, my spoon in mid-air. My uncle Tony's face came into my head.

"Take a situation like this. It's a Saturday night, you've got a couple of drunks causing trouble, one of them is six foot tall and well built. Are you telling me that an average woman, five six, five seven, could deal with that?"

I opened my mouth to answer but he carried on.

"Of course not. It takes a man in a physical situation like that. Now you're quite well built, Patsy, but look at little Suzy here. How could she deal with that?"

We all looked at Suzy and she gave a silly little smile. She was tiny, four or five inches shorter than me and very thin. Helen Driscoll had been small, Heather had said. Perhaps Roger liked that type; the word "petite" came into my head.

Brian cleared the plates away.

"That was really good!" I said to him, meaning it. He smiled with pleasure and didn't seem to notice the half-full plates he took from Suzy and Roger.

"I was in the station yesterday," I said, trying to direct the conversation towards Helen Driscoll. "Everyone there still seems very involved in the Railway Murders. Of course, Roger, you went out with poor Helen Driscoll. I hope you don't mind, but I was asking Brian about it last night."

"Poor Helen," Roger said, picking up a crouton and popping it into his mouth.

"Was it long ago that you and she finished?"

Roger looked at Suzy.

"The end of the summer," she said and gave his hand a squeeze.

"Brian said it finished badly," I said. "That must

have been awful for you, Suzy."

"You're not kidding," she said and sat forward at the table. It was the first time I had seen her alert. "She never left us alone, did she, Roger? She used to wait for us to come out of school in the afternoon and then follow us home shouting things, horrible, abusive things."

"Poor Suzy," Roger said.

"She tried to spread rumours in school about me, didn't she, Roger?"

"Cake?" Brian put a plate on the table with an oblong cake on it. It was dark and heavy-looking, like a slab of earth.

"Yes, please," I said, unsure. Roger and Suzy both shook their heads.

"It's banana." Brian cut off a piece that was at least three centimetres thick.

"The funny thing was," Roger said, "she wasn't like that when we first broke up. She was quite haughty then. Wouldn't speak to me, ignored me when she saw me. Even when I started seeing Suzy she just went her own way; she started hanging round with that older girl, you know, the kid who moved to Bethnal Green."

"Fay Norris," Suzy said.

"Then suddenly, overnight almost, she got nasty, started with the name-calling."

"And the phone calls. Don't forget those."

"Phone calls?"

"She kept phoning me up, at all hours." Roger was tracing an invisible pattern on the table with his finger. "Threatening, my dad called it. In the end he went round to her house and warned her."

"How awful," I said, breaking off a piece of cake and gingerly putting it into my mouth.

"If you think that's bad, you should hear about the way she treated her brother."

"Her brother?" I said, though my mouth was full.

"Poor Joe, she teased him and made him feel miserable, didn't she, Roger; even when you were going out with her."

"Because he was adopted?" I said.

"She was just plain horrible to him. He wasn't very bright, was he, Roger? And she felt embarrassed, you know. He was in a special slow class and had extra help."

"He's a bit odd-looking as well. Nice bloke – well, I like him."

"He's much bigger than he should be for his age, really good at games and stuff. You took him climbing once, didn't you, Roger? He liked it, was really good at it you said."

"Yes, he was," Roger agreed.

"One of her mates told me that she used to taunt him because he was adopted and she wasn't. She used to tell him that she'd arrange for him to go back into care, didn't she, Roger?"

"Poor Joe," Roger said.

"He didn't really fit into that family at all. After Roger and Helen broke up he spent a lot of time here. Used to hang round Roger's dad, said he wanted to be a policeman."

"My dad took him into the station, just the other week. I haven't seen much of him since then. Nothing since the murder, of course."

"I never liked her," Brian said.

"She never liked your cooking, that's why," Roger said and gave Suzy a sly look.

"I understand that Joe Driscoll is really upset about his sister's death, though."

"Really?" Suzy said, getting up from the table.

"So they said at the station," I lied.

"Don't suppose it'll affect his game though," Roger said.

"Game?"

"Squash. He might not be very bright but he's brilliant at squash. Junior champion down at Valentines sports club. Plays virtually every day."

"You nearly beat him once!" Suzy said, looking up at Roger.

"That's true," Roger said modestly.

After they'd gone we sat on the settee. Brian had the football teletext pages on the screen of the TV but there was no sound. We sat for a while staring at the match scores. Interestingly enough Brian never said a word about football, just talked about other things;

his job in PHOTOKWIK, his car, his plans. Then he started to talk about his mum.

"I'm more like she is really. She hated the police force, left at the first opportunity. She's a caterer now, makes the food for weddings and functions. Sometimes I help her. I suppose that's how I got interested in cooking. My dad doesn't approve, of course; it's not a man's job. Neither does Roger; that must have been clear. No, I don't suppose I'm what you'd call close to my dad. Your parents are divorced, aren't they?"

"Yes, five years ago." I started to tell him about my mum and dad's break-up.

The living room was getting darker although neither of us made a move to put a light on. The fact that the TV was on without any sound made the room seem unnaturally quiet; as if there was a definite absence of noise. It was churchlike; my voice telling a story, him sitting listening, interrupting now and then to ask something.

After a while we both became silent. I glanced at my watch and thought that I ought to go. I was leaning against him on the settee. It was almost dark in the room except for the glow of the TV screen.

"This is nice," he said and rested his hand on my hair.

I knew that it was time to tell him, to be straight with him, to say: *I like you, Brian, but I don't feel attracted to you.*

I didn't though. The strangest thing happened. I sat up and leant over to kiss him. I pressed my lips on his and put my hand into his hair. My eyes were closed and I turned my head to the side and let my tongue touch his teeth.

He sat forward and kissed me again and after a few moments he put his arm around me.

A little voice in my head was asking me what I thought I was doing and the answer was I didn't know. It was warm, it was comfortable. He had made a nice cake and I was lonely.

He suddenly sat up.

"Look at that!" he said. I turned and looked at the screen; West Ham had scored a goal.

I began to laugh, more at myself than anything else.

Brian dropped me off at my house at about six. I said I'd ring him.

When I got in I went straight to my bedroom and wrote down as much as I could remember about what had been said. I made a heading – "ROGER" – and put all the stuff I'd heard under it. I underlined the bit where he had said he'd gone *climbing* with Joe Driscoll. I remembered all the photos of the lengths of rope that had been used to strangle the girls.

The I made another heading – "JOE DRISCOLL" – and wrote down all the information I'd heard; that he was adopted; his sister made his life a misery; he was not very bright but big and fit; he played squash almost every day at The Valentines squash club.

Finally, I wrote the name "FAY NORRIS". Underneath it there was just a blank space. She was someone I had yet to find out about.

Then I closed the book and put it away in a drawer. I really had had enough of it all for one day. I shut the drawer as tightly as I could, as if that might keep it there, out of my head for a few hours.

I kept thinking about Brian Martin though, a vague feeling of guilt lining my stomach. Was I using him? I liked him more that I had before, I especially liked his kisses, but was I being unfair? I knew the answer and it didn't make me feel very good.

I went downstairs with a heavy heart and told my mum I was going to get a video.

"Oh," she said, as I opened the front door, "Billy rang. He's coming back from Norfolk tomorrow."

"Is he?" I said, my spirits suddenly lifted at the thought of seeing him again.

"Yes, he asked where you were. I told him you were out on a date."

"What?" I said with dismay.

"I said you were out with a new boyfriend. That was all right, wasn't it?"

"Oh, hell," I said. The honest truth was I didn't know whether it was all right or not.

13

Joe Driscoll

The next day was Sunday. I put Billy and Brian Martin out of my mind and thought about Joe Driscoll. I rang The Valentines squash club and asked whether the junior champion was playing that day. I said I wanted to watch him for tips on technique. After a bit of paper-rustling the receptionist came back and told me he was playing at two-thirty.

I put the phone down and looked at my watch. I had plenty of time.

I went into the kitchen. My mum was there with her friend Sheila. On the table were several Sunday newspapers laid out. As well as our usual broadsheet papers I noticed a couple of the tabloids as well. Sheila was poring over the details of the Railway Murders.

"Look here, imagine this," she said and started to read out bits. I clicked the kettle back on and waited for it to boil.

"'*COP'S SON'S SWEETHEART LAST VICTIM OF RAILWAY KILLER*'," she went on as my mum looked up from her newspaper. "'*Helen Driscoll, the last victim of the crazed Railway Killer, was romantically linked with the son of a police inspector, it was revealed last night.*'"

So the press had got hold of the story. I only hoped that Des Murray and Stevie didn't think it had been me who had told them.

"It's in here as well," my mum said from behind her giant paper. "'*POLICE INSPECTOR'S DISMAY AT IDENTITY OF VICTIM*: *Although uniformed inspector John Martin was not directly involved in the Railway Murders investigation, he was shocked and upset when told that the last victim was fifteen-year-old Helen Driscoll. The inspector's son, Roger, had been at school with the girl and the pair had been dating some months previous to the murder.*'"

I looked over her shoulder at the report. There was a small picture of a uniformed officer. Underneath it said: "Inspector Martin". He had a peaked cap on and only a small portion of his face was visible. He looked ordinary; just like any other police officer.

"Look," Sheila said, "here's a picture." She held up her newspaper. It was a school class photograph and the editor had ringed two faces; one was Helen Driscoll's and the other Roger Martin's. Underneath there was a caption: "*Tragic lovers*".

I skimmed the article. It was factually inaccurate, suggesting that the relationship between Roger and Helen Driscoll had still been going on at the time she was killed. I suppose it made a better story. I wondered what Suzy would make of it.

Sheila was immersed in the article. When she'd read it she closed the paper and flicked through the one underneath. In that I could see another angle the journalists had taken: "*I LIVED IN FEAR OF 'RAILWAY KILLER' exclusive by ex-wife Brenda Knight.*"

"Why do you read this stuff, Sheila?" I asked, pouring some boiling water on to a tea bag.

"I like to see what my students are reading," she said, her eyes scanning the pages, her mouth slightly open, her tongue licking her upper lip.

"Sure," I said and looked at my mum, who was hidden from Sheila behind her paper.

She sucked in her cheeks and raised her eyebrows. "Course you do, Sheila," she said.

I'd only been to The Valentines squash club once before. My uncle Tony had asked me to deliver a letter to a solicitor who had been playing a game there.

The club was a two-storey brick building that was

surrounded by a lawn. It was pristine, the windows glittering and not a bit of litter in sight. The doors in the reception were automatic and really did open when you walked up to them.

I had my sports bag with me and poking out of it was the end of my mum's squash racquet. I hoped that I looked like someone coming to play. I'd also put my hair into several small plaits and stuck on a basketball cap that I had. In my pocket I had a large lump of chewing gum that looked like pink play-doh. I was hoping to appear younger than my age.

I walked straight through reception towards the changing-room area and the squash courts. No one stopped me; no one even noticed me.

Once inside the building I looked for the sign that said "Spectators' Gallery". It took me up a flight of stairs.

There were eight squash courts. The spectators' gallery ran between them – four on one side, four on the other. I was above the players, looking down on them. Three of the courts had women playing on them, two had older men and on another two Asian men were playing. On the last one a young boy was playing an older man. The young boy appeared to be winning.

It had to be Joe Driscoll. The boy was big; three or four inches taller than the man he was playing. He looked muscular as well and was quick on his feet. He seemed to fly from one edge of the court to the other. The man he was playing managed to return the ball three or four times before missing it. Then he leant over, his hands resting on his knees. When he stood up his mouth was strained and his face a beetroot colour.

He said something to the boy but I couldn't catch it because of the noise from the other courts. After a few more minutes' play the man picked up a towel that had been in the corner, put it round his head and walked towards the door. The boy followed him and they disappeared into the changing-room area.

I went to the seating area just outside the changing rooms and sat down. I looked at my watch a number of times. After about ten minutes Joe Driscoll appeared at the door. He was dressed and his hair was wet and combed back. I stood up, knowing that if I didn't approach him then, I'd never do it.

I walked away from him at first, then "tutted" to myself and turned round quickly, as though I'd forgotten something from the changing rooms. I deliberately kept my eyes on the ground and allowed myself to walk straight into him. It was quite a collision. My head hit him somewhere in the chest and my bag fell to the ground. My mum's squash racquet slid out and bounced a couple of times on the parquet flooring.

"Oh, no," I said, without looking at him. I retrieved the racquet and stood up apologizing profusely.

"I'm so sorry. I wasn't looking where I was going; did I hurt you? I'm really sorry."

"No, no."

He said the words slowly, completely unflustered. I looked up at him.

"I just don't look where I'm going. I'm always doing this."

I stood looking deep into his face for a few seconds. I got out the chewing gum and poked it into my mouth. I creased my forehead as though I was trying to work something out.

"Don't I know you?" It was a corny thing to say but it was all I had up my sleeve. "You're Helen's brother Joe, aren't you? Joe Driscoll. My God, fancy seeing you after all this time. And in these awful circumstances. Poor Helen. It was so awful."

He was still standing in the same position looking at me. His face didn't give a lot away.

"It's me, Patsy Page. I was in your sister's class at school. I left a couple of years ago. I read about Helen in the paper. It was dreadful."

He stood looking at me unsurely. Close up he looked his age, even though he was bigger than me by about six inches. He had mousy hair and his skin was pale with the stirrings of acne. We had to move out of the way so that a man with a trolley of canned drinks could get to a nearby machine.

"Patsy?" he said, a look of incomprehension on his face.

He didn't believe me. Maybe he thought I was a newspaper reporter. With some panic in my chest I surged on: "I saw Roger Martin a couple of days ago and poor Suzy; they're really upset. I couldn't believe it when I heard. You never think it's going to happen to someone you know, do you?"

"No," he said, softening a bit at the mention of Roger and Suzy.

A couple and their children passed us by and we had to move up against the wall.

"I was just going for a cold drink," I said. "Why don't you come?" I looked him straight in the eye, hoping somehow to mesmerize him into joining me. He avoided eye-contact though and I thought I'd lost the gamble. But after a few seconds he shrugged his shoulders and said: "OK."

We went to the far end of the cafeteria. I bought the drinks and as I paid for them I watched him sitting at a table. He seemed unperturbed about being there. A couple of people passed him by and said hello and he nodded in reply, all the time with his eyes averted. It wasn't just me he was avoiding looking at.

I chatted for a while, making up stories about me and Helen Driscoll, and then talked about my new school. He didn't say much, I wasn't even sure that he was listening. I was getting nowhere. After about ten minutes I decided to get to the point.

"Poor Helen. It must be over a year since I last saw her and now it's too late. How are you coping, Joe? And your mum; Elizabeth, isn't it? She's grief-stricken, I suppose."

I looked up from my drink and caught a fleeting expression on his face. I couldn't have said exactly what it meant because it faded so quickly. His eyelids had closed with irritation and his lips had stretched across his teeth. Then his face just slipped back as it had been: blank.

"And you Joe, I know you and Helen didn't always get on that well, but I bet it's hit you badly as well."

I looked straight at him, caught his eye for a mini-second, then he looked away, at his cup, at the table, anywhere but at me.

"I'll tell you what though, Helen was really fond of you, she was always talking about you; Joe this, Joe that."

"Don't make me laugh!" he said and rolled his eyes.

"Oh, she was, Joe," I continued.

"Helen never cared for anyone but herself."

He said the words distinctly but slowly. He was looking down at his fingers, using his thumbnail to push at his cuticles.

"I know she used to rib you, Joe, but it was never serious…" I said, feeling uneasy about opening this up with someone who was clearly unconfident and ill at ease. What if he was innocent? Did I have the right to upset him like that?

"You weren't there," he said. He turned round to his bag and I had the feeling that he wasn't going to stay there much longer.

"No, but Helen always said…"

"'You're not really part of this family,' she said to me. 'Mum got *paid* for looking after you.'" He put on a high voice when pretending to be Helen.

Then he looked me straight in the face, his eyes locking on mine for a few seconds. I could see he was angry.

"She was proud of your squash-playing," I continued, grabbing at straws.

"She didn't care about anyone but herself. She might have fooled you into thinking… You ask Fay Norris…" He lost his thread and unzipped his bag. He rummaged around for a few minutes and then said: "I sorted her out though, didn't I?"

"What do you mean?" I said.

"I sorted her out. I put her right."

His hands were flat on the table. Close up I noticed how big they were, his fingers thick and powerful.

"Helen?"

"'Oh Joe, how could you be so horrible,'" he mimicked her voice again. Then lowered his voice: "I sorted her out."

He stood up, towering above me, his hands

hanging heavily for a moment; then picked up his bag and said: "I've got to go."

I watched him walk out. A number of people at other tables were looking at him, nudging each other. Whether it was because he was the junior squash champion or had a murdered sister, I didn't know.

14

Visitors

When I got home the house was empty. There was a note on the kitchen table: *Gone to cinema, be back about eight, love Mum.*

I got out my notebook and wrote down as much as I could remember of what Joe Driscoll had said. I even tried to put his exact words down: *She didn't care about anyone but herself… You ask Fay Norris… I sorted her out.*

I pulled the plaits out of my hair and looked in the fridge for something to eat. I got out some cheese and made a sandwich.

There were two young men, Roger Martin and Joe Driscoll, who both had reasons for disliking Helen. One of them, her adopted brother Joe, hated her.

They both had links with the police station, although Roger's was much stronger than Joe's. Roger wanted to be a policeman, often spent time with his dad talking about the job; surely something as serious as the Railway Murders would have cropped up in conversation, the fact that it was called "Operation Rose". *Why's that? Oh, the murderer left roses on the dead bodies.* Maybe that was why the rose was the wrong colour. Only half the information had got through.

I sat, feeling uneasy about this; Roger Martin simply didn't look the type. Then I pictured Joe Driscoll sitting opposite me in the squash club, his muscular shoulders and arms, his giant hands that seemed to fill the table, his eyes shifting here and there, unable to look me in the face.

Inspector Martin had taken him recently to visit the police station. Like me, maybe he had had a look round, wandered into the conference room. Perhaps he saw the words from a distance, written on the white board, "OPERATION ROSE", glanced at the photographs of the bodies, the roses. Perhaps he was quicker than people gave him credit for. *You can't go in there, son,* Inspector Martin may have said, *that's the nerve centre for the Railway Murders, highly confidential.*

Perhaps, perhaps, perhaps. I picked up my sandwich and bit into it just as the doorbell rang. I carried it out to the front door with me.

It was Billy.

My mouth was full of bread and cheese and it was a minute before I could speak. Usually he would have just walked past me, straight into my kitchen. He didn't though. He stood waiting for me to beckon him in. Eventually, after I'd finished my bite, I said, "Nice to see you," and immediately regretted it. It sounded false and anyhow we usually didn't bother with such niceties. He followed me through to the kitchen and I clicked the kettle on again.

"Tea?" I said and he nodded.

"Good journey?" I said and he nodded.

After a further few seconds of saying nothing he looked at my notes, lying across the table and said:

"So you're carrying on with it, Detective Kelly?"

I stiffened at the tone of his voice. He was mocking me and my unimportant work.

"Billy, if you're annoyed about something come out and say it. And yes, as a matter of fact, I am continuing with the investigation."

I had my hands on my hips and my tongue was pushing against the back of my teeth. For the first time I noticed a brown paper bag that he had on his lap.

"So let the police deal with it. It's their job."

"But … but what if…"

"What if you're wrong? You're not sure then!"

"I am sure."

"But you don't want to look an idiot. For

destroying the photos, for not going to them before now."

"I don't know."

"You want all the glory. After the Judy Hurst case you want to be the centre of attention again." Billy was sitting forward in his seat.

I pulled out a chair and sat down. "No, I don't know," I said miserably.

There was silence for a moment.

"I bought you this," he said abruptly, in the same tone that he'd just been arguing in. He handed me the brown paper bag.

It was a pottery vase.

"Thanks," I said, feeling awkward. We didn't usually buy each other gifts; it was strictly Christmas and birthdays with us. I placed it on the table and he put his hand out and caught my wrist. I looked up at him and without a word he pulled me across and started to kiss me.

I was leaning across the tiny kitchen table. Billy's hands were holding my arms, pulling my mouth on to his. I was still tense from the argument and the angle was uncomfortable. After a few seconds I stopped noticing.

He drew back for a moment and looked at me. I thought he was going to speak but he didn't and I went round the table, sat in the chair next to him and kissed him hard on the mouth, my fingers on his face.

Somewhere in the back of my head I heard a nagging sound. Billy's hands were on my shoulders, one of them running up and down my arm, sending a shiver across my chest.

The nagging noise continued and after another moment I drew back, my mouth wet, and realized that it was the front doorbell.

I got up, smoothing my hair down and walked along the passageway, my head still slightly dazed, wondering what on earth Billy and I were going to say to each other. It had been over a year since we had first kissed. Were we going to be able to talk about it? Refer to it?

I opened the front door. Brian Martin was standing there. Dismay must have been written all over my face because he said: "Don't look so pleased to see me, Miss Patsy Kelly, I'm not stopping, just passing," and then, without another word, he gave me a hug.

I'd turned slightly as he came in, and over his shoulder I could see Billy, standing at the kitchen door watching me. I tried to make a face, to signal that I wasn't enjoying or hadn't asked for such an affectionate display, but my mouth was pushing into Brian's coat and my arms were pinned to my side.

Eventually, after what seemed like ages, he let me go. Billy had disappeared from sight. I heard a sound from the kitchen, as though something had fallen over. Billy appeared, buttoning up his coat.

He walked towards us along the hall.

"I must go, Patsy," he said, ignoring Brian.

"Not on my account," Brian said, looking a little disconcerted as Billy brushed past him.

"My friend Billy," I said, holding my hand out weakly.

"Hi," Brian said, as the front door banged shut. I turned and walked down the hall towards the kitchen.

"Your friend was in a hurry," I could hear Brian's voice from behind me.

In the kitchen, on the floor, were the pieces of the vase that Billy had bought for me.

I felt like crying.

Later, when Brian had gone, I thought about Billy's kiss and the way he had left in a huff as soon as Brian had arrived. Did that mean something *real* was happening between us? I put my hand on my shoulder and rubbed it up and down my arm the way that Billy had done, letting a picture of it come back into my mind.

Did I want something to happen between us?

It was perplexing and I began to sort through my stuff when I heard the front doorbell ring again.

When I opened the door Heather Warren was standing there. I immediately tensed, a feeling of guilt developing, even though I wasn't sure what I had to feel guilty about.

"Patsy," she smiled, "we need to talk."

"Really?" I said, full of innocence.

"About Helen Driscoll, Patsy."

"Oh," I said and held the front door open. She took off her coat and handed it to me. Then she walked past me towards the kitchen. I hung her coat over the banister and hurried after her, wondering what on earth she wanted to see me about.

"A coffee would be good," she said and took a packet of cigarettes out of a bag.

"Milk?" I said timidly. I tidied up the table, tucking my notebook under a pile of magazines.

"Absolutely not, no sugar either," she said and lit up. I silently hoped my mum wouldn't arrive home and find her kitchen full of smoke. I scurried round making the coffee and talking about the weather, the weather and the weather.

Eventually I placed a mug of boiling coffee in front of her. A splash of the liquid came over the side and landed on my hand. It felt like molten liquid. I rubbed the spot with my fingers.

Heather sat looking at me crossly, then picked up the cup and took a mouthful. The steam divided around her face. She never flinched as the liquid went into her mouth. She held it there for a few seconds and then swallowed.

"Lovely," she said and I swallowed a mouthful of saliva. I sat down and forced myself to speak.

"What did you want to see me about, Heather?"

"Well, let me see. Yesterday one of my officers came to see me because a neighbour of Helen Driscoll's parents phoned and said that a strange girl went round to see the family yesterday. The girl was hanging around, asking questions, said her mother knew Mrs Driscoll and so on.

"The neighbour phoned Mrs Driscoll but she knows no one at all fitting the description. The visitor was about your age, Patsy, and had glasses and an unusual hat on."

I sat very still, said nothing. There was no proof that it had been me.

"Then today, not half an hour ago, another of my officers came and told me about a phone call from Mrs Driscoll herself saying that her son, Joe, had been approached by a young girl claiming to be a friend of the late Helen. This girl was not unlike you, Patsy, and guess what? Said her name was Patsy something."

"I…" I started to speak.

"No, no, Patsy. Don't say anything, let me finish. At that very moment my colleague Des Murray was round and he said that when you spent time with him you were very inquisitive about the Railway Murders, about Operation Rose in fact. Now why would that be?"

"I… It's just that…" I blustered, not knowing which words, if any, were going to come out of my mouth next.

"No, no, Patsy, let me finish." She stopped for a moment and took another mouthful of the scalding coffee. "Thing is, I know you're a good detective. I know that because of the Judy Hurst case. I know how enthusiastic you are, Patsy, but the trouble with this investigation is that it's already been solved! We have the murderer. He's on remand, behind bars. You don't have to solve this one, Miss Nancy Drew, it's already been done."

"Right," I said, nodding, as though I'd accepted my telling-off. I looked down at my lap, then at my hands, then back at Heather.

"What's happening, Patsy? I want to know it all."

I sat very still for a moment, then it started to come out. The whole thing: the photographs in the precinct; recognizing the girl; the day at the police station; the contact with Roger Martin; the meeting with Joe Driscoll.

She listened to me without speaking. She lit up three cigarettes, one after the other. When I'd finished, I sat back and looked at her.

"Is that it?" she said.

I nodded and she stubbed out her last cigarette.

"Why didn't you come and tell me, as soon as you recognized the girl?"

"Because I'd thrown the photos away. I had no proof!"

"But I'd have listened to you, Patsy. We could have checked it out. Asked the girl who was sitting in the square to come forward. We could have sorted it."

"But she can't come forward, Heather. She's dead. It was Helen Driscoll. I'm as sure as I can be."

"Then you should have come to me! What did you think you could do? All you've managed to do is upset the Driscolls and they've been upset enough already."

She had raised her voice.

"But Heather," I said, "did you widen your investigations at all, around Helen Driscoll?"

"No, the MO was the same as for the other victims. Why should we? We caught the guy red-handed."

"Both these boys, Roger and Joe, had strong animosities towards Helen."

"But that doesn't mean they killed her!"

"But did you even ask them where they were on the afternoon that she was killed?"

"No, because we have the murderer, in custody." She let out a sigh, as if I was being a nuisance. There was an angry silence. Eventually she said: "What about if I personally find out what these two boys were doing when Helen was killed. You can call it an alibi if you like. When we find out that they had nothing to do with it, will you be satisfied then? Will you drop it then?"

I heard the front door open.

"Yes, of course. I was only…"

The kitchen door opened and my mother came in, Sheila behind her.

"Mum, this is Heather Warren," I said. "Inspector Warren."

My mum smiled but her nose crinkled up and her eyes focused on the plate on the table with the cigarette-ends. Then she looked at me questioningly.

"Heather's just popped by to give me a message for Tony," I said, as though I'd been asked a question.

Sheila came round, her eyes glittering.

"Inspector Warren, of the Railway Murders? Oh, I am pleased to meet you…"

I looked at Heather and raised my eyebrows. She smiled at Sheila.

"I'll be off now, Patsy. Nice to meet you," she said and drained the cooled coffee from her cup. I took her to the front door.

"I'll ring you tomorrow evening. Remember, no more detective work on the Driscoll case, right?" she said in a loud whisper, a glance over my shoulder at the kitchen.

I nodded my head and watched her go off to her car.

15

Fay Norris

I tried to take my mind off the case at work the next day. I spent all morning tidying out the filing cabinets and threw out a lot of dead paperwork. Tony asked me to get out his diary and write in some meetings he had arranged for himself. I noticed that he was meeting Heather Warren on Wednesday morning.

"Why are you meeting Heather?" I said, curious. I knew how much he disliked her.

He was filing his nails and blowing on them. Suddenly I noticed how dark his hair looked, almost jet-black. My aunt Geraldine had been colouring the grey again.

"I'm looking into an old missing persons case. The police and I may be able to help each other. Anyway, now that she's been promoted, I ought to get to know her a bit better. I thought of taking a gift. A box of chocolates? Some flowers?"

He really was serious.

"Would you do that if it was a man?" I said, handing him his diary.

"That's it," he said half-joking, "bring women's rights into everything."

"We are half the population," I said.

"The prettier half, by far," he said. He had a smirk on his face. It was his bull-fighting look. He was going to wave a red rag at me until I charged at him. I wasn't in the mood for playing.

"I'm going to lunch," I said.

"By the way," I could hear his voice as I walked into my office, "how did the date with young Brian go?"

"Never you mind," I shouted.

Brian Martin. He was another thing I was trying not to think about.

Late in the afternoon I got out my notebook and had a flick through. I wondered how long it would take Heather to find out the alibis. I looked at all my work; blocks of writing, lists, words circled and underlined. At the top of a page I noticed the name "FAY NORRIS". Underneath it there was nothing. I took my pen and wrote "BETHNAL GREEN". It was about four stops on the main line into Liverpool Street.

It could take Heather ages to get back to me. She was a busy woman, probably had dozens of other cases to attend to. It could be days or even the end of the week before she rang me.

I made a decision.

It didn't take me long to ring the six Norrises in the phone book. I asked for Fay each time. Only on the last call did I get the answer I wanted: *Fay's not in from college yet. She'll be in at about six.* I copied down the address from the phone book. If only everything else in the case had been as easy to find out as that had been.

I went straight from work to Bethnal Green. I had Fay Norris's address in my bag and an A–Z of London.

I told myself I wasn't really investigating anything, just clearing up some loose ends. All I'd heard about Helen Driscoll had been bad stuff. I wanted to see if her friend had another story to tell.

I walked up her street and decided that I was going to be honest with Fay Norris; no more dramatics, pretending to be a long-lost friend of the family. If she refused to speak to me, then I'd have to leave it at that.

A young woman opened the door of the address that I had. She was older than I had expected, about eighteen. She had long blonde hair, the type you see in the TV ads for hair shampoo.

"Fay Norris?" I asked.

"Yes?" She peered out into the dark street, looking first one way and then the other.

"My name's Patsy Kelly. I work for a private investigations company and I'm doing some personal research on Helen Driscoll. I'd very much like to talk to you."

She frowned at me for a moment and then, pushing the front door to, she said:

"Are you with the newspapers? I've got nothing to say."

I put my hand against the door to stop it closing.

"I'm not a reporter, Fay. Look, I think I was one of the last people to see her before she was murdered. It's sort of important to me to know what she was like." It was honest, even if it didn't tell her everything.

She stood for a minute, her hand playing with the straw-coloured hair.

"You'd better come in," she said.

We went up to her bedroom which was right at the top of the house. It was a small attic room with a bed in the corner and an easy-chair by the tiny window. I looked out and saw the beginnings of splashes of rain on the window. I heard Fay calling something downstairs and then she came into the room.

I sat on the chair and she sat on the bed.

"I wasn't really close friends with Helen, I wasn't

even in the same year. It was just that before we moved here we used to live close to her and she and I walked to school in the mornings. I don't think she had many friends. I kind of felt sorry for her. What do you want to know about her?" she said.

"Why don't I tell you what I know. Then you can fill in anything that's been left out."

"OK." She lay back against the wall and I began to talk. She looked away from me and plaited the ends of her hair, letting it come undone and then starting again. Once or twice she shook her head at something I said but most of the time she just lay, lifting her leg occasionally to look at something on her foot. When I'd finished she sat up and said: "It doesn't surprise me that Roger and Joe should talk about Helen like that. She wasn't always that easy to get on with."

The door of the room opened unexpectedly and a woman brought in a tray with two china cups and saucers on it.

"Some tea for your friend, Fay," the woman said.

"Oh, Mum, there was no need." Fay stood up and took the tray, then gave her mum a hug. The woman went out humming a tune and Fay offered me a cup.

"Helen wasn't happy in that family. At least she had been until Joe came. He was fostered, as you know, then adopted. He was ten when he first went to live there and had enormous problems, learning

334

difficulties I think they called it. Helen said her mum and dad stopped being interested in her. They just became obsessed with the boy, Joe. I think she was exaggerating, you see what I mean?" Fay left the words in mid-air, then drank some of her tea.

"She started to see Roger Martin I suppose about a year ago, maybe not so long, I'm not sure. Anyway, she was dead happy when he started to go out with her. I never knew what she liked about him, he was a real bore...

"Things were all right between them, I think, but I didn't see that much of her then, I was hanging round with some other kids. I'll tell you what though; it was common knowledge that Suzy Peters had her eye on Roger Martin. She started to hang around with their set long before Helen and Roger split up. She was always there, Helen told me, being nice to Roger: 'Isn't that right, Roger? Don't you think so, Roger?' Everyone noticed it."

I smiled, remembering Suzy's way of including Roger's opinion in her conversation.

"I was away when it finished, on holiday I think. There'd been a big party down at the council estate. Helen said something bad had happened; she wouldn't go into it. I assumed she'd caught Roger and Suzy; like I said, we weren't that close then. I was about to move, you see what I mean?"

"She came to visit you though," I said.

"Yes, things started to get much worse at home.

She started to get into trouble at school. She began to bunk off. I'd frequently come out of college in the afternoon and find her there, waiting for me."

"Is that when she began to torment Joe, about him being adopted?"

"No, no," she said impatiently, "she and Joe always had a kind of mickey-taking about that. She'd say he was the new kid in the family, tell him not to get on his high horse. It was a joke, you see what I mean? At least it started that way. I think it got worse in the autumn though. Joe started getting upset about it and instead of leaving it she became serious about it too. Who does he think he is? she'd say. It got worse after Roger dumped her, much worse."

I was getting a different picture of Helen Driscoll. She was mixed up, confused. Someone who had lost her way.

"What about her parents," I said, "didn't they notice?"

"No, it was Joe they focused on, not Helen. Helen was the stable one, the one who could cope; Joe wasn't."

"And Helen was their own daughter, more secure than the adopted boy," I said.

Fay was silent and looked at me for a minute. Then she said: "Helen made me promise not to tell anyone but now, I suppose, it doesn't matter." She shrugged her shoulders. "Helen and Joe were rowing all the time. Helen told me that one afternoon she was really unpleasant to him. She came round here and said, 'I've gone too far, Fay, I've really upset Joe.' She said she was going to go home and make it up to him.

"I didn't expect to see her for a while but she was outside my college, the next afternoon. She was in a terrible state. I brought her home here and she told me everything. It seems that Joe was so upset with her taunting that he went to their mother and told her. Mrs Driscoll was furious and called Helen in. She told Helen then and there, that Joe hadn't been the only adopted child, that she, Helen, was also in fact adopted."

I didn't say anything. It was a piece of information I hadn't expected.

"Apparently the Driscolls had adopted Helen at birth. They'd never told her, thinking they'd never need to. But the adoption people asked them to have Joe, and he'd had such an awful life that they'd taken him. He knew he was adopted but they couldn't suddenly tell Helen. She was ten, after all. So they just left things the way they were."

"So Helen found out that she was just the same as Joe."

"Yes, it changed her. She became really bitter towards them, you see what I mean? She seemed to hate everyone. That's when she started to get nasty towards Roger and Suzy."

"Oh."

"She stopped coming to see me for a while. She started to write me letters. Here, I'll get you the last one she sent, just before Christmas."

Fay got up off the bed and went to a small chest of drawers. She pulled out a small envelope and gave it to me.

Dear Fay, [it said] *just two weeks to Christmas and I'm almost there. I've found out that my real mum and dad both come from north London; the adoption agency have suggested that I write my mother a letter through them. Maybe she will want to see me.*

Things are just the same at home, Joe is walking round like he owns the place. My mum and dad are still angry at me for the way I treated Joe. I can't blame them.

Everywhere I go I see Roger and Suzy. They make me sick. Everybody thinks he's such an angel. If only they all knew him like I do.

Hope all is well with you, I'll try to get over before Christmas. Love, Helen.

"She was looking for her natural mother?" I said.

"Yes, had been ever since her mum, Mrs Driscoll, told her."

"I wonder if that's why Joe Driscoll was so cocky about Helen when I spoke to him." I remembered his words: *I sorted her out.*

"Joe was always dead odd."

"So she was adopted too," I said quietly to myself. I wondered if it meant anything. The window was glistening with raindrops. Every few minutes I could hear a bus splashing along the wet street outside.

"She wasn't all bad, you know," Fay said. "She had a kind heart, but you know lately she just seemed bad-tempered all the time and when she found out about her parents, well…" Fay held her palms upwards and shrugged her shoulders. I stood up, handed her back her letter and walked downstairs. When I got to the front door she said:

"When you saw her, you know, before that maniac got her, how did she look? Did she look happy?"

I thought about it for a minute, remembering Helen's rigid face, her slumped posture, her stare, through the playground, through me. I opened my mouth to speak.

"It's OK," Fay said, using her hands to pull her long yellow hair back behind her ears. "You don't have to say. I can guess what she was like."

I got home at about eight. There was a message on the answer-phone from Heather.

"This is for Patsy. I'll be brief; if you want to ring me for more details I'll be in the office in the morning. Roger Martin was in school on the afternoon of the tenth of January, taking internal exams; mathematics, I believe. Joe Driscoll was absent from school because he was playing in the local semi-finals of the under-sixteen's squash championships.

Like I said, I'm here in the morning if you want to go over it. Bye-bye."

It was all a dead-end. My murder victim had turned out to be quite different from what I had thought and my two suspects, Roger Martin and Joe Driscoll, had cast-iron alibis.

Maybe Heather had been right. I should have dropped the case.

16

Relatives

I had my lunch the next day in the precinct where I had last seen Helen Driscoll alive. Billy was going to meet me there. It was cold and icy but I sat with a packet of chips on the same bench that I had sat on the day I was following Mr Black.

Tony had given me the afternoon off. Business was slack and he said he was going to meet some of his insurance friends.

There were a number of schoolkids lounging around the playthings in the square. A boy of about fourteen was on a tiny swing and some loud girls were sitting flicking sand at each other. Everywhere there was debris from the chip shop; bits of paper, chips thrown away carelessly on the pavement. I began to feel very old, wishing the teenagers could just use the bins.

Billy turned up at about one. He took a chip and said: "What's happening? Why are we meeting here?"

"I just thought, now that it's all over, you might like to see where it all happened, where I saw Helen Driscoll."

"It's all over?" he said and looked at me. He knew what I meant but there was a mischievous look in his eye, as though he was referring to the events of Sunday evening. Maybe I was just being too sensitive.

"Heather Warren came, after you left. She gave me what you might call a major telling-off."

Billy raised his eyebrows. Looking down at my knees I told him about Heather's comments and her phone call the previous evening informing me of the alibis. From time to time I lifted my head to look at him but his head was turned away, or his eyes were fixed on some point in the middle distance. I also told him about my visit to Fay Norris.

"So Helen Driscoll's life gets more mysterious at every turn," he said unexpectedly. He sounded serious. A small surge of hope rose in my chest. He looked me straight in the eye for the first time. I couldn't help but think of the kiss. It sat there between us, huge and unmentionable.

"Yes," I said.

"And you're absolutely sure it was her you saw here on this bench at two thirty-two." He had adopted a businesslike voice, as if he was on the brink of suing someone.

"Absolutely. Utterly. Without any doubt."

"But it looks like the boyfriend and the brother are definitely not involved."

"It looks that way," I said grudgingly, still not completely convinced. He had leaned back on the bench and his shoulder was touching mine.

"If you're right, and she was here at the time that Leslie Knight was caught, there's only one other explanation. Someone else killed her for some other reason."

"Um…" It was unlikely; even someone as mixed up and difficult as Helen couldn't have had that many enemies.

"Let's go through it all again, from the beginning."

I was surprised. There wasn't a hint of sarcasm in Billy's voice. I wondered what he was up to. Had he decided to humour me, let me get it all out of my system the way a parent would go along with a child, or was he genuinely interested? Either way I needed the audience.

I leant back and started at the beginning again; the photographs, the realization that it had been Helen I had seen. I got out my notebook and told Billy about my day with CID, my trip with Heather to the place where Helen's body had been found.

Billy took the book and flicked through the pages

asking me about the notes: What's Operation Rose? Who's Inspector Martin? Who said the words: *Helen, you should have got to know me better?*

I told him about the evening with Brian Martin (omitting the kisses) and my meeting with Roger and his girlfriend Suzy. Finally there was Joe Driscoll's story; the rest he knew.

We sat, idly flicking through my notebook, as though the answer might jump up out of a page. I looked round the precinct and noticed that the schoolchildren had gone; the swing was hanging listlessly and the sand was deserted; an empty can of Coke was rolling down the incline towards the shops.

The man from the chip shop had come out and was gathering up some of the bits of paper and rubbish left by the schoolchildren. Just along, past Majestic Dry Cleaner's, outside the Asian shop, I noticed a bucket full of cut flowers that were for sale. It reminded me of the sad bouquets that had lined the pavement outside the railway warehouses where Helen had been found. The words, *Helen, you should have got to know me better*, kept going through my head, like the chorus of a song.

Finally Billy spoke.

"You know there's something important that you've left out of all this."

"What?" I said, mildly miffed. Over the last few days I'd covered a lot of ground, even though it had left me in the middle of nowhere, quite literally back where I had started.

"You saw her here, in the square, on her own, right?"

"Yes."

"When kids bunk off school they usually do it with mates. They do it to be with their mates, right?"

"Mostly, yes."

"But she was here, on her own."

"Yes." I couldn't see what Billy was getting at. My attention was taken by the Asian woman, coming out of the shop and picking up one of the bunches of flowers. I watched as she shook the water from the bottom of it before taking it inside the shop.

"So perhaps she was here, on this bench, for some particular reason."

"What though?" Why should a cold bench in the middle of a tatty square of shops hold any clue to Helen's death?

"Thing is," Billy sat forward, "remember that girl in the year above us, at school, Rosemary someone? The kid who had been in care; you know, the one who arrived in the social worker's car every day."

"Rosemary Lewin?"

"Yes. I heard, I can't remember exactly when, but I heard that she'd started to look for her real mother."

I didn't say anything.

"I heard that she'd found her through some agency or other. The thing is she went to see the woman and…"

"It was awful, I remember, the woman didn't want to know her."

"That's right. The woman had a family of her own, a husband; I can't remember exactly but the point is that she didn't want Rosemary around."

"Helen Driscoll was looking for her mother, Fay Norris said; in fact she was close to finding her; it said so in a letter that I read."

"Exactly," Billy said. He opened the pages of the notebook and went on: " *'Helen, you should have got to know me better.'* What if that bouquet was from her natural mother?"

"You think her mother killed her?" I said incredulously.

"No," Billy said, exasperated, "but it might explain why she was here, in this square. If someone else knew that Helen was here that would back up your story. The police might reopen the investigation."

I had a blank look on my face, but in my head a picture was moving into focus. I remembered Helen sitting on the bench, her body relaxed, her head rigid, as if she were *looking at something*. She had been staring past me, preoccupied even when the toddler fell over.

I looked round and saw Majestic Dry Cleaner's. I

remembered the day I had been there, my camera in my bag. There had been a woman, in a grey overall, looking out on to the square, at the same moment that Helen had been looking in.

I stood up and grabbed Billy's arm.

"My God," I said, "she was here, in this square, because it was where she'd found her mother. That's why she was sitting on the bench, staring into that shop." I pointed to the dry cleaner's.

"Don't get too excited. It's just a guess," Billy said.

But it wasn't. I felt suddenly that it was right. That it had been staring me in the face. Helen had no other connection to that square. It was miles from her school and she had no friends there.

Helen, you should have got to know me better. The note must have been from her mother.

"Maybe there's some connection with all this and her murder," I said, excitement sizzling through me. Billy put his hand on my arm.

"Patsy, slow down. Take it one step at a time. You can't go rushing in accusing people of murder."

"I know, I know. What do you take me for?"

"We'll have to think of some way to find out, without asking the woman straight out. What if her family's there?"

"She may not want everyone to know that she's Helen's mother."

"Slow down, take it easy. We won't rush into it."

We walked towards the dry cleaner's, talking

quietly. Just before I opened the door I squeezed Billy's arm and whispered:

"Billy, you're brilliant. You've cracked this case."

The heat from the dry cleaner's hit us as we walked in the door. It was a relief to be out of the cold but it quickly became oppressive. We waited for a moment while the woman behind the counter served someone else.

She looked familiar, not unlike my own mum, perhaps a bit older. She had a short grey overall on over jeans. Her dark hair was hanging round her face and she had no make-up on. She looked hot and red-faced. She had glasses on that had slipped down to the end of her nose; every few seconds she pushed them back up again with her middle finger. She talked constantly to the woman she was serving, about the weather, the price of apples and the government. When the woman left with her dry cleaning she said, "I'll just be a minute and then I'll be with you." She walked into the back of the shop and I could hear her talking to someone. A male voice answered indistinctly and then she came out again, carrying an armful of clothes on hangers and, puffing slightly, she laid them down on a section of the counter.

I noticed then, with a flicker of concern, that she was not at all like Helen; she was much bigger, taller and broader. What had I hoped for? That she would be Helen's double? Only twenty years older?

"Now." She held out her hand and looked expectantly, first at me, then at Billy. I realized after a second that she was waiting for our dry cleaning ticket. Billy spoke:

"Sorry to bother you, only our friend left her dry cleaning in here the other week and we've come to pick it up. We've got no ticket though."

"Oh," the woman said, pulling a giant, dog-eared book out from under the counter. "Name?"

Billy looked at me; I held my breath.

"Her name was Helen Driscoll; D.R.I.S.C.O.L.L. It was about a week ago. She lived on The Valentines estate."

The woman's head was bent over the book. Her eyebrows crinkled for a moment and she continued to point her finger on the page and move it downwards.

"About a week ago?" she said, turning back through the book.

I looked closely at her, to see if there was even a flicker of recognition at Helen's name, but there was nothing. I decided to push it further.

"Yes, it's very sad. Our friend was killed last week, murdered I should say."

"How awful," the woman said, looking at me, then at Billy. She used her finger to push up her glasses. "Driscoll, did you say? I'm sure I haven't got any dry cleaning here under that name. I'll just check in the back. I don't work here all the time, only part-time you see; my husband might remember something."

She disappeared for a minute and I could feel disappointment beginning to lean on my shoulders. Billy was looking round the shop, avoiding my look.

"No, I'm sorry," she said from the back, her voice reaching us before she did, "my husband doesn't remember anything about it. I'm so sorry. Do you thing it might have been another dry cleaner's?"

We said yes, probably, and left the shop, hearing the "ting" of the door as it shut behind us.

"Maybe it wasn't the dry cleaner's," Billy said. "Maybe it was one of the other shops."

We looked around but there was only the Asian grocery, the Chinese fish and chip shop and the car parts place that was over on the far side. I had distinctly remembered Helen looking to my right and that was where the dry cleaner's was.

My memory. It was the only thing holding me on to this case. It was like a thin thread that was being pulled and stretched and was at breaking point.

"I've got to go and deliver a car this afternoon. Why don't I run you back home?" Billy said. I must have looked suicidal because he put his arm round my shoulder in a big-brother hug. I followed him round the corner to the car, a black hatchback with a crumpled side-wing.

"I'm taking it to get it priced for an insurance

job," Billy said, opening the door. He stopped mid way, looking past me, towards the precinct. I turned round. A man was walking towards us. I stood still as he came closer. He was tall and very thin. He was wearing a grey overall, the arms of which were too short. He stopped and said nothing; then looking as though he had just made a decision he said:

"Can I talk to you?" He clasped his hands and I noticed his bony wrists and knuckles, the skin only just seeming to cover the long fingers. "It's about what you said, in the dry cleaner's. It's about Helen Driscoll. I knew her, you see. No, be perfectly honest," he seemed to be talking to himself, "she came to see me last week. She's…" He stopped speaking for a moment, then lowered his voice. "She says she's my daughter. That I'm her father. That I *was* her father."

17

Daughter

We drove away from the precinct with the man in the back of the car. We parked a couple of streets away. He talked most of the time.

"My name's Ron Carpenter. My wife, you see, she doesn't know anything about this. Sarah, my wife, would be very upset. She has no idea that I have a daughter at all. That's why I've not contacted anyone, the police…"

He had one of his hands over the back of my seat. It sat there, almost touching me, pale and skeletal. I moved closer to the window.

When we pulled up he stopped talking and took an inhaler out of his pocket. He sucked on it and after holding his breath for a few minutes he said, "She just turned up one day and said, 'Hello, Dad', bold as brass."

He kept looking out of the car windows, up and down the street we were parked in.

"My wife and I, we've been running the dry cleaner's for about five years now. We've no children of our own. My wife couldn't have them. It's one of the reasons why I don't want Sarah to know."

"But did you see Helen, there in the park, on the day she was murdered?" I said, remembering my hope that he would back up my story.

"On the day she died? You mean the Tuesday? The day she went missing? No, no. I'm sure I didn't. I was at the wholesaler's that afternoon."

I turned round and looked out of the front window of the car. It was no use. Ron Carpenter hadn't been in the square that day, hadn't seen his daughter when I had seen her.

"How did she find you?" Billy said. I had given up talking. I was imagining myself walking round a maze. Every time there seemed to be a way out I came to a dead-end.

"Through her mother. Lord, what a day that was, when Helen turned up in the shop. It was sheer luck that Sarah wasn't there. She's standing in front of me, cheeky as anything. Good-looking girl too. Just like her mother."

"Her mother?"

"A woman we knew from way back. It was a sleazy business, truth to tell, sneaking around. I don't know why I'm telling you all this anyway.

Annie, her name was, Annie Wilson. Funny thing was, we met through this support group, for childless married couples. Me and Sarah and Annie and her husband. Me and her just sort of hit it off. When she got pregnant it was obvious that it wasn't her husband's. They split up and Annie kept the baby. At least I thought she had. She never said anything, see, not to her husband – or to anyone – that I was the baby's father. That's how come Sarah never knew."

"Presumably Annie didn't keep the baby after all," Billy said.

"No, she was adopted at six months. Annie probably found it too hard-going, on her own with a small baby. Helen found her, I don't know how. She's living on the other side of London. Didn't want to know Helen apparently. She told her my name though and the address I'd previously been living at. It didn't take Helen long to find me here."

It was getting steamed up inside the car and I opened a window. I imagined Helen Driscoll walking the streets, searching for her natural father. Ron Carpenter continued. I noticed he kept his inhaler out, his finger cupped over it, ready for use.

"It got harder to keep it from Sarah because Helen started to get difficult. First couple of times she came to see me she was fine. I explained to her the circumstances, that Sarah couldn't know about her. But I said we could be friends. She could visit me occasionally, maybe go out. Sarah need never know, I said, and with all honesty she seemed to like that, thought it was fun." He was speaking faster and faster. "The trouble was, as the weeks went by, she started to come round more often; sometimes instead of going to school. I'd look out the window and see her sitting on the bench. Sometimes I'd slip out and talk to her but more and more I'd just have to ignore her. Truth to tell, it was very awkward."

It was *awkward*. I found myself looking at Ron Carpenter with growing dislike. He left his daughter sitting on a freezing cold bench because he was afraid to own up to his wife.

"And she started asking me to do things. She was having some problems with a previous boyfriend's father. He was threatening her, she said."

My ears pricked up at this; Billy looked around as well. Ron Carpenter looked startled to be the centre of our attention again.

"I shouldn't really be telling you this. I think I've said enough."

"Ron, please go on."

"I can't go to the police about any of this. I can't have any of it out in public. It would kill my wife."

"You don't have to go to the police, just tell us."

"She said her boyfriend's dad…"

"Inspector Martin," I said.

"Yes, that's him; she said he was threatening her. Something about getting her in trouble with the police for something that had happened with a car. I don't know. I said I'd see if I could speak to him. Thing is I often go to the police station. I deliver dry cleaning, you see. I've got a regular visitor's card. It's easy for me to see most of the officers who work down there."

"And did you see him? Inspector Martin?"

"I was going to. I was in the station the day after she told me but…"

"What?" Billy said.

"He was … no, to be perfectly honest I got cold feet. If I had had a word with him, I'd have had to admit to being Helen's father. I was sure, I was positive it would get back to Sarah."

"So you didn't bother," I said. I couldn't keep the disdain out of my voice. He didn't seem to notice, just carried on.

"And then a few days later she was dead. I couldn't believe it. I didn't know what to think or feel. She was my daughter, true enough, but I didn't have any deep feelings for her. No more than for any other teenager…" Ron Carpenter held the inhaler up and sucked out of it. He sat, his lips tightly closed and looked from me to Billy and back again.

Billy started the car up; he had had enough.

"I mean if I had told Sarah, what good would it have done? Just upset her. And in the end, it would all have been for nothing. Poor Helen's dead."

We dropped him off at the end of the road. He

looked around again as he got out of the car. It was as if someone was following him. I watched him walk up the street and wondered how he could sleep at night. *Helen, you should have got to know me better.*

Maybe it was better that she hadn't.

Billy spoke first after we drove off.

"There was some trouble with a car," he said. "I don't remember seeing that in your notebook."

"No, it's the first time I've heard of it. Come to think of it, Fay Norris said something bad had happened down on a council estate. There was a party and it was when Helen and Roger had finished."

"So you need to talk to Roger again?"

"Oh, I don't know," I said, "maybe this is all a waste of time." I was tired. I wanted the whole thing to finish. Nothing was emerging from all the investigations; if anything, the story got more complicated every time we uncovered some new detail.

"You're not giving up now. Let's make this our last call. We'll talk to this Roger Martin and then tonight you can ring Heather Warren and wash your hands of the whole thing. If they don't think there's enough evidence to start the investigation, then it's no skin off your nose."

Billy was organizing me. I felt so grateful I could hardly speak.

"Where will Roger Martin be?" he asked.

"In school probably. Here, I've got the name of it under Helen's details. Westpark High."

"If we're quick, we might get there in time for the end of lessons."

18

The Party

Roger Martin came out of the school gate amid a stream of other kids, some running, some walking closely in twos, some, hands in pockets, whistling along the road. A few metres behind, running to keep up, was his girlfriend Suzy.

I was leaning against a shop opposite the gate of the school. As soon as Roger got free of the crowd of schoolkids I walked across to him. He saw me coming and smiled slowly. It was a controlled look. Suzy didn't smile, not at first. Her lips moved rapidly, saying something I couldn't hear. Then, as she came closely to me she smiled as well.

"Patsy," Roger said with a great show of pleasure, "is Brian around?" He looked up and down the street even though it was perfectly clear that I had been standing alone.

"Roger," I replied, "we need to talk about Helen Driscoll." I had decided to be completely straight with him.

"We've already talked about her. Anyway what's it to you?"

"I'm following up the case. There are some things that don't add up." I was overdosing on the clichés; any minute the words *the butler did it* were going to come out of my mouth.

"We told you everything about Helen, didn't we, Roger?" Suzy said, her arm linking Roger's.

"Not quite. You didn't tell me about the party or about the trouble with the car." I looked straight at Roger as I said this. He turned immediately to Suzy and said:

"You've told someone; I knew you couldn't keep your mouth shut."

"I never, Roger, I never said a word." Suzy was looking bewildered.

"Just keep quiet. That's all you had to do."

"Roger, I haven't…" Suzy had raised her voice. A number of younger kids were standing around us. Some of them were nudging each other.

Roger looked across me, out into the distance. He had shaken Suzy's arm away from his.

"What's it got to do with you? I don't have to talk to you about anything."

He looked so different from the first time we'd met. He'd been friendly, warm; now the joviality had gone; he was apprehensive, guarded.

"That's right, we don't have to talk to you, do we, Roger?" Suzy said, agreeing with him. I noticed her trying to slip her hand through his arm but he was holding his elbow flat against his side.

"Roger, last night I talked to Fay Norris who told me some things about Helen and you," I said. I took off my glasses and rubbed my nose. "I have a feeling that very soon the investigation over her death will be reopened. If you've got some secrets, then it would be better if you were to tell them before they come out by themselves."

I turned and started to walk away. I could see Billy, in the car, a few metres ahead on the other side of the road. After a few moments I heard footsteps.

"Wait, Patsy," Roger's voice came from behind, "I'll talk to you." Suzy was puffing a few metres behind him, her heels making it difficult for her to keep up.

"We'll talk to you, won't we, Roger," she said unnecessarily.

We went back to Billy's house. It was empty but after he had put his calor gas fire on it was warm. He put the kettle on and we all sat round the kitchen table.

"All of what I told you about Helen was true."

"It was," Suzy said.

"Shut up, Suze," Roger said and Suzy pursed her lips.

"She did harass us. She hated the idea of me and Suzy going out together."

"What about the car and the party. What happened there?"

"We'd been going downhill, her and me, rowing and stuff. I knew I was going to have to end it but it was difficult. She was always depressed and whenever I raised the subject she'd just start to cry."

Billy put the tea on the table and sat down.

"Fay Norris said that Helen knew Suzy was after you, had known for months; maybe that's why she was depressed."

"No," Roger said. He did look genuinely surprised. Suzy said nothing.

"Some kid from our class's parents were away. He was having a party. It was the end of last summer. We all went, most of the class. Helen was difficult all evening. She kept sniping at me, taking the mickey out of my dad. In the end I told her it was over. She started to drink, there was stuff around, I had some wine. Most of the kids from my class were gone by this time. Suzy had gone. There were only about five of us left."

Suzy was silently playing with her fingers, tapping them together, making shapes with them, a triangle, a circle, her palms together as if she was praying.

"Someone suggested that we went for a drive. Helen was all for it. She was loud by this time, very drunk. I wanted to go home but I didn't want to leave her there, on her own. Anyway the long and short of it was that we got into a car that was parked round the back of the estate. I thought, I honestly thought, that it belonged to one of the kids' brothers."

It was a stolen car. Roger Martin had got into a *stolen* car.

"Everyone took a turn to drive, just up and down the road. It was pitch dark, you know the road that leads down to the river, where all the empty houses are. We weren't doing any harm, no speeding, no messing around, no hand-brake turns or anything stupid like that."

"But you'd been drinking," Billy said.

"Yes." Roger stopped speaking.

"They'd all had more than you, hadn't they, Roger. He was the most sober," Suzy said.

"That's true. That was the trouble. If I had been really drunk I'd just have done what the others did and left the car down by the river. Trouble was I was still thinking it belonged to one of their brothers. I wasn't drunk but Helen was. She was lying across the back seat. I decided to return the car to where we'd got it from. I don't know why I did it. I could have just left it there and no one would have ever known."

Roger Martin had his eyes closed and his hands were shaped into fists.

"What happened?" Billy asked.

"I drove it back towards the flats. Helen was awake by this time. She kept saying 'don't leave me, Roger, don't go'. I must have looked round into the back seat or something because somehow I lost control. There was this cat, see, in front of me. It hadn't been there before. All I saw were these eyes in the headlights of the car and I swerved to avoid them. I don't know why I didn't just brake, maybe I did, but whatever, the car crashed into this other car that was parked at the side of the road. It made a massive bang and then there was this even bigger silence."

"Didn't you get hurt?" Billy said.

"I had a seat-belt on. Like I said we weren't joy-riding. I was taking the car back."

"Returning it," Suzy said, her voice shaky.

"And?" I was impatient to hear the rest.

"I got out of the car. I pulled Helen out and we ran. I just panicked. I just ran until we got home. My dad was there. I don't remember much. I think I might have even been crying. I just remember not knowing what to do and then he was there and he took it over."

"He covered it up?" I said, surprised, remembering the stern photograph of him in the newspaper.

Roger said nothing, he just shook his head from side to side.

"If only I'd just left the car down by the river."

"Nobody lost out of it," said Suzy. "The car owners will have got their insurance and it's not as if anyone was hurt."

"For a while Helen was quiet about it. Like I said, after we first broke up she seemed OK, really quite aloof, like she didn't care. I saw her a couple of times, on her own."

"You never said," Suzy said, looking down at the table.

"She was quite pleasant. Mentioned the crash once or twice, but it was like, 'thank God we got out of that, I'll never be able to thank your dad for keeping us out of trouble,' and then one day, like overnight, she just changed."

I thought about Joe Driscoll's words: *I sorted her out*. He had. The revelation of her having been adopted had changed her character.

"She came to me and said she wanted to go out with me again. Then she would keep her mouth shut about the crash. She said she would go to the police station and say what had happened. It would have been the end for my dad and for me. I'd never have got a job in the force then." He sounded much more concerned for himself than for his dad.

"He'd have lost his career just for one little mistake," Suzy said.

"My dad said he would warn her off. He did. He went to see her about a week before she died. I don't know what was said but he told me it would be OK, that he had sorted it out. He said he'd told her about the trouble she'd get into if she said anything. In the end, none of that really matters because she died anyway."

"We were shocked, weren't we, Roger?" Suzy seemed to feel a need to say.

"No, no, not shocked. I was relieved and that's the truth."

"No," Suzy said.

"Shut up, Suze."

It was quiet in the room and in my head I kept thinking of Inspector Martin; a troublesome girl on his hands, a series of murders that were being followed up by his colleagues. What if there was one more, would it matter? If he made it look like all the others?

Roger and Suzy sat for a while talking. Then they went out into the dark night. As they walked up the path I could hear his voice, flat and dull; over the top, high-pitched, I could hear Suzy's words: "Won't we, Roger, shouldn't we, Roger, doesn't it, Roger."

Roger seemed shell-shocked by all of it. I wondered how he would feel if he thought that his dad had murdered Helen Driscoll in order to keep himself and his son in a job.

I went back into Billy's kitchen.

"I'm going to do what you said."

"Really?" he smiled, rinsing the cups under the tap.

"I'm going to unload all of it on to Heather Warren. She can deal with Inspector Martin."

Billy came towards me, drying the cups with a tea towel.

"Take care, Patsy," he said. "It's an awful big jump, from being a decent police officer to a murderer. There's no real evidence that it was him."

Billy was being cautious again.

"I know, I know, but he's got the motive and the means. Think about it; this police inspector's under-age son drives a stolen car while under the influence of drink and then crashes it. This police inspector covers it up, allowing his son to get off scot-free. If it had come out it would have cost him his career, not to mention his son's. Helen Driscoll certainly had a wild, unbalanced side to her. Perhaps he tried to keep her quiet but in the end she kept on. Look how she found her mum and plagued her dad. She could be relentless. Perhaps, in the end, he couldn't stand it any more."

"OK, perhaps," Billy said. "Just be careful when you're talking to Heather."

"I will," I said.

19

The Wrong Man

Heather listened in silence while I spoke. There was no expression on her face as I described my visit to Fay Norris and my discovery of Helen Driscoll's natural father. I had my notebook on my lap and my voice was racing with excitement. As I went on though I could see there was no surprise or astonishment in her eyes about my findings, my revelations or my solution.

I had had to get her out of a meeting, had told her my information was urgent.

"It had better be," she'd said testily as she led me up to her office. As she listened I noticed the absence of cigarettes. In her hands she had a pencil that she kept playing with, weaving it in and out of her fingers, tapping it lightly on the desk in front of her, holding it up in the air, the end of it in her mouth like an imaginary pipe.

At the mention of Inspector Martin she seemed visibly to stiffen. She put the pencil down and picked up a small Plexiglas ruler which she proceeded to bend and then straighten. I began to feel like a naughty schoolgirl, summoned to the Head's office, trying to explain away my rôle in some major school mischief. When I'd finished I sat waiting for a few seconds. My throat seemed full of something that I couldn't swallow.

There was a knock on the door and a young man came in.

"Excuse me, marm, but your car is ready."

"Thanks, John," Heather said and started to gather things off her desk into an attaché case. When the door had shut behind the young man she said:

"Patsy, when you and I spoke the other night we made a deal. That deal was that I would find out about alibis and you would drop this investigation. You agreed to that, right?"

I nodded glumly. She was angry with me.

"Now I find you haven't kept your side of the bargain, that you're still meddling in it all, poking your nose into the lives of the people I work with."

I listened with a sinking heart. *Poking your nose.* The words stung me.

The interview hadn't gone the way I had hoped it would. I think I had imagined myself being the centre of a lot of back-slapping. *Well done, Patsy* was the phrase I had thought might be directed at me. Instead I was being treated like a first-year who had been caught smoking behind the gym.

I began to feel angry with Heather. I said nothing though, I let her speak on. She was standing up pulling paper and files together, talking to me at the same time, no eye contact, just a steely edge to her voice.

"For your information, Patsy, John Martin did come to me at the time that his son crashed the car. He did not, as you put it, *cover it up*, he came and told me exactly what had happened, not quite as graphically as you just have. I, personally, followed it up. John Martin is a valued colleague here. I felt I owed it to him to try and help when he was in trouble.

"The car in question had been stolen, some months before. It was an old car that the insurers had written off and sent to the breaker's yard for spare parts. One of the boys from the estate had presumably stolen it from there."

My redrafted notes were lying on my lap. I turned a page and saw line after line of slanted blue handwriting. I'd even underlined some things. I almost laughed out loud. How important I'd thought I was.

"The car he crashed into was a derelict car. It hadn't even got any wheels, had been parked in that spot for weeks." She clicked her attaché case shut. She went to a coat stand and took a silk scarf and wrapped it round her neck.

"Theoretically you're right. John Martin's son did break the law but you know, Patsy, sometimes you have to give a little. No one had been hurt, no one had lost money. If we had charged Roger Martin all that would have happened is that he would have received a caution or, at the very most, if it had gone to magistrates, some community service. I, myself, felt sure that he would never offend again. The end result would have been that a young man who had wanted to be a policeman all his life wouldn't have been able to join.

"I took a decision. I think it was the right one."

"But Helen Driscoll was trying to blackmail Inspector Martin…" I said weakly.

"But she had nothing to blackmail him with! The case was closed, and anyway," she was buttoning up her coat, "even if what you're saying is right and John Martin did have a motive for murdering Helen Driscoll, he has an alibi. In fact John Martin has an alibi for the whole of that afternoon. He was with me. We were at a liaison conference. We were sitting with one of the members from the local council when my bleeper went off and I was informed that my officers were chasing a suspect down along the railway. We both left the meeting and were there, minutes later, when Knight was caught. He was beside me, Patsy, so he couldn't have murdered anyone."

She stood by the door, stiff and formal. Misery must have been written all over my face because after a few moments she softened and put her case on the floor. She came across and sat on the edge of the desk.

"Don't think I'm not impressed with your determination, Patsy, but you've got to stop playing at this. If you want to be a real detective, come and join the force; otherwise you're just playing around in the dark, embarrassing yourself and other people. You'll end up a laughing stock. I don't know what your uncle would think."

She looked at her watch and got up to go. I stood up and looking through the windows of her office I could see the CID detectives milling around in the room outside. There were one or two faces I thought I recognized and over by one of the computer monitors was Des Murray's back. As I walked out they were all looking away, at bits of paper or thumbing through files, and one or two were on the phone. Even the cleaning woman seemed to turn away from me. I turned and walked to the door and felt every pair of eyes on my back, boring into me; they all knew I had messed up, every one of them.

It was dark and cold outside and I pulled my collar

up and the woolly brim of my hat down. This case had been like a Russian doll. Every time I had lifted one off there had been another underneath; one solution had led to another set of problems.

Inspector Martin had been with Heather.

I should have listened to Billy Rogers.

My mum was in and so was her friend Sheila. They were both sitting on the settee, in front of the TV, eating an Indian takeaway meal.

"There's some chicken biryani in the fridge for you," my mum said in between mouthfuls. "Put it in the microwave."

I went to the kitchen and took the food out of the fridge even though I wasn't very hungry. I didn't fancy joining my mum and Sheila. Sheila was bound to make some comment about the murders or Leslie Knight and it was the last thing I wanted to talk about. I tipped the food on to a plate and slid it into the microwave.

Just then the doorbell rang and I shouted, "I'll get it," and went to the front door. It was Brian Martin.

"Brian!" I said. In all the rush and hurry to go and see Heather Warren I'd completely forgotten about Brian. No doubt his brother had told him all the things I'd said.

"Can I come in?" His face was long. "I won't be long. I'm not stopping."

I took him into the kitchen. The buzzer sounded in the microwave but I left my food there.

"A cup of tea?" I said lightly, nervously. I had a feeling that I was about to be told off again. Twice in one day; I was getting used to it.

He ignored my offer.

"Why didn't you tell me you were investigating Helen Driscoll's death?"

"I wasn't really," I said, still lying. I looked at Brian Martin's face. His expression had a hard edge to it. I'd been unfair to him. I should have told him the truth.

"You used me," he said, as if reading my thoughts. "You could have been honest with me. I wouldn't have minded you talking to Roger. If he'd had anything to do with Helen's death, then I'd have wanted to find out the truth."

"I'm sorry," I said. "It did start off that way, me wanting to find out about your brother and Helen but…" I was stumbling for words, "but I really did get to like you."

It was weak even though it was true.

"It's all right; you don't have to be nice to me any more. You don't need any more information."

"Brian, I'm…" I put my hand on to his arm but he shook it off.

"You could have been honest. Maybe I could actually have helped you."

"I'm sorry." It was all I could say. He was right. If

I had been honest from the start, then maybe the misunderstandings, the mysteries, would have been cleared up more quickly.

"You weren't really interested in the truth," he said, "you just wanted to be the hero."

The door opened and my mum came in carrying two empty plates. I could hear the TV from the other room.

"Sorry, Pat. I didn't know you had company."

"She hasn't," Brian said. "I'm just off."

I walked to the front door with a dozen things to say rushing round my head. I never got the chance though; he opened the door and went through it without so much as a backward glance. I stood looking out into the dark as his back disappeared into the night.

Even though I hadn't really wanted him I felt as if I'd lost something. I leant up against the door jamb, weary with the whole thing. *You just wanted to be the hero ... you weren't really interested in the truth.* The words settled in my head like lead.

"Your food's ready, Pat," I could hear my mum's voice.

"I don't want it," I said and walked off upstairs.

20

The Letter

I got up on Wednesday morning feeling as though I had a bad hangover, even though I'd had nothing to drink.

You just wanted to be the hero were the first words that came into my head when my alarm woke me up. I also remembered Billy's cutting words: *you want all the glory; you want to be the centre of attention again...*

Was it true? Had I been more interested in my own position than in solving the case?

As I was getting dressed I told myself that it hadn't been like that. My tights got twisted though and the zip stuck on my jeans; a button came off my shirt and the jumper I wanted to wear was in a crumpled heap on the floor from the previous day. Frustration was simmering inside me and when I couldn't find the scarf I wanted I slammed the wardrobe door shut and broke the magnetic catch.

The door swung idly back and hung dismally open.

It wasn't going to be my day.

My mum handed me a letter when I got downstairs. It was a large brown envelope with my name and address written in block letters on the front. I picked up the mug of tea she'd made me and sat down at the table. Inside was another smaller envelope addressed to Fay Norris in Bethnal Green. There was a note with it. It read:

To Patsy Kelly. I got this in the post yesterday with a note from Helen's mum, Mrs Driscoll. She said she'd found it in among Helen's things. It had been stuck down and was ready to send so she thought it was probably private and forwarded it to me.

Helen must have written it on the day that she died, meaning to post it to me. I thought, after the things you said, that you might be interested in it.

Poor Helen, she wasn't all bad. I wish I'd been kinder to her now. Fay.

My mum was making the breakfast and talking about her day at college. I said "um" a couple of times and opened the letter from Helen Driscoll, dated the tenth of January.

Dear Fay, I haven't been over for a while because I've been busy trying to find my real mum and dad. I spent some time looking through my mum and dad's papers and found some information on a group they used to belong to, Childless Couples Support Association. It seems they used to go there regularly before I was born. While they were there, they heard of a woman who had a baby she couldn't look after. Me!! They have a letter from this woman, Annie, her name is. There was an address on it and I went there and got a forwarding address. Annie, my real mum, lives in north London now. I went to see her a couple of weeks ago. She is so nice. There's a problem; her present husband doesn't know about me, so we're not going to see each other for a while until she tells him. It's only fair that I give her some time. The other good thing is that she gave me the address of my real dad! I've been to see him; he works in a dry cleaner's in a local precinct here. We've had a few chats, he's really nice, although a bit nervous about his wife finding out. I've kept going to see him though. He likes me a lot, I think. His wife's a bit unstable apparently. She's had some kind of breakdown and has been in hospital.

Today though I got a big surprise. He sent me a letter asking me to meet him at two-thirty in the square. He wants to tell his wife about me so that it's all out in the open. It'll be great. In a few months my real mum will have told her husband, then I'll have all sorts of relatives!

By the way, I'm getting on better with Mum and Dad at home; even daft Joe isn't annoying me so much now. I even saw Roger Martin the other day, with his puppy dog Suzy, and for the first time I didn't feel like crying.

Things are looking up for me. See you soon. Love and kisses. Helen.

I put the letter down on the table. In front of me was a mug of tea and a plate of toast that my mum must have put there while I had been reading. I found myself breathing very shallowly.

Helen Driscoll's father had arranged to see her on the afternoon of the tenth of January. That's why she'd been sitting there, on the bench. She'd been waiting to meet him.

I remembered him hurrying after me and Billy as we'd left the dry cleaner's: *she says she's my daughter. That I'm her father, that I was her father.*

He'd said nothing to us about having arranged to meet his daughter that afternoon, not a word. I sat with my head in my hands and tried to think back over the conversation. I'd taken no notes. I'd only picked up on the stuff about Helen being threatened by Inspector Martin. I'd not really held on to what he'd said at all.

Phrases kept coming back to me; no, to be perfectly honest, in all honesty, truth to tell. He was constantly emphasizing the fact that he was telling the truth. But he'd said nothing about meeting Helen on the tenth of January.

I got up and walked around the room. I heard the radio on upstairs and the sound of the shower running. I picked up a bit of cold toast and nibbled at it.

I went through it all, trying to imagine what might have happened.

Ron Carpenter and his wife Sarah couldn't have children. They met another couple at a support group and Ron had an affair with the woman, Annie. Helen was born although no one knew about it. Annie moved away; eventually Helen was adopted by Mr and Mrs Driscoll.

Helen was fifteen and had found her real mum and dad. Neither of them seemed to want to know her. She left her mum alone but continued to approach her dad, not realizing (or maybe ignoring) the fact that he wasn't very keen to take her into his life.

He was desperate that his wife shouldn't find out but Helen continued to sit out in the square, a ghost from his past.

Ron Carpenter worked for a dry cleaning company. He had a contract with the local police station to launder and clean uniforms. He had a regular pass there, delivering stuff that he had cleaned. The newspapers were full of the Railway Murders. At the station Ron overheard or even saw the information about Operation Rose. Because he was not closely involved he didn't get all the information; he only knew that a rose was left on the bodies, not what colour it was.

Helen continued to plague him and he was terrified that his wife Sarah would find out. He had no real feelings for the girl; he had said so, to me and to Billy. He asked her to meet him at two-thirty, perhaps took her away, in his van, to a deserted railway yard. In the back of his van he had a piece of climbing rope and a single yellow rose.

I was eating my toast as though it was a piece of chewing gum. I let it go and swallowed.

What could I do about it?

I could hardly go to Heather Warren, not after what she had said to me.

I couldn't just leave it though.

I would have to go and see Ron Carpenter.

21

Yellow Roses

I found Billy at home. He was in his overalls, getting ready to start work on a car he was servicing for a man down the road.

I showed him the letter and brought him up to date on my meeting with Heather Warren. I half expected him to try and talk me out of going to see Ron Carpenter, to suggest some other course of action. He didn't though. He got changed into his jeans and a jacket. On his way out of the front door he picked up a large spanner and put it into his jacket pocket.

It was only eight-thirty when we got there. The shop was closed. We rang the bell for three or four minutes. I looked around the square while I was waiting. The newspaper hoarding outside the Asian shop said: "RAILWAY MURDERS: *Psychologist comments on mind of serial killers.*" It was just over a week since Helen Driscoll had been murdered and yet Leslie Knight was still making the headlines.

Eventually we started to knock on the glass, looking through into the interior of the shop before Ron Carpenter appeared. He came forward with a quizzical expression on his face and unbolted the door at the top and bottom; then turning the key, he opened it.

"What's going on?" he said, looking at his watch. "We're not open yet."

He stopped for a minute, looking closely at us. Then he said:

"You're the two I spoke to the other day about Helen. What do you want? It's lucky my Sarah's out. What do you want?"

"Can we come in, Mr Carpenter? I've got something very important I want to say to you about Helen."

Ron Carpenter looked cross. He looked out into the square, as if to see whether anyone was watching.

"You better come up then," he said grudgingly.

The flat upstairs was tiny. The three of us walked single file along a narrow hallway into a small living room. There was a settee and an easy-chair with several cushions scattered about. On the far wall were a number of framed photographs, all of groups of adults.

"Where's your wife?" Billy asked.

"She works part-time, cleaning," Ron Carpenter said. "What's all this about?"

It was while looking round that I saw the bowl of yellow roses.

I walked across to it. It was one of those crystal glass bowls that had a steel mesh fitting across it so that the roses could stand up separately. I put my finger out to one of the blooms and the petals came off at my touch and floated down to the table top, where they joined several others. The flowers had been there for some time.

There was something unsettling about the roses being there. It gave me a shiver. Had Ron Carpenter bought a bunch of roses, selected one for his purpose and saved the rest as a gift for his fragile, over-protected wife?

Billy looked over at me and the roses and walked towards the door. He had his hand inside his jacket. I wondered if he thought we were going to need a weapon.

"What is this? What's going on?" Ron Carpenter said.

I decided to be blunt, more for shock value than for anything else.

"Did you kill your daughter, Ron?"

His mouth fell open and he took a step back as if the very sentence had knocked him from his spot.

"What do you mean?" he said. He pushed his

hand deep into his pocket and came out with his inhaler. He held it by the side of his face and looked at me with apprehension.

"We think that Helen was murdered by someone who wanted her out of the way; to stop her being a nuisance."

"But she was killed by that, that madman, that bloke they caught!" He was looking aghast. He put out his arm and leant on the back of a chair.

"No she wasn't. I have a letter here, in my pocket, that she wrote to her friend on the day she died. She said you had asked her to meet you, at two-thirty. She said you were going to tell your wife about her."

At each thing I said, he seemed to grow weaker. I looked across at Billy. He had his arm across the door as if he was expecting Ron Carpenter to make a run for it. The way he was standing, the expression on his face, it didn't look as though he could make a run for the settee, let alone for anything else. A tiny doubt began to take root in my head.

"You wanted her out of the way, Ron. You didn't want your wife to know about her. She wouldn't go away though, would she? Every time you looked out of the window she was sitting there in the middle of the square staring across at you."

He put the inhaler into his mouth but didn't use it. I walked across the room to the wall that was full of photos.

"No, I was … cross at her … but –" the words

came out of Ron Carpenter's mouth as if he was speaking in a foreign tongue and searching for the right vocabulary – "my wife … she…"

My attention was taken by a photo on the wall of a woman in an overall in the middle of a group of men, one of whom I recognized. It was Des Murray, the CID officer I had spent the day with. I was still talking to Ron but part of my mind was wondering why Des's photo should be there.

"You had access to the police station and could have found out about the roses that the murderer had left on the bodies of the other victims. It was easy for you to make it look like it was the work of the Railway Killer."

Then I realized where the photo had been taken. It was in the CID room and some of the other male faces looked familiar. The woman even began to look like someone I knew. It was Ron Carpenter's wife, Sarah, who had been behind the counter on the day we'd come into the shop. She looked different in the photo, her hair tightly pulled back from her face.

"You bought roses, even though they were the wrong colour, Ron," I could hear Billy's voice finishing off the line of questioning.

I looked round at Ron, suddenly sure that we'd made a mistake. He was ashen, rubbing his hands together.

"Truth to tell," he said, "I didn't buy those roses;

my Sarah did."

"My God," I said, "your wife bought the roses."

I had a flashback to the day I had seen Helen in the square. I was looking over my shoulder at the shops behind me and I saw Majestic Dry Cleaner's. Inside there was a woman peering out through the glass. Helen was watching the shop but it was a *woman* looking out, a *woman* who had made the appointment to see Helen, not a man.

"Where is Sarah, Ron?" I almost shouted at him.

"She's at work, at the police station. Why?"

I walked swiftly past him, down the stairs and out of the flat.

When I got to the station I asked to see Heather. She wasn't available, was actually in a meeting with my uncle Tony. Stevie came down to the front desk.

"Patsy!" she said, when she saw me. "How have you been?"

"Fine, fine. This is my friend Billy Rogers," I said impatiently, pointing behind me. "Stevie, we need to come upstairs…" She was screwing her mouth up. I went on: "We desperately need to see my uncle Tony. I've got some important stuff to tell him. I've got to do it personally. Heather won't mind."

She looked unsure but she got a couple of visitors' badges out anyway. We followed her through the entrance and into the building.

When we got up to the CID suite I saw Sarah
Carpenter immediately. She was polishing some of
the desktops down at the far end of the office. She
was the cleaner who had helped me mop up my spilt
tea on the day I'd spent with CID. She looked
different from when she'd been behind the counter
in the dry cleaner's, less hot and bothered, her hair
neatly tied back.

Walking through the long room, Billy behind me,
I was aware of people stopping their work to look at
us. Through the glass I could see Heather's face
although it was clear that she hadn't seen me. She
looked as if she was deep in conversation with my
uncle. I could see the back of his head, nodding at
something she had said.

I walked up to the woman and said:

"Sarah, remember me? I came into the shop the
other day and asked you about Helen Driscoll."

Stevie was alongside me.

"What's going on?" she said, touching my elbow.

Sarah Carpenter had stopped cleaning, had put
her duster and spray can down on the desk. She
looked at me straight, eye to eye.

"Sarah," I said softly, "did you arrange to meet
Helen on the afternoon she was killed?"

The office was going quiet. From behind I could
hear whispers and the sound of a door opening.
Heather Warren's voice came from far away.

Still Sarah Carpenter said nothing, just gave me

an unblinking stare.

"Did you buy the yellow roses, Sarah? Did you kill Helen?"

"What on earth?" Stevie said. I could hear Heather's voice, crossly: *What's going on?* and my uncle Tony: *Patricia, what's happening, have you gone mad?*

"Did you kill her, Sarah? And leave the yellow rose behind to make it look like the Railway Killer?"

Sarah Carpenter sat down slowly. The chair she chose was a swivel one and she had to steady herself by leaning on the desk. She mumbled something that I couldn't quite hear.

"What, Sarah, what did you say?" I said, holding my breath. The tension in the room was so strong you could have stopped a train with it.

"She was going to take him away, like her mother tried to. Every day I watched her sitting in the square, looking into the shop, trying to catch his eye. He thought I didn't know, but I'd always known. Annie Wilson had told me about the baby. I just dared her to try and take my Ronnie away. The daughter, the dead one, I'd have known her anywhere. She was the spitting image of her mother; tiny, skinny. A puff of wind would have blown her away. I knew it was her. I'd been waiting for her for years…"

"Sarah," Heather said, "do you know what you're saying?"

"I know. I know what I've done. Don't think I could ever forget it."

I heard a male voice from behind me.

"I think you should read her her rights, marm." It was Des Murray.

Heather looked flustered. After a moment she started in a calm voice:

"You do not have to say anything, but anything you do say…"

I turned and, pulling the sleeve of Billy's jacket, started to walk out of the room.

My uncle Tony's head was turning back and forth, looking from me to Heather and back again.

"Let's get out of here," I said.

22

Copycat

The newspapers were full of it.

"*RAILWAY KILLER'S LAST VICTIM KILLED BY JEALOUS WIFE*" – and – "*COPYCAT MURDER IN BID TO FOOL POLICE*".

Heather Warren was quoted extensively:

"*We became aware, as the days went by, that the evidence and facts in the Driscoll death were not exactly the same as those in the previous murders. It was important to keep our investigations secret as we realized that only someone with a link to the station could have broken the security of Operation Rose and concocted such a scheme. We did, in fact, have help from the public on this case.*"

I was sitting on the floor of Billy's living room

with the newspapers spread out in front of me. Billy was on a chair just behind me. Every few minutes I leaned back and felt his knees poking into my shoulder blades.

"There's not a mention of me anywhere!" I said, making a small pile of the newspapers that we'd bought.

"Not that you're worried," Billy said, reaching across and picking up one of the papers. "It's not as if you wanted to be the hero or anything."

"No," I said. His mention of the word *hero* made me thing of Brian Martin. I'd seen him just the previous day. He'd been coming out of PHOTO-KWIK as I'd been passing. I'd started to smile at him, determined to make friends again, but he'd steadfastly ignored me and walked on as if I wasn't there. I'd felt a pang of something; whether it was guilt or loss I couldn't have said.

"What I don't see is how Sarah Carpenter got Helen Driscoll to go to the railway warehouses with her," Billy said.

"Oh, Heather told me," I said. "Apparently Sarah met Helen, probably just minutes after I'd left the square, and said that Ron was making deliveries and had broken down. She told her that they'd go and pick him up and then they could have their talk about the future. She was very pleasant and chatty to Helen; she must have been, to put her at her ease. Helen probably didn't even notice where they were going until it was too late."

I felt a little shiver saying that. At what point had it become *too late*? When she'd got into the car? When she'd got out of the car and walked into the warehouse? Or when she'd first found her dad and sat in the square, watched by Sarah Carpenter?

I leaned back, my neck aching from bending over. I could feel Billy's knees behind me.

"Here," he said, and put his hands on my shoulders and started to rub them. I closed my eyes and felt my shoulders relax and the muscles in my neck soften.

"That's good," I said and I thought, for the five hundredth time, about the kiss we had had and not mentioned. We were like partners in a medieval dance, coming together and then pulling apart; a little twirl here and a curtsy there, now and then a touching of the hands.

It was frustrating.

"So, Detective Kelly," he said softly, "what are you going to investigate next?"

I turned round to look up at him. "I'll think of something," I said.